BILLY PARKER
AND THE MYSTERY OF THE
LOST CONFEDERATE GOLD

AUGUSTUS BRIDLE

Belleville, Ontario, Canada

BILLY PARKER AND THE MYSTERY OF THE
LOST CONFEDERATE GOLD
Copyright © 2013, Augustus Bridle

ISBN: 978-1-4600-0194-3
LSI Edition: 978-1-4600-0195-0
E-book ISBN: 978-1-4600-0196-7
(E-book available from the Kindle Store, KOBO and the iBookstore)

Cataloguing data available from Library and Archives Canada

To order additional copies, visit:
www.essencebookstore.com

Epic Press is an imprint of *Essence Publishing.*
For more information, contact:
20 Hanna Court, Belleville, Ontario, Canada K8P 5J2
Phone: 1-800-238-6376 • Fax: (613) 962-3055
Email: info@essence-publishing.com
Web site: www.essence-publishing.com

Printed in Canada
by
Epic
Press

Dedicated to those who came of age in the '60s.

Chapter 1

The Dowager,
Rosedale, Toronto—May 1964

The brand new, 1964 Pontiac Parisienne wound its way through the tree-lined streets of Rosedale, passing the mansions of Toronto's elite. Billy's father, Bert, punched the buttons of the radio tuner, trying futilely to find his favourite station as the speaker blared a mix of music and noise.

Billy hated this neighbourhood. To him it felt like a giant, gloomy graveyard. The mansions were all brown stone or brick, darkened by years of pollution. Everything was buried under a canopy of leaves from the massive oak, elm, and maple trees. The architecture felt medieval—like something out of a horror movie. Billy was a suburban boy, born and bred. The suburbs, where the sun shone unobstructed on the rows of bungalows and ranch-style homes, is where he felt at home.

The Pontiac seemed out of place as it rolled up the laneway for number 99 Castle Frank Road. This was a narrow thoroughfare designed for a horse and buggy, not a pressed steel and chrome behemoth blaring rock and roll. They glided through the grandeur of the covered portal and back to the old stable, which had not seen a horse since the 1920s. Billy and his dad jumped out of the Pontiac and made their way to the imposing oak front door, which looked designed to keep out invading armies. Bert Parker pulled the door bell, which was still a mechanical rope and pulley device.

"You don't like it here much, do you, Billy," Bert said, knowing the answer.

"Nope," was the reply.

"Someday you'll look back and be thankful we had this visit. Just think of it as a walk back in time...a visit to the past."

"Gives me the creeps." Billy was not persuaded.

One half of the large door was swung open by a diminutive, stooped old woman in the attire of a maid. "Please come in, Mr. Parker and Master Billy...Madame awaits your visit."

"Thank you, Paintie, and how are you on this fine spring day?" Bert replied. He was fond of the old girl.

"Just as spry as a lamb," she said with a trace of an English accent and a twinkle in her eye.

"Well, if I was as young as you, I would be too." Bert knew how to stroke old Paintie, who was beaming at the attention.

"Young Billy and I will see our way up to her room. I know the route," he added.

Billy cringed as he reluctantly followed his father through the interior of the old mansion. It was dimly lit and darkened even more by the ubiquitous walnut panels and wainscoting. Ornate frescos, marble mantelpieces, and the long, curved, exquisitely carved balustrade leading to the second floor all felt like some kind of gothic horror movie set. Even the people in the paintings, most of which were men in some foreign uniform, all looked dour and foreboding. To top it off, the place smelled musty and old, as though any fresh air was sucked out of it long ago.

Bert and Billy made their way up the staircase and along a second floor hallway to a closed bedroom door at the end. They entered the room without knocking. Billy was astounded by the size of the bedroom. Along one wall was a full-sized fireplace, floor to ceiling bookshelves along another, a small alcove with a bay window looking out over the grounds, and several smaller adjoining rooms. At the far side of the room, across from the entrance, sat a huge four-poster bed with canopy, the likes of which Billy had never even dreamed of, let alone seen. In the dim light from across the room, they could make out the female occupant of the four-poster, who appeared to be sleeping while partially propped up by pillows.

Bert moved silently across the floor with Billy in tow, trying not to startle the old dowager, but Billy resisted as they neared her bed. She was a sight he would not soon forget. What was left of her hair were only strands of grey drooping over a wrinkled face that had a creamy pallor. Her hands were skeleton-like, veiled in thin splotchy skin. Billy quietly retched as all his forward motion was now being supplied by his father's firm hand. Bert was losing patience with his reluctant son.

As they approached the bed, the old lady detected their presence and slowly opened her eyes. Billy recoiled against his father's grip. Her eyes were a milky colour and seemed to lack pupils.

"Who is there? Is that you, Bert?" she asked. Her voice was deep but not quite masculine.

"Yes it is, Aunt Emily. I'm here with my son Billy, who I would like you to meet. He is a mischievous twelve year old."

"Please come here, boy." She raised her hand off the bed, but in no particular direction.

By now it was quite obvious to Billy that the old lady was quite blind as he stood frozen at her request. Bert mouthed calming words of encouragement to his son along with a gentle push in her direction.

"Let me feel your face. I can tell a great deal about a person from their face." Her long spindly hand gently felt its way up Billy's chest to his petrified visage. She meticulously maneuvered around all the features of his face as if reading a Braille document. "Ah, fine features...a strong jaw...you are quite a good-looking lad." She seemed to take great satisfaction from her explorations. "Youth was so long ago and such a glorious time. Don't ever think that it will last forever, and don't waste a second of it, lad."

"No ma'am," was all Billy could muster.

"Let me tell you about my week," Bert said, sensing that it was time to relieve Billy. Bert proceeded to recount his week's events in a stentorian tone, and the old dowager listened raptly.

Relieved that he was no longer the centre of attention, Billy began to survey the parlour more thoroughly. Over top of the fireplace mantel a large portrait of a girl caught his gaze and instantly all of his attention.

"Go take a closer look," Bert said to his son in a low voice that the old lady could not hear. Billy slowly ambled over to the fireplace, transfixed by the painting. The young lady was dressed in a blue velvet hoop skirt. She had long dark hair, a peaches-and-cream complexion, and the most deep blue penetrating eyes that he'd ever seen. She was perhaps the most beautiful girl that he had ever set eyes on. Billy's jaw dropped and his breathing was shallow—spellbound by her beauty.

"Time to go, pal. Come say goodbye to Aunt Emily," Billy's dad called across the room. Billy struggled to break free of his enchantment. The beauty of the young girl had transcended the gloomy ambience of the place, and Billy felt relaxed for the first time since he had arrived.

"It was a pleasure to meet you, Billy, and please come back to see me again," said the old dowager, who was clearly being sincere.

"Thank you, ma'am, and I will," Billy was beaming. Bert smirked at his rejuvenated son.

The trip back to the suburbs was a much quieter affair with both Billy and his dad seemingly lost in their thoughts. Bert even refrained from his annoying habit of fumbling with the preset buttons on the radio.

"Do you know how old she is?" Bert broke the silence first. "She is one hundred and four years old," he said not waiting for an answer.

"One hundred and four! She can't be" Billy mulled the numbers over in his mind. "That would mean she is ninety-two years older than me...no way."

"Well she is...born in 1860. And you know that picture over the mantel? That is a painting of Aunt Emily when she was twelve years old."

Billy fell silent—like he had the wind knocked out of him—but in a good way. The angel was now real and she had a name. He smiled as he watched Rosedale slip by through the car window. Life was full of marvels—at least for a twelve year old.

Chapter 2
The Civil War, Sandersville, Georgia—1864

The Old South was falling, slowly being crushed under the weight of the vastly superior numbers of the Union forces. Atlanta was under siege by General Sherman, and Grant was in a stalemate with Lee at Petersburg, Virginia. That was soon to change.

The Reynolds plantation outside Sandersville, Georgia, had been operating for most of the war without the supervision of the master of the house, Colonel William Reynolds. Colonel Reynolds was mobilized shortly after the first shots were fired on Fort Sumter and rarely had the opportunity to return to his beloved plantation. His wife, Susannah, was now at the reins, and any pretense to her past life as a spoiled Southern belle had long since vanished.

The plantation, verging on a thousand acres, was a typical Old South cotton operation with a Greek revival big house at the end of an oak-lined laneway. It had a workforce of upwards of fifty slaves as well as house servants and big, old Mammy, who was ostensibly a senior servant but in reality was second in command of the whole operation.

With the cotton blockade in full force, very little revenue was finding its way into the plantations' coffers, and the whole place was slowly slipping into disrepair. The

Reynolds plantation was a microcosm of what was happening to the grandeur of the Old South.

The Confederate captain rode his horse at a trot up the laneway to the Reynolds mansion. His gut told him to urge his steed into a full gallop, but not wanting to alarm the residents of the plantation, he held her back.

For several days now, Susannah had tried her best to ignore the roar of far-off guns, but deep down she knew that the war was coming to her doorstep. She was terrified, and there was nothing in her genteel upbringing that had prepared her for her present life. But there was a code in the South that demanded stoicism and courage, and that code applied to women as well as men.

The captain dismounted and gave his horse to the care of a footman as Susannah, under the close watch of Mammy, made her way across the verandah. The sight of a grey uniform no longer lifted her spirits the way it did at the start of the war and only paralyzed her with dread. A visit from a Confederate soldier these days usually only meant one thing: a loved one was dead.

"Good afternoon, ma'am," said the captain as he removed his hat. "My name is Captain Benton, ma'am." The captain knew full well what his presence meant to residents of the South these days and did not wait for any polite rejoinder from Susannah. "Let me set your mind at ease right away. I am not here to tell you about any deaths in your family, but I do bear bad news."

The colour instantly returned to Susannah's now-smiling face, as if the trigger had been pulled in the game of Russian roulette and the chamber was empty. No news could be bad now—the colonel was still alive.

"Welcome, Captain. I am the wife of Colonel William Reynolds, and I am honoured to offer our hospitality to a captain of our beloved Confederate forces. Please come into the drawing room."

"Thank you, ma'am, but what I have to tell you is very urgent, and neither of us has time to engage in the social niceties to which we were both accustomed. No doubt, you have heard guns over the past several days."

"Yes, Captain, unfortunately I have."

"Well, Atlanta has been under siege for four months now, and she has fallen to the Yanks." Susannah knew that the writing was on the wall. Any hope that she had of returning to her genteel plantation life after Johnny Reb had whipped the Yanks was quickly vanishing.

"The Yank general is a scoundrel named Sherman," the captain continued. "Sherman is a butcher and leaves a trail of destruction behind him. He has no regard for civilian property or civilians, for that matter."

"Can you stop him, Captain?"

"Ma'am, we are severely outmanned and outgunned. I believe that the best that we can do is slow him up a little. At the moment, we do not know where he is headed next...be that Macon, Savannah, or Augusta."

"Sounds like Mr. Sherman will be paying us a visit sooner or later, Captain," Susannah said, trying to appear stoic.

"Ma'am, something that you should know about Sherman...he seems to harbour a particular dislike of the cream of Southern society...the plantation owners such as yourself." His words created a whirlwind of fear in Susannah's soul. "Ma'am, there is no way to sugarcoat this. You must abandon your plantation, free your slaves...leave

12

nothing that could be of value to the Yanks. Destroy what food you cannot take with you, shoot any extra horses, mules, or livestock, and burn all wagons or carts that will be left behind. You must be out of here within the week."

With every ounce of stoicism now used up, Susannah was openly weeping. "Captain, we will do what you request, we will head for Savannah...but...could you please grant me one request...could you somehow notify my husband, Colonel Reynolds, that we have left for Savannah...please, Captain?"

"Ma'am, I will do my best. I am very sorry, ma'am." The captain remounted his bay mare and this time galloped back down the laneway.

There was a strange calm in the early evening as Susannah sat on the verandah exhausted physically and emotionally from a day of dismantling a home that was the centre of her life. Somehow the gentle ambience of the Southern evening transcended everything—she felt a strange peace.

"Mammy, do all the Negro folk hate us?" Susannah asked her trusted house servant.

"I don't believe so, ma'am," Mammy replied, trying to skirt the question that had clearly taken her aback. "I certainly don't hate you."

Susannah gently smiled, appreciating Mammy's attempt to shield her from the truth. "I know that it is no excuse, but I was born into this system. They always told us that this was God's will...that we were the superior race. Strangely...when I was a little girl, I had the hardest time accepting it. As I grew older I no longer questioned that owning someone was wrong...it somehow seemed okay," Susannah said philosophically. She paused for several minutes, deep in her thoughts. "I guess that I should have listened to that little girl."

"It's a very strange system indeed, ma'am, cuz ah was bo'n into it too and ah don' know no other life," Mammy replied, starting to open up. "It must sound mighty strange...but ah's scared now that it's lookin' like it might end...ah just don' know what to do."

"Tomorrow, Mammy, little Emily and I will start out for Savannah. I have relatives there, and I would be honoured if you would come with us...but for the first time in your life, the choice is yours. If you choose to stay, I will give you what money I can and a horse and wagon."

They were both quietly in tears—both not realizing until now, how close they actually had become, and what a bond of love there was between them.

"Tomorrah, Miss Susannah...it's you, me, and little Emily off to Savannah. We's family, and ain't nothing can break us up."

Chapter 3

Don Valley, Don Mills—May 1964

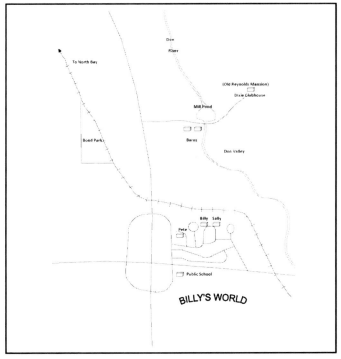

To North Bay

Don River

(Old Reynolds Mansion)

Dixie Clubhouse

Mill Pond

Bond Park

Barns

Don Valley

Billy Sally

Pete

Public School

BILLY'S WORLD

The Don Valley was a virtual paradise for any young
buck fortunate enough to live within spitting distance of its
slopes. It stretched to about one half of a mile at its widest
point down to a few hundred yards where the embank-
ments grew steeper. The river, lined by huge willows,
looped lazily back and forth through the valley.

The valley was a huge toy box for a kid. It was a playground that would keep a young guy either in trouble, running from trouble, or planning trouble. The railway hugged one slope if hopping trains or climbing trestles suited a kid's fancy. The golf course supplied a decent income from golf balls and lots of exercise running from irate golfers and staff. The nineteenth century barns let a city kid experience the joy of tumbling in a hay mound, and a guy could actually swim in the old mill pond or skate on it when the freeze up came.

Every spring the river had the good sense to flood and sweep away kids that got a little too close on a dare or others who thought that riding a chunk of ice might be fun.

Then there was the old, heavy gauge rope that someone had tied to the upper branches of a huge old willow clinging to the bank. At the peak of the swing, a writhing ball of youth could be ten feet above the river, all desperately clinging to the rope or each other. And there were always casualties that could no longer hang on and dropped into the four feet of water covering the rocky bottom.

If the railroad or the golfers or the rope swing did not get a young guy, the gangs would. One of the laws of youth states that if boys can find some way to differentiate themselves from other boys, then they will form a gang. The south side of the valley naturally was the territory of the South Side Gang. The part of the valley where three tributary streams merged into the river was the domain of the Three Valleys Gang, and just about every other notable piece of geography had a gang named after it.

Billy was a member in good standing of the South Side Gang. The South Side Gang spent most of any gang conflicts running away from the Three Valleys Gang, who always seemed bigger and more numerous. Conflicts were usually never premeditated, and only occurred when gang members going about the normal course of their activities in the valley came across rival gang members. On the rare occasion that there was a pre-planned event, it would usually be fought by throwing rocks and firing projectiles with slingshots, with both sides taking shelter behind sheet metal garbage can lids. The potential for injury was there, but somehow no one ever seemed to sustain much damage.

The grand old farm in the valley was bought up by a golf club sometime in the late '50s. The club felt that they had an idyllic spot to put a golf course, but it became a lot less idyllic when they found themselves in a turf war with the local youth. Things deteriorated to the point where the golf club felt obliged to hire their own security staff who would cruise the course in tractors and golf carts in search of the young miscreants that got their members so irate. To Billy and the guys, these were the golf course Nazis, known derogatorily as the "workies."

On more than one occasion, the South Side Gang would be running from the Three Valleys Gang when the whole sordid mess of them would inadvertently run into a platoon of workies. This would change the whole dynamic of the chase, with the two rival gangs now running side by side to escape the much-feared wrath of these golf course Nazis. When the workies snagged one of their prey, which they would do occasionally, they would throw him in a golf cart and take their screaming, blubbering victim to workie headquarters in the old barns. What happened there, Billy and his buddies did not want to even speculate. All they knew was the captive never returned. An hour or so later, his father's car would pull up to the barns and take away the prisoner. The next day in school, the victim would relate to the others all the heinous torture that he had endured at the hands of the workies. They left him with one dire warning—if they ever caught him again, he would not be coming back. Workies were to be feared and hated.

It was a beautiful Saturday morning in May—one of those mornings when Billy could not get out of the house fast enough. Something about Saturday morning and spring and the sunshine—it gave him a sort of rapturous feeling, like everything in the world was perfect. It might have been spring fever, but Billy felt no need to explain it, he just wanted to soak it in.

"Hey Billy," Pete Mills yelled from the crest of the valley. "Let's get goin'."

Pete, like Billy, was a rambunctious, twelve-year-old but a touch more reckless with a strong propensity to act on impulse. Act first and ask questions later was the constant bane of his existence. Pete had a perpetual just-got-out-of-bed look to him with a proclivity for wearing the same torn T-shirt day after day, along with a broken set of eyeglasses held together with hockey tape.

"Hey Pete," Billy answered, "great golf ball day."

Finding lost golf balls and selling them back to the golfers at twenty-five cents apiece was a great source of revenue for Billy and his buddies. It sure beat cutting lawns and shovelling driveways. The golfers did not want the boys anywhere near the course, but they were quite happy to buy the balls at a cut rate. Billy could never figure out their logic.

By far the best way to come out of the valley with pockets full of balls was to wade in the river, because most golfers would give up a river ball as lost and the river wound around every hole. The problem was, wading through the river down the middle of the course made a guy very vulnerable to workies.

"Let's try the bend in the river by the ninth hole," Billy said. "I got a ton of 'em there last week."

"Lots of workie jerks around there too," Pete warned. So off they went making sure the fairway was clear of golfers and workies as they made their way into the river.

Taking your running shoes off was a huge mistake that only rookies made. If a guy had to make a run for it, there was no chance of getting them back on, and running in sloshing shoes was still better than pounding through the brush and gravel in bare feet.

"Billy, this stinks. Somebody cleaned this place out." Pete was getting frustrated at the slim pickings after an hour and a half of wading and ducking into the embankment to dodge workies.

"Yeah, you're right. Let's head up to the barns." Right in the centre of the stretch of valley that Billy and the guys claimed as their own was a cluster of old barns and worker's cottages built back in the nineteenth century. The livestock operation had ended years ago, and some of the barns were used for storing golf course equipment while others sat abandoned.

The day was not going well. The new golf ball fishing hole proved to be just as fished out as the previous location. Pete and Billy lay out of sight under a fallen old willow alongside one of the fairways discussing their bad luck. "You know what the problem is?" Billy said.

"There's no golf balls...that's the problem."

"No, the problem is that there are too many guys lookin' now...we used to have this river to ourselves. Now those idiots from Three Valleys are cleanin' everything out..." Billy continued on with his monologue, unaware that Pete had lost all interest in what he had to say and was eyeing a couple of balls that had landed on the fairway about ten yards from them. Shortly thereafter, two more landed. This was like dangling a steak in front of a starving coyote. Looking at those beautiful little white gems lying in the grass was just too much for a guy who had little to show for a day's hunting.

Billy ended his monologue only to realize that there was a potential catastrophe brewing as he watched his partner drooling over those diamonds on the fairway. "Don't even think about it!"

It was too late—Pete was off and running. In a short little arc around the fairway, he deftly scooped up the four balls and was now headed full bore back to a horrified Billy at the river bank.

"Are you nuts? They're gonna kill us," Billy was right. The racket coming from the four screaming golfers that were now pounding down the fairway echoed all over the valley. The cacophony had now alerted the dreaded workies, who had their golf carts headed full steam ahead to the scene of the crime.

There was really only one direction for the two fugitives to go now—across the river. It was tough slogging because the river was deeper there, but they gambled that a river crossing would be the end of the chase for the genteel golfers. Unfortunately they underestimated the ferocity of golfers, who had watched their perfect tee shots absconded by two punks. It was the ultimate act of blasphemy for a golfer.

Now the workies picked up the chase on the other side of the river with their carts roaring down the opposite fairway. Billy and Pete had another quick decision to make—either try to outrun the carts up the slope of the valley and head into the neighbourhood or head into the compound of the barns and try to lose them there. Billy chose the latter, while Pete headed for the hills.

Billy, running into the compound, had a few hundred yards on his closest adversary as he turned on what afterburners that he had left. From previous forays into enemy territory, Billy knew his way around the barns pretty well, inside as well as out. He ducked into the old horse stable, which was a big old building that was quite elegant in its day but was crumbling from neglect. He charged up the aisle past the stalls, leaping over all the collected detritus to an old tack room at the far end. This was the end of the line, and his only option now was to find somewhere to hide. At the far end of the barn, Billy could hear his pursuers crashing through the stable as they threw open all the stall doors. "That little bastard is here somewhere...we got him this time."

Billy struggled to get behind old saddles and harnesses that were stacked up beneath a bench alongside one wall. All was quiet in the tack room as three scruffy workies entered, smelling victory. "There's not a lot of places to hide in here, kid, so we're gonna get ya." These guys were not known for their polite, refined mannerisms. They proceeded to throw tack around, kick over benches, tear open cupboard doors, taking great pleasure in moving in for the kill. But the kill did not come—nowhere was there any sign of Billy.

Chapter 4
Confederate Spy Camp, Don Valley—1864

The four men emerged from the narrow passageway into the dimly lit room. "Okay, gentlemen, you may remove the sacks and blindfolds now," an unfamiliar voice instructed them. After a two-hour coach ride, it was a great relief to remove the gunny sacks and blindfolds.

There was a long oak table in the middle of the room with a black chalkboard along one wall. A Rebel flag was the only piece of adornment in their austere surroundings.

"I know you may find it a bit demeaning to be treated this way, but it is a fact of life in our business. You will only know what you need to know, and your present location is not on the 'need-to-know' list. Let me introduce myself. My name is Robert Lacy, and if you believe that, then you should be in some other line of work." There was a chuckle throughout the room. "We will go around the table, and you can introduce yourselves along with your home state. Remember...what you call yourself here tonight will be your name for the duration of our operations."

The first of the four gentlemen rose. "The name is Johnny Reb from South Carolina," he said, followed by another chuckle throughout the room.

"Well Johnny, there are a million Johnny Rebs due south of here, so maybe you should think of a less-common moniker," Lacy replied.

"Then, sir, you can make that Peter Williams."

The introductions went around the room with pretty much the same results among the other three. Lacy had to admonish them that Abraham Lincoln was probably not a good alias for a Southern agent. He was pleased with their cockiness, exactly what he needed in a spy.

"Okay, let's get back to business. First something about your present environment. For all intents and purposes, Canada is a neutral country in our current war. But if you scratch beneath the surface, you will find a definite senti-ment towards the Confederate States of America. British Canada does not trust the Yankees. After the War of 1812, Canadians are still a little gun shy and suspect that Mr. Lincoln has one eye on the north. So they hope that we will win—which we will—but they cannot show any obvious signs that they are helping the Confederacy. As far as our spy operations out of Toronto...you can be fairly confident that they will look the other way, providing that we are not too blatant about it."

"Running around town with gunny sacks over our heads could arouse some suspicion, I would think," commented one of the four, eliciting laughter from the others.

"Enough!" Lacy had his fill of senseless humour. "Let me give you another ugly fact. If you are caught by the Yanks, you will not be considered prisoners of war. You will be considered spies, and spies have no rights except the right to be executed." He paused for a few moments of awk-ward silence to let the idea sink in. "The greatest threat to us on this side of the border is Yank spies. Toronto is crawling with them, and their only purpose is to intercept and sabotage our operations here. Fortunately I have some Canadian contacts that keep me informed of any new Yanks coming to town."

For the next several hours, the group went over every minute detail of a plan to break out Confederate prisoners of war from a Union POW camp on Johnson's Island on Lake Erie. If all went well, the freed Johnny Rebs would be quickly re-armed and would join up with a secret society of Southern sympathizers known as the Sons of Liberty. Lincoln would then have another battle front in the northwest.

In the early hours of the morning, the meeting adjourned and the conspirators donned their blindfolds and sacks for the return journey into the city. Robert Lacy, also known as Colonel William Reynolds, sucked on his cigar in the cool night air. He thought about Susannah and Emily and longed for their idyllic plantation life before the war.

Chapter 5

The Second Visit with Aunt Emily, Rosedale, Toronto—May 1964

"Billy, I'm proud of you, son. I wasn't going to ask you along to see Aunt Emily today, and you even volunteered to come." Bert was sincerely impressed.

"I think that you were right, Dad, I kinda find her interesting," replied Billy, beaming from ear to ear.

"She was an old friend of my mother's. We used to live in this neighbourhood, you know, but on the other side of the tracks, so to speak. I bet that I was about your age when I first met her too."

As they entered the laneway of the old mansion, Bert had a test of his reaction time as he jumped on the brakes to avoid a gardener who appeared out of nowhere. The Pontiac skidded to a stop as the startled gardener jumped out of the way. His snarling face was inches away from Billy's window as the Pontiac slowly proceeded up the laneway. Billy locked his gaze straight ahead, trying to ignore the icy stare.

Billy and his father approached the huge arched doorway of the mansion and pulled on the old rope device that operated the doorbell. The door began to slowly creep open.

"Morning Paintie...still spry as a lamb, I trust?" asked Bert.

"Good morning, Bert and young Billy—not quite a lamb today, I'm afraid, more like an old, tired mare—the arthritis you know."

"Well you are a darn sight more cheerful than your gardener. That guy needs a happy pill."

"Gardener, sir?" a bemused Paintie asked. "He is not due until next week."

"Anyway, we are off to see my girlfriend—or I should say, my other girlfriend." Bert, the consummate cad, always left her blushing.

As they entered the old dowager's bedroom, Billy instinctively headed over to the fireplace, mesmerized by the painting, while Bert gently announced their arrival to Aunt Emily. "I am afraid, Aunt Emily, that Billy has fallen in love with the beautiful lady over the fireplace." Bert was amused at his son's infatuation.

The old lady was clearly enervated by the thought of a young man's attentions to her former self. "Well, Master Billy, if you have come a-courting, I am certainly available." Billy blushed as he approached her bedside. Bert had never seen her quite so perky and was delighted with the effect that his son was having on the old dowager.

"Now Billy, we must get to know each other. Tell me about you."

"What do you want to know?" Billy replied feeling a bit awkward.

"I am sorry...that was not a fair question, I will be more specific. I know what you do in school. I suspect that it has not changed a great deal, so tell me what you do after school. That is much more interesting."

"I need to make a quick stop into the office if you two would excuse me for about half an hour," Bert interrupted.

Bert sensed that Billy was quite comfortable now and would be fine alone with her. It would be a good experience for him to learn the art of polite conversation, he thought as he left the room.

"I usually spend time in the valley."

"That would be the Don Valley?"

"Yes, that's right. It's right behind our house. We have a rope swing there and a fort that we dug out of the hillside, and we look for golf balls...it's a great place."

"And you never bother the golfers, of course?" she asked rhetorically.

"How did you know about that?" He shuffled awkwardly from foot to foot.

"Oh...your dad mentioned a few things to me."

"There are some barns in the valley too, that my buddies and I go into sometimes."

"Well, tell me more about the barns," she asked, appearing much more curious.

"I was in one last weekend, but don't tell my dad. I'm not supposed to go there because he says we will get charged with break and enter, or something like that."

"Your secret stays with me," she reassured him.

"I have something I wanted you to see, 'cause it's just like the one on your mantel." Billy pulled out a small brass ornament with a symbol overlaid with the letters RP. He placed it in the old lady's hand, and she began to stroke it as if she were reading Braille. She fell silent, appearing lost in thought. Her eyes moistened.

"Do you know what this is, Billy?"

"No, ma'am."

"It is called a horse brass...it hangs on a leather strap across the chest of a horse. The letters stand for 'Reynolds

Plantation,' and there were only three made like this...one for Mother, one for Father, and one for me, which is on the mantel. Where did you find it?" she asked, much more seriously now.

"I was hiding in this room in one of the barns...from the workies," Billy replied with a touch of guilt in his voice. "And I found it under a bench."

"The workies?"

"Yeah, they're the guys that try to catch us on the golf course. We hate them," he answered. "And there is one other thing that I haven't told anybody because I was scared. There's a secret passage in the barn. I pulled on a leg of a bench to try and get underneath it and a small door opened up in the wall. I was really scared, but I was more scared of the workies, so I went in it to hide. I don't know where it goes. I got out as fast as I could after the workies left."

The old dowager pondered in silence for a moment. Billy thought for sure that he was going to get a lecture. "Billy, there is much that I must tell you, but we don't have time now. Promise me that you'll return and promise me you won't tell anyone else about your secret."

"Sure, Aunt Emily. I'll come back...and I won't tell a person."

Chapter 6
The Casket,
Washington, Georgia—1865

The old buckboard pounded and clattered its way along the road going south out of Washington, Georgia. The road was heavily scarred from the heavy guns and cavalries of both sides of the conflict either going into battle or retreating to fight another day. For the South, that other day was no longer coming. General Lee and the Confederate army were just about spent from fighting too many lopsided battles. A few soldiers wanted to fight on as a guerrilla force, but too few to pose anything but a nuisance to the North.

Hamish was at the reins of the buckboard with Willy riding shotgun, without the shotgun. In the back were six caskets with the bodies of young Johnny Rebs, whose combined ages would barely crack a hundred. Both Willy and Hamish were good Southern boys who had fought for the Confederate States of America. Taking the boys to be laid to rest in their home towns was a labour of respect and homage because there was no money in it.

About a mile down the road, Hamish could see dust rising and hear the faint clatter of hooves. "Here comes trouble, Willy," he said, assuming the worst.

"Ain't very likely that they're Rebs...not anymore anyway," Willy replied. Willy was right—a cavalry platoon came into sight wearing the dreaded blue uniforms, all crisp and clean, like they never did much fighting.

"Well, we ain't in uniform and we ain't armed...suppose that makes us fair game for a Yank." Hamish shook his head in disgust.

The captain signalled his troops to pull up as they approached the wagon. Hamish attempted to run the buckboard around their side knowing full well that the Yanks had no intention of letting them pass unharassed. He hated the sight of Yanks and would do anything to provoke them, even if it meant putting himself in a precarious position.

"Where in hell's name do you two think you're going?" the captain barked. Hamish made a desultory effort at stopping his team, clearly showing his annoyance. "We're off to Sandersville. Anything else I can do for you?" Hamish sneered contemptuously.

The captain ignored Hamish and walked his horse around the buckboard. "Of course you only have bodies in these caskets. Is that correct, sir?"

"I don't know what you Yanks use caskets for...but down here in the South, we use them to bury people in."

"Then maybe you would like to open one up for us."

"Maybe I wouldn't want to open one for you. These are courageous men that deserve the respect due the dead."

The captain pulled out his revolver. "Open one." Hamish, mumbling under his breath, grabbed a crowbar from under the buckboard seat and began to open a box on the top row.

"Not that one," the captain ordered, "The one on the bottom."

"God damn it," Hamish started in.

"Hamish, shut up. Let's just get it over with," Willy said, getting concerned about Hamish's increasing arrogance against an armed foe. Hamish and Willy unloaded the boxes until the bottom casket was visible and began to pry the lid off. As the lid was opened, they both recoiled at the sight and the stench. The captain walked his horse to the side of the buckboard and viewed into the casket. Sure enough, there were the remains of a young Confederate soldier, barefoot but still in a tattered uniform.

"Close it up," he said, wincing from the sight. "Proceed with your journey." The platoon carried on by the buckboard while Willy kept a strong arm on Hamish, fearful that he might do something that they both would end up regretting. He knew that the Yanks could have shot them both with impunity.

"God damn Yankee bastards...they got no respect for nothing," Hamish started into his tirade, which lasted pretty much the rest of the next hour.

Around midnight, the buckboard was several miles outside of Sandersville, travelling under the light of a beautiful full moon. "The old Reynolds plantation's got to be pretty close to here," Willy said as they passed the laneways of plantation after plantation with only foundations and fireplaces left to show for the big houses. "Colonel Reynolds wants us to drop off this here top box with Pvt. MacIsaac written on it...says he's a local boy that he wants buried on the plantation."

"Here she be," Hamish announced as he directed the team up the laneway of the Reynolds place. The sign from a big oak tree still hung despite being full of bullet holes. At the end of the laneway, like a ghostly apparition, were the silhouettes of two men waiting by the ruins of the old mansion.

"Welcome, gentlemen. Good of you to come by for a visit," Colonel Reynolds announced tongue in cheek. "My name is Colonel William Reynolds, and this here is Major Josiah Evans...not that rank matters much anymore."

"It certainly does, Colonel," Hamish replied reverently. "Your reputation precedes you, and we are honoured to do this chore for you...aren't we, Willy?"

"Certainly are, sir," Willy shook his head eagerly.

"Thank you, boys...I trust that the Yanks did not give you any trouble."

"Nah, except for one patrol...they made us open up a box...the heathen bastards."

"And which one would that be?" Colonel Reynolds cocked his head askance.

"Naturally the one right on the bottom…Yanks being Yanks," Hamish replied.

The colonel and the major exchanged wry smiles. "Then let's get the private down," the colonel said. The four of them struggled to lower the casket to the ground. Willy and Hamish bade them farewell, and the wagon headed off down the laneway for Sandersville, lighter by one casket.

"Sure ain't hard to fool a Yank, is it, Colonel," Major Evans smiled.

"We'll see," replied Colonel Reynolds as he pried off the top of the box. He beamed at the sight. "You're right, Major...it's sure not hard to fool a Yank," They both looked down on the box of gold bullion. "The rest of it we got out before the war ended. For now, we will bury it here. The Yanks think that the war is over, but I don't, and this box of bullion doesn't either. The South will rise again."

Chapter 7

Aunt Emily's Story, Rosedale, Toronto—May 1964

Billy jumped off the streetcar a few blocks shy of Castle Frank Road and broke into a run. Running was the normal gait for Billy, and usually at this time on Saturday afternoon, running would be a necessity to escape whomever he and his buddies had happened to provoke in the valley. But today was different. For the past week, all he could think of was what Aunt Emily needed to tell him.

"Welcome, Bert," said Aunt Emily as Billy approached her bed. If she was awake, her diminished senses would only detect someone when they were within a few feet of the bed.

"No, it's Billy, Aunt Emily...I came to see you by myself."

"Well, young man, it is a true honour that you chose to spend your Saturday afternoon with me," she said, visibly pleased. "Tell me about your week."

"Nothing much...I went to school and practiced with my basketball team. We really beat Fenside on Tuesday. I fouled out of the game. The coach wasn't happy about that."

"Why, Billy? You do not strike me as an unsportsmanlike player. What would cause you to foul out of a game?"

"The coach says that I get too excited and then I start to forget the rules, but I'm trying."

"Just make sure that you do not lose your enthusiasm, young man. That is much more important than fouling out of a game."

"Yes, ma'am," Billy replied, not quite sure what she meant.

"Billy, I suspect that you are not here to talk basketball."

"That's right, ma'am."

"Well, I did say that I had more to tell you, so where should I start?" The old lady paused to collect her thoughts. "Do you know anything about war, Billy?"

"I know some things about World War II, ma'am, because my dad was in it."

"I am referring to an older war, even before World War I...a war that was fought on American soil."

"That must be the Civil War, ma'am. I know a little about it too, from comic books."

"Written by the North, no doubt," she frowned. "We will have to get one thing straight right now. The correct name for the Civil War is the War of Northern Aggression. You must remember that."

"Yes, ma'am," replied a mildly admonished Billy, not knowing why.

"I was born in Georgia at the start of the War of Northern Aggression in 1860, on a big beautiful plantation...the Reynolds plantation...the initials on that horse brass that you found. My maiden name was Reynolds." Being blind, the old lady could not see the astonished look on Billy's face. "The first year or two of the war did not affect us much, except that I rarely got to see my daddy, Colonel William Reynolds, who was off fighting the Yanks. I was really too young to have an appreciation of what was going on in the world or that our world was about to end."

She paused to re-energize. "Life on the plantation seemed idyllic, at least now looking back on it. And yes, we had slaves," she said, as if it was a question going through Billy's mind. "Don't you get caught up in the slave issue. Mommy and Daddy were not at peace with slavery either, but they were born into a system, you know. And the North did not care one hoot about freeing the slaves. All they wanted was dominance over the South. Am I going too fast for you?"

"No, ma'am," replied Billy, which was not altogether true.

"As you can see, I get very excited about this issue, just like you and basketball." Billy smiled. "When I was four years old, we had to flee the plantation. I do not remember much except a very rough wagon ride to Savannah. Savannah is a city southeast of our plantation. We had to flee because of that butcher Sherman, who you have probably never heard of."

"No, I haven't, ma'am."

"Well, Sherman was a Yank general who liked to fight civilians because he was a despicable coward. His men would go onto plantations, steal anything of value and kill all the livestock at a time when people were starving, then burn the place down. That is what he did to the Reynolds plantation." She paused again, almost out of breath. "Even that was not good enough for him. He would go into town, get all the deeds and records for the county, then set them ablaze. Can you guess why, Billy?" Billy, aghast at the story that he was hearing, shook his head, forgetting that the old lady was blind. "He burned them so that after the war no one could prove ownership—the Yanks could take our property by default because officially no one owned it." She paused again, to try and calm herself down. "Billy, I apologize, but every time I recount this story, it saddens me, it angers me, and most of all, it tires me. Could you come see me again to allow me to continue...perhaps next Saturday?"

"I sure can, Aunt Emily," Billy eagerly replied.

"And Billy, can you come alone again? Your daddy is a fine man, but he has been brainwashed by Yankee propaganda and we cannot have a congenial conversation about these issues."

Billy said his goodbyes and left the old mansion in a flat-out run back to the streetcar.

Chapter 8

Brothers of the Gray Ghost, Sandersville, Georgia—May 1964

The pickup trucks rolled into the old schoolyard and parked anywhere on the grass without much regard to order. The trucks were a collection of Jimmies, Fords, and Dodges, but the culture of the owners was unmistakably the same. Every rear window was adorned with the Confederate battle flag and in most cases sported a rifle hung to be conspicuously intimidating. The "Brothers" were in good spirits as they hopped out and let out rebel yells whenever someone would hit their Dixie-playing horns.

Over top of the door on the red brick schoolhouse was a limestone plaque with "Brothers of the Gray Ghost" carved into it. The "Gray Ghost" was the moniker given to a famous Confederate commander, Colonel John Mosby, who was known for perfecting the ambush. The boys had chosen Mosby to be their spiritual leader. The plaque was old and weathered, but the school was even older, dating back to pre-Civil War times. It was built to serve the plantation children in the rural areas around Sandersville.

The building was a museum to all things Confederate, or even more like a shrine. There were swords, muskets, rifles, and regimental flags hung on every available piece of wall. At the front of the room, behind the stage, was a mural of General Lee leading his glorious troops into battle. The

South had lost the war a century before, but the ambience of this place was all victory.

Frank Mackay, dressed in Civil War garb, mounted the stage and took his place behind the podium to address the crowd who were slowly taking their seats. There was no question about who was in charge here as his presence sent a wave of silence over the membership.

"Let us pray." They bowed their heads, and Frank Mackay led the pseudo congregation in a Christian prayer that was equally infused with Southern sentiments. He paused for several seconds and surveyed the room. "We all know the code of secrecy, and we all know the consequences of violating that code. I need not say more."

He paused again. The message was loud and clear to the men who fidgeted nervously. "Today, I am going to tell you of some very interesting developments in something that is very near and dear to all of our hearts. At the end of the War of Northern Aggression, most of the gold in the Southern treasury fortunately disappeared, and I say fortunately because it meant that the Yanks didn't get it, but unfortunately neither did we. We have no doubt that our forefathers have hidden it, and it was hidden for us to carry on the cause—never forget that!"

He paused to take a sip of water. "Most of us have spent the last twenty years following leads and digging holes all over the South. Our fathers and grandfathers dug holes all over Dixie, and what do we have to show for it? Dirt...piles of lousy dirt." He shook his head in disgust. "What we have never considered is that maybe the treasury is not in the South, maybe the treasury is not in the North. Maybe—just maybe—it is hidden in a foreign country. We all know that many of our brave Confederate soldiers left this land for

Europe, for South America, for Canada, so that they would not have to live under Yankee rule. And with the premise that the treasure left with them, I have asked Brother Cyril here to research soldiers who headed for foreign lands, but primarily the higher ranks because they would have had access to the information." He nodded to a studious looking, bespectacled gentleman in the front row. "Brother Cyril, please come up and tell us your findings."

He stepped down and Brother Cyril made his way to the podium. "A year or so ago, Brother Frank asked me to investigate high-ranking expatriate Confederate soldiers," he began, "with the purpose of getting leads into the disappearance of the Southern treasury. As you can imagine, due to the high numbers of expatriates, it would be a very arduous task unless I could narrow it down a little. Now to do that, I used a couple of criteria: first of all, it would make sense that only the rank of colonel and up would be privy to treasury information, and secondly, since it is common knowledge that the treasury was moved to Washington, Georgia, then a Georgia boy would have a better lay of the land to keep clear of the Yankee troops. There were several Georgia officers who left for South America and Europe, but one who caught my eye was a Colonel Reynolds, who left for Canada.

"Now Colonel Reynolds never made any secret of the fact that he planned to regroup and take the war back to the Yank in due time, but many of our brave boys did the same. What caught my eye was a shipment of six dead Confederate boys who were signed out of a morgue in Washington, Georgia, by Colonel Reynolds, for shipment to Sandersville and burial in a small church yard there. Well, the records from the church show that only five caskets were put into the ground from that shipment." There was a murmur throughout the room. "Where did the sixth one go? The route to Sandersville goes right by Colonel Reynolds' old plantation. Coincidence? Maybe, but it also turns out that Colonel Reynolds set himself up in a very opulent lifestyle in Canada at a time when even the wealthy were left in poverty. Gentlemen, I will let Brother Frank take it from here."

There was applause as Frank remounted the stage. "Thank you, Brother Cyril. Now you may be inclined to think that we are up against a dead end in Canada, and we would be if it were not for one fortuitous fact—Colonel Reynolds had a daughter, and that daughter is still alive in Toronto, living among Toronto's elite in an old mansion." The membership let out a collective gasp, astounded at what they had heard. "We have operatives in Canada, but we must act quickly."

Chapter 9

Dixie Farm, Don Valley—1872

The stable boy led two beautiful Irish hunters from the stable to the cobblestone courtyard, one a sixteen-hand sorrel and the other a bay, smaller at fifteen hands. Colonel Reynolds took the reins of his favourite steed, the sorrel named Stonewall. "Where is his brass, James? The Reynolds plantation brass," inquired the colonel.

"It seems to be misplaced, sir, but it will show up."

"And where is my daughter? She is never on time."

"Emily seems to be misplaced as well, sir, but I won't guarantee you that she will show up."

No guarantee was needed. Twelve-year-old Emily came skipping down the cobblestones, happy as a lark. The colonel was overjoyed to see his carefree daughter, seemingly unscathed from all the upheaval and horrors that she had seen. He often worried that she may have missed her youth, but just the sight of her today dispelled that concern.

"Good morning, Father, good morning, James, good morning, Dolly."

"And what about Stonewall? Do you want to hurt the feelings of a loyal Confederate horse?" the colonel pretended to admonish.

"And good morning to you too, Stonewall," Emily gave the sorrel a pat on his muzzle.

"We have a lot of exploring to do, girl. This is all new country to us. We'll ride the river trail to where that small creek feeds into it. Then we'll come back on the other side and ride the fences in the west pasture. I think the cattle have broken through some of the rails, and if the Indians don't get us, we'll end the day at the mill pond."

"Indians don't scare me...Dolly can outrun anyone."

Father and daughter mounted up and cantered down the trail into a world that was similar in some ways to their South but so different in others. The valley was teeming with game: deer, fox, coyotes, and the occasional black bear. Trout and even salmon from the great lake downstream swam the river. Massive willows hung lazily over the banks, and a mix of pine, oak, and maple covered the hillsides that had not been cleared for pasture. The landscape was harsher than the bucolic scenes that the Southern family had been raised on but breathtaking just the same. The river flowed through the city about ten miles downstream, and as they progressed down the trail, signs of civilization became more frequent as they passed farms, mills, and abandoned pioneer log cabins. The landscape reminded the colonel of riding through Pennsylvania and the subsequent recurring nightmare of Gettysburg. He still rode with the subconscious vigilance of a soldier in foreign territory and had to constantly remind himself that he was no longer in a war zone. He longed for the day when he could ride relaxed again, like Emily.

As they reached the confluence of a small stream and the river, they dismounted. The colonel laid out his long, lanky body against the trunk of a tree while chewing on a sprig of grass. He kept a close eye on Emily at the water's edge. "How do you like your new home, Emily?"

"I like it just fine, Father," she replied, not entirely convincingly. "I sure like it a whole lot better than Savannah. I hated Savannah."

"Savannah was a casualty of the war. It was, and is, an occupied city, and occupiers are not known to be generous people, especially if they are Yanks," the colonel spat his sprig of grass into the dirt.

"I miss our plantation. Even though I was only four when we left, I still remember it well."

"So do I, Emily, but it is gone and we won't be getting it back. That's why I designed our new home after the plantation."

"But why did we have to leave the South, Father? Why could you not have built our new home in Sandersville?" she asked sadly.

"There are several reasons, my dear. First and foremost, I promised your mother, and I promised myself, that we would never live under Yankee rule. Some day you will understand." He paused to gather his thoughts. "It took me several years to get us set up in our new country, Canada. I had to leave you and your mother alone in Savannah, and for that I am very sorry."

"I understand, Father," she replied. She could feel his remorse.

Chapter 10
Aunt Emily's Story II, Rosedale, Toronto—May 1964

"You see, Billy, the barns that you play in—or should I say hide in—they were part of our farm a-way back. It was called the Dixie Farm as homage to the South. Father was going to call it the Dixie Plantation, but plantations had acquired such a negative connotation after the war that he decided against it."

"And the golf course clubhouse was your home?" Billy asked incredulously.

"That is correct, Billy," replied the old lady, clearly revelling in nostalgia. "It was designed as a replica of the old Reynolds plantation, a magnificent place."

"I've never seen a home that huge, and Dad never told me."

"That is because I never told him—it was so long ago—even before this century began. I just wanted to forget it because of what happened…" her voice trailed off.

Now Billy was hooked—he needed to know more. "Please tell me what happened."

"Then. Billy, I need to give you some more background," replied the old lady, starting to perk up again. "Life went very well in the first few years after we moved onto the farm. We raised cattle and bred horses…some of the finest in the country. Dolly and I were a common sight in the valley, just like you are today, only for different reasons," she smirked. "I loved working on the farm with the farmhands, and even Mammy came north with us, but the winter was very hard on her...she never got used to it."

"My parents cultivated a life that was very similar to what they had left behind on the plantation, with galas and balls and parties. Our laneway would be filled with buggies, most coming up from the city but some from neighbouring farms. I loved to watch them dance in the ballroom." The old lady began to drift off in her memories.

"But what was it that happened, Aunt Emily?"

"The curious thing about my parents' friends was that a lot of them were from the South. They had come to Canada to avoid the Yankees like us. And almost all the men folk were ex-Confederate soldiers, and high ranking, you know. My father was very close to a Major Josiah Evans, a wonderful man and my godfather."

"But what happened?" pleaded Billy.

"Not all the gatherings at Dixie Farm were so pleasant. Oftentimes only a group of men would come, sometimes in uniform, and they all looked very serious. Father would quickly shuffle them into the drawing room where they would stay for hours. Then they would leave without saying goodbye, and some weeks later, it would happen again. As these meetings carried on, shouting and anger became more and more common. I know because my bedroom was right above the drawing room. It was muffled, but I found that if I sat near the hearth, I could hear their voices more clearly." The old lady writhed in pain, overcome with great waves of emotion. Billy was wracked by pangs of empathy and guilt for pushing her to relive something very ugly.

She continued on. "Most of the arguments seemed to be about gold—gold bullion that was hidden—but I could never hear clearly enough. During their last meeting, the shouting was the worst I had ever heard it...it was something terrible." She began to sob. "The only thing that I heard distinctly was Father yell...saying that—" she paused, "that no one would be executed."

She was now crying profusely. "There seemed to be a struggle, and the whole lot of them stomped out of the drawing room and down towards the barns." The old lady paused for several minutes and seemed to regain her composure. She became very quiet and solemn, as if the worst of the storm had passed, but she was left battered. "Billy?"

"Yes, Aunt Emily," he muttered emotionally.

"That was the last day that I ever saw my father."

Chapter 11
The Meeting, Dixie Farm—1875

Colonel William Reynolds and Major Josiah Evans, both in full Confederate uniform, sat by the fire in the drawing room, shifting restlessly in their chairs.

"So how do we deal with O'Donnell, Colonel?"

"Major, there this only one way to deal with him and that is to expose him, which I intend to do. Problem is...I'm not sure that I trust the other two much more. They seem more concerned with the bullion than getting their country back. For now, I am the only one that needs to know where it is, and when the time is right, you will be the second to know. If this information gets into the wrong hands, then this whole operation won't be worth a pinch of coon shit."

"I have never had a problem with that, William," replied Evans.

The sound of boots on the verandah brought the colonel to his feet. Answering the door would normally be a function for the staff, but for these meetings he made sure that everyone had the night off. "Good evening, gentlemen," said the colonel, as he welcomed First Lieutenant Henry Barksdale of Alabama, Captain Andrew Lumsden of Virginia, and Sergeant Nathan O'Donnell of Alabama into his home.

Barksdale was a bit of a firecracker, a shoot-from-the-hip type of guy with no lack of courage but a great lack of scruples. Lumsden was cut from the same cloth but much more taciturn. O'Donnell was a bit rough around the edges and somewhat out of place among his higher-ranking colleagues. They all supposedly had two things in common: they refused to live under Yankee rule after the war, and they were dedicated to fomenting another armed insurrection that would free the South. Their dream was of a Confederate Foreign Legion, made up of the Confederate diasporas that had emerged after the war. All operations would be financed by gold bullion salvaged from the Southern treasury at the war's end.

"Sure is a damn sight nicer than when we used to meet in the barn during the war," commented Barksdale as they entered the drawing room.

"Yeah...and we don't have to wear sacks to get in," added Lumsden, which elicited a stifled chuckle. Except for O'Donnell, they were all veterans of the Southern spy ranks.

All but Colonel Reynolds took their seats. As a brandy bottle and box of cigars were passed around, a tension hung in the air that belied their pretense of comrades in arms. With a brandy snifter in one hand and a cigar in the other, the colonel sauntered over to the hearth. Every second of his silence heightened the apprehension in the room and spoke volumes about the seriousness of the business to come.

"Sergeant O'Donnell, of the Third Calvary Regiment, Alabama," said the Colonel. "Is that correct, sir?"

"That is correct, Colonel. Why do you ask?" replied Nathan O'Donnell.

"Got beat up pretty bad at Decatur...fought Hood through Georgia?"

"Yeah, that's right." O'Donnell's brandy glass slipped from his hand and shattered on the floor. Both Barksdale and Lumsden looked on with bewilderment.

"Where did the regiment surrender, sir?"

"Everyone knows that...we gave it up to Hood in Georgia," O'Donnell replied. He was sweating profusely. "I demand to know what this is all about," he added with belligerence.

"The Third surrendered in North Carolina, sir. I have contacts in the South that have informed me that they found the body of Sergeant Nathan O'Donnell in a shallow grave dug by the Yanks. No identification on him, but like most of the boys, but he had his name sewn into his uniform. You are an imposter, sir!" O'Donnell's hand leaped for his holster, but two six shooters pointed at his head by Barksdale and Lumsden, who had anticipated his move, dissuaded him.

"You low-down Yankee spying scum," growled Barksdale. "You know what we do with spies, we shoot em."

"That will be enough, Lieutenant," the colonel ordered. "I will decide what we do with him."

"They strung up two of our boys in New York and Buffalo...have you forgotten that, Colonel?" Lumsden sneered in disgust.

"You cannot spy on a country that does not exist, and the Confederate States of America does not exist and we are not in a state of war. I am not a spy, and I am acting only on my own accord," O'Donnell pleaded.

"You are a spy, and we are going to execute you," Barksdale shot back.

"There will be no execution!" the colonel yelled. Pandemonium broke out. Barksdale and Lumsden, guns still out, grabbed O'Donnell and started dragging him to the door. The colonel and Major Evans leaped to his defense only to find themselves staring down the barrel of a gun.

"Everybody outside. I'm in charge now," Barksdale ordered. Barksdale and Lumsden dragged O'Donnell, now white as a ghost, down the verandah steps while keeping one revolver on the colonel and the major.

"Colonel, we no longer report to you, and I'm sick of you keeping your own little treasure. That gold belongs to all of us," Barksdale said. "Let's take them down to the barn, Captain." No one in the colonel's family or among his staff knew anything about the secret room, nor did they know the history of the farm during wartime; the need-to-know rule still applied.

The coal oil lamps cast an eerie, flickering glow on the walls of the old hideaway, which had not seen any occupants since the end of the war. The colonel and Major Evans were held at gunpoint by Lumsden under the tattered Rebel flag. Barksdale lined O'Donnell up against the wall to their left. He began to recite a list of charges against the imposter to try and give the whole morbid affair a semblance of justice being served—or at least to fool himself that this was not a summary execution.

"And therefore I find you guilty as charged and sentence you to death by firing squad." He raised his pistol.

"Barksdale, you are committing murder!" the colonel screamed as he made a courageous attempt to stop the atrocity. Barksdale and Lumsden fired simultaneously. The colonel fell to the floor holding his stomach, and the man who was O'Donnell collapsed with a hole in his forehead. The two gunmen and Major Evans stood frozen in horror at the sight. All three men had killed and seen their share of death, but an execution had a special level of evil about it, even to the perpetrator.

"Leave them here; no one will ever find them," Lumsden finally said. "And Major Evans, you are now our prisoner and I would advise you to remember where the bullion is hidden." Lumsden had ice water in his veins.

Chapter 12

Aunt Emily's Story III, Rosedale, Toronto—June 1964

Billy skipped up the stairs of the old mansion as if he lived there. It was no longer the foreboding place that made his skin crawl just a few short weeks ago. Visiting the old lady on his own gave him a sense of pride in his new-found independence, like he was no longer just a kid.

"Good day, Aunt Emily, and how are you on this fine day?" he asked, taking the words right out of his father's mouth.

The old lady gave a slight smirk, amused at her juvenile friend's new-found maturity. "Why, I am fine, Master Billy. And you are the same, I trust?"

"I am fine too, Aunt Emily...but I am a little scared."

"And why would that be, Billy?"

"Well, Paintie was wondering about me coming to visit you without my dad. I'm scared that he might be mad if he finds out."

"Leave Paintie to me, Billy," she reassured him, "but this must be the last time that we meet without your father. Bert is a fine man, and I don't feel right about going behind his back. The things that I tell you are our secret."

"Sure, Aunt Emily."

"On your last visit, I was quite upset. I apologize, but unfortunately the years have not diminished the pain." She paused. "I just do not know why Father left me...was it something to do with the gold? I just don't know, and I *need* to know. Billy...I don't want to die without an explanation."

"I really understand, Aunt Emily. Sometimes I wonder what I would do if my dad died, and I can't even think about it." Billy instinctively placed his hand on the old lady's.

"After Father disappeared, Mother's health took a turn for the worse; she became very depressed. We stayed on with the farm for a few more years...until they declared him officially dead, and then we sold out and moved to the city—to this house, to be exact."

She laid her head back and remained silent for several minutes. "Mother passed away soon after...she had lost all interest in living. When they settled the estate business, I inherited everything—everything except happiness, that is. Sometimes I wish that I had been born into a working-class family. I used to envy the children of our staff; they seemed so much happier than me. Being born at the eclipse of the plantation era and on the eve of a war...I wouldn't wish it on my worst enemy."

Billy felt that he had an obligation to console her somehow, but it was not in his twelve-year-old repertoire. "I am very sorry," he blurted out sincerely, mimicking a line that he had heard in a movie.

She smiled—the first time he had seen her smile—appreciating his honest sentiments. "Billy, you are a brave, adventuresome boy, and I do not expect that anything I say will keep you from returning to that secret passageway that you stumbled on—but be very careful—the farm has secrets."

"What do you mean?"

"Major Evans was my father's closest friend and confidante. A year after my father disappeared, the major's body was found washed up on the shores of the lake. He had been murdered. Billy, these things happen for a reason...there is an ugly secret, and it has not died with the passing of the years. In the last few months, I have received phone calls. They were from a man who purported to be from the South...probably saying what he thought that I wanted to hear...a confidence man. He said that he had read about my father and that he was a great fan of his, and he went on and on in this vein, all the while trying to steer the conversation towards a secret that supposedly we both shared. You do not get to be one-hundred-and-four years old without learning a thing or two about people, and I could smell a con man with ulterior motives right away, so I bade him good day. The next call was not so pleasant, and he got right to the point. He said that I had an obligation to the South to tell him where the treasure was hidden. I hung up on him."

"Why don't you tell the police?" Billy asked.

"Because, Billy, the police cannot investigate every prank phone call, and that may be just what this is. If my father was involved in something, I do not want his good name besmirched after all these years." The old lady's story seemed surreal to Billy, like a mystery he had seen on TV. But the reality of it gave him chills and an adrenalin rush of adventure.

Chapter 13

School's Out, Don Mills—
June 27th, 1964

Sally Olmstead laid out the beach towel on the grass of her back lawn, tuned in her transistor radio to the local AM rock and roll station, then laid back with her red Hollywood sunglasses on, to soak up the sun. School was out, and the summer had officially started. Her home backed onto the valley, just a few doors away from the Parkers', where the infamous Billy lived. Billy had been her good buddy for years, but now as they both were on the verge of teenagehood, she was finding him just a little too juvenile. Her childhood crush on him was wearing thin, and she knew that there was no future in a guy who spent all his spare time running through the valley with his delinquent buddy, Pete. She wondered, in her condescending way, if he would ever grow up.

Unfortunately for Billy, he was about to confirm all her worst beliefs about him, which he excelled at doing. Just as Sally was getting settled into a state of solar bliss, her reverie was shattered by a ruckus coming from the valley's slope leading up to her house. Shortly thereafter, one head appeared, followed by another, rising from the embankment, both in a state of sheer panic and in a flat-out run. Neither Billy nor Pete paid the slightest attention to her as they raced by and dove headlong into a bed of thick shrubs alongside of her house.

"Another day in the valley, boys?" Sally lackadaisically raised her sunglasses to peer at the shrubbery.

"Sal...shut up...they're after us!"

Some things never change, she thought to herself as two apoplectic golf course workers crested the hill in a dead run. "You seen two punks run by here?"

Billy and Pete lay paralyzed in the bushes, praying that Sally would back them up, just this time. Billy was not so confident about Sally these days—she was not the girl she used to be. It was hard to figure. "They went that way," she replied, pointing to the street. With nary a thank you or an acknowledgement, the two workers were off and running again.

"Thanks, Sal," Billy said as the pair re-emerged from the bushes.

"You're a pal, Sal," Pete chuckled, amused at his poetry.

Sally was not amused by these two guys still living their childhood. To Billy and Pete, she was still tomboy Sal, and they showed no interest in the girl that she had developed into. *Their loss,* she thought.

The boys sauntered down the railway tracks, trying to balance on the rails as they headed to Bond Park, looking for a pickup game of ball. They had two months of glorious, lazy, hazy days of summer ahead of them and enough energy to launch a rocket.

"Now I remember," Billy blurted out for no apparent reason.

"Remember what?" Pete asked.

"I've seen one of those workies before."

"So what...I've seen them all before."

"No, not here in the valley...he was the gardener at Aunt Emily's place."

"Yeah, so what?" Pete was thoroughly engaged in walking the rail.

Billy was now struggling with the coincidence that the same guy would show up in two different locations. Or was it a coincidence? He thought back to his last visit with Aunt Emily and about the threatening phone calls she had received.

A few miles down the track, the horn of a freight train let loose as it wound its way through the valley. There was always something about an approaching train that instantly raised the excitement level with the pair; a rush of adrenalin that came no matter how many freights passed by them. They both instinctively dove for the brush along the ballast to keep out of sight. From experience they knew that some trains carried railway police looking for kids like Billy and Pete who had the bad habit of hopping freights. A freight train could not develop much speed as it snaked through the valley, and any kid worth his salt could keep up. Normally the engineer would not throttle up until he passed Bond Park, where there was a railway yard, so some guys would use the train as a free ride to the ball park.

Billy and Pete lay just feet from the track as the train approached, with heads down and hearts pounding out of their chests. As the locomotive bore down on them, it was a moment of sheer terror and, paradoxically, sheer bliss. The time to spring into action was imminent. Their adrenalin peaked as the first engine passed by them and gave them that spark of energy to begin their sprint alongside the cars. Running on the ballast while concentrating on the passing ladders was not easy, and the occasional thought about the guy at school who had a hook where his hand used to be did not help. Billy watched his buddy successfully commit to a ladder and instantly get accelerated to train speed and then he made the leap himself. Billy always felt an enormous surge of relief and accomplishment as he got a firm grip on the ladder and pulled himself up—as if he had beaten fate again.

Normally the rest of the trip would be a pleasant ride hanging off the ladder to Bond Park, with that wonderful feeling of just having survived a game of Russian roulette. But today was different. With a blast of black exhaust, the engines started to throttle up, well short of Bond Park. This would be the boys' last chance to hit the ground running without becoming a tumbling mass of limbs. With both Billy and Pete at opposite ends of a flat car, each looking for some sort of decision from the other, the point of no return passed them by. Fortunately for the pair, they had boarded a flat car with half walls that could easily be climbed, and the ride to their unknown destination would be more or less comfortable—at least more comfortable than hanging off ladders.

"What'll we do now?" Pete asked as they met in the centre of the car. That was a question that they frequently asked each other while going from one self-imposed crisis to the next, and it was one that neither of them ever had an answer for. Billy attempted to compose himself but had little success. A trace of a smirk appeared on his face. Pete looked away, trying to retain an air of seriousness at their predicament, but he could not fight a smile. All it took was a short giggle from Billy to trigger a mutual eruption of pure, joyful, ecstatic laughter that went on well after the freight had left the city's limits. Gallows humour was always the best.

Things could have been worse. It was a beautiful summer's day, and the boys were getting a free tour of the countryside while on route to who knew where. They leaned up against the wall of the freight car, watching the clouds scuttle by and occasionally standing up to see if they recognized anything. At that point, it did not actually matter anymore; the chances of getting home for dinner were zero, and the chances of getting home that night were slim.

"Pete...remember when I told you about that secret door?" Billy asked.

"Yeah, and I haven't told anyone, like I promised."

"We've got to go back there with flashlights...find out where it goes."

"Won't be doing it today, and if we don't get home tonight, I'll be seeing a lot of my bedroom for the next few weeks."

"That makes two of us." Billy shook his head and sighed.

The afternoon was now slipping into evening, and as the temperature dropped, the free ride was now much less pleasant. The freight slowed down through a few towns but never slow enough to get off without extensive personal damage. Finally in the twilight of the evening, the train entered a rail yard and the cars banged together like dominoes as the engineer applied the brakes. Billy and Pete knew that it was time to go, and they leaped off, hitting the ground in a dead run, never looking back until they were clear of the yard. At the entrance to the yard, they walked past a large railway sign that read "North Bay."

"Ho-l-y crap, Billy! You know how far away North Bay is?"

"We're screwed...my old man's gonna kill me." Billy ignored the question and plodded on resolutely. "Let's find a phone booth."

All Pete could hear from outside the phone booth was a series of "but Dad" and parts of Billy's lame excuse. It would be at least three hours before a livid Bert Parker could have the Pontiac pulling into North Bay, but it would still be a much better three hours for the boys than the ride home.

Chapter 14

Grounded, Don Mills—July 1964

Billy laid out the beach towel on the fresh cut grass of the back lawn, took off his beat up T-shirt, put on his dad's aviator sunglasses, and laid back, waiting for whatever it was that Sally found so appealing about sunbathing. For the life of him, he could not see what the attraction was, but Sally Olmstead spent all day every day doing it, so maybe he was missing something. It was not like he had a lot of options, and with four days left on his sentence, it was worth a try.

The thought occurred to him that maybe this was the ideal time to show Sally his other, more mature side; after all, he even had a book to read. Billy climbed up three rungs of the fence and took a gander over two backyards to see Sally hard at another day of sunbathing. "Hey, Sal."

With a desultory roll to her side, she lifted up her sunglasses in her best starlet manner to see who was bothering her. "Yes, Billy?"

"Come on over...I'm sunbathing too."

"You come over here."

Billy didn't want to tell her that he'd been grounded because that was not something that happened to mature guys, so he had to find some sort of attraction. "I'm making Kool-Aid." Billy figured that was the hook that no girl could refuse, and he was right, she started breaking camp and heading in his direction.

The day was starting to look up for Billy—he had some company, and for the first time, he started to notice that Sally was turning into a pretty nice-looking girl.

Arriving in his backyard, Sally surveyed Billy's body from head to foot. Her slight smirk made Billy feel very uncomfortable. "You look weird."

"Why?" Billy looked like a deflated balloon.

"Because your arms are brown and the rest of you is lily white."

Billy had never been self-conscious about his appearance before; it had never even been on his radar. With one cutting blow, Sally had sent him careening into that adult world of self-consciousness, where there was no turning back.

"You're reading a book?" Sally gave a look of mock incredulity.

Her observation gave Billy a chance for redemption— a chance to show that he was a book reading kind of guy. "Yeah," he replied proudly. "It's called *Gone with the Wind*. It's about the Civil War, the South, plantations, all that kind of stuff. My mom recommended it because I wanted to find out more about that stuff. It's about a thousand pages long and—"

"Billy, who's that?" Sally interrupted him, looking in the direction of the valley. Just beyond the back fence, behind the underbrush was a half-shaved, scruffy man peering ominously in their direction. Billy recognized him instantly. It was the same workie that he had seen in Aunt Emily's yard and who he had narrowly escaped from the previous week.

Enraged at this voyeur who seemed to keep popping into his life, Billy ran screaming towards the back fence.

"Get out of here, you pervert!" By the time he had reached the fence, there was no sign of the intruder.

In his show of rage and bravado, Billy in one fell swoop had inadvertently changed his image in the eyes of Sally from a boy to a courageous young warrior, and this caused no small tug on her heart strings.

"Billy, that was great...I didn't know you were like that," Sally swooned. She left for the afternoon with a promise to sunbathe with him anytime he wanted.

Billy was feeling pretty good about himself as he began the first chapters of *Gone with the Wind*. The buggies and riders were coming down the oak-lined laneway of Tara for the big social event of the year. The war drums were beating, and the confidence and bravado of the South's finest was pervasive. The young men fawned over a stunning Scarlett O'Hara, who treated most of them with indifference. Billy, in his crisp, grey uniform, rode down the laneway on his favourite black stallion. As he dismounted and the servant took his horse, he spotted Emily seated on the verandah looking very coy. Her long black hair flowed onto her blue velvet hoop skirt. Her radiant blue eyes were accentuated by a flawless peaches-and-cream complexion. He removed his white gauntlets as he climbed the stairs, his boots echoing crisply off each step. As he approached her, she looked to him with pleading eyes. "Billy, you must help me...help me to find Daddy...please, Billy," she begged.

"Billy! Wake up!" Barb Parker stood over her snoozing son, shaking her head in disgust. "You've laid out that towel over fresh cut grass, and I'll never get the stains out...honestly, Billy." He opened his eyes and surveyed the real world, wishing he was back at Tara.

Chapter 15

The Swing, Don Valley, July 1964

The big, old willow tree clung to the embankment of the river, about ten feet above the swimming hole. Every year its hold became more tenuous as weather eroded the bank and more exposed roots gave up their grip on the earth. No one knew who had originally tied the thick, old rope to one of the willow's larger branches, which hung conveniently over the river. It was as if the old tree had just come equipped with a rope and tire dangling from it. Whoever it was could take credit for scores of bruises, broken bones, and hours of entertainment for generations of the Don Valley neighbourhood kids.

The swimming hole was kind of a no man's land, neutral territory for the all the rival groups that met there. There was sort of an unwritten rule that all animosities should be left behind when you arrived at the swing, but if you met at the trail going there, that was different. Everyone had a common interest at the swing.

The beauty of the swing was that it was simple and exciting. One guy would start out sitting in the tire, which gave him the security of never falling off, but also made it impossible to get off until all others had de-boarded. Each time the pendulum made its trip back to the bank, a guy would have to make a split second decision whether or not to board, and erring on the side of caution was not the strong point of most young guys. Most would inevitably commit to the ride across the river with a death grip on anything solid. More and more boarding parties (swing vernacular) would grab to whatever was left available to cling to. When things got desperate and the visible rope disappeared, this usually meant hanging onto someone's head, arm, shoulders, or even belt. Inevitably someone would not make the round trip and would take a ten foot plunge into the shallow swimming hole.

After he had his fill of the action, Billy sat on a log watching his buddy Pete slowly lose his grip on the return swing of the rope and take the plummet onto the water cushioned, rocks below. It was always amusing to watch someone else take the fall. Pete clambered up the embankment, wet but relatively unscathed, and took a seat beside Billy.

"Nice one," Billy said with a smirk and obvious lack of sympathy.

"Shut up...I almost killed myself. Some idiot was rippin my head off."

Billy giggled with amusement. "You still in for tomorrow?" he asked.

"Maybe, maybe not," Pete replied, still smarting over his friend's enjoyment of his fall.

"Why not?"

"Because every time I do something with you, I end up grounded for a week...but yeah, I'm in."

"Good. Bring a flashlight with good batteries. We leave at zero eight hundred, before the course gets crowded," Billy said using military lingo that he had heard on *Combat*, the World War II television show.

"Roger—Wilco," Pete replied, mocking his friend.

Chapter 16

The Barns, Don Valley—July 1964

The boys lay in the waist-high grass on the ridge, overlooking the barns in the valley below. Both had their war surplus rucksacks on, and Billy scanned the scene with a pair of binoculars that he had borrowed to "bird watch" from his astounded mother. At this time of the morning, golfers were still scarce, but the workies were busy firing up tractors and lawn mowers for their morning chores. The equipment clattered over the narrow cobblestone laneways between the barns. From experience, both Billy and Pete knew that the place would soon clear out except for a few stragglers left behind to work on the machinery. These were the ones that they had to watch out for.

"First we head for that bunch of trees, then when it's all clear, we make a run for the corner of the big barn," Billy barked the orders with military precision. It was always inevitable that the pair would make their misadventures into a World War II military operation. They were in Italy, the workies were the Germans, and the tractors were tanks. It just added to the excitement.

Their first sprint took them to cover behind a copse of trees at the bottom of the valley. The next leg was a traverse across a wide open fairway to the barns. This one was a crapshoot—there was no telling when the enemy would appear.

Billy and Pete took off with rucksacks flying, hearts pounding, and legs just a blur of motion. A twelve-year-old kid's greatest assets were his legs.

They reached the complex of barns unseen, and now it was a matter of zigzagging across the cobblestone laneway, like the soldiers did on TV, until they reached the old horse stable. Billy and Pete, agile as cats, glided through the stable door unseen, both beaming a satisfied smile. They had outwitted the Germans once again.

Billy led the way through the maze of stalls to the room at the end of the alleyway. "I ran into this room and pulled on this leg here to try and get underneath the bench," Billy explained, reliving his last visit to the tack room. He hauled back on the support, which pulled freely like a lever, and as it rotated, a panel began to open up in the wall.

"H-o-l-y crap," Pete's jaw seemed to drop all the way to his chest.

"I told ya, Pete...I told ya! Get your flashlight." With the wall panel fully open now, they nervously shone their lights into what seemed like an abyss. Just beyond the wall panel, they encountered a short set of steps leading to a narrow passageway. Billy inched his way down the staircase, reluctantly shining his light down the passage, afraid of what it might reveal lurking in the darkness.

"Pete, start talkin' to me and keep talkin'...this gives me the creeps," Billy walked slowly, deliberately—like he did in the House of Horrors at the Exhibition.

"This is really weird, Billy...I think I saw this in a horror movie," replied Pete, his usual bravado now absent. As they progressed in a slow motion, lock step, the darkness closed in behind them. The passageway was lined with planking and had dusty coal-oil lamps fastened to its walls.

The air had a musty, stale odour that made their nostrils cringe with protest.

"We're coming to a door," Billy said nervously. They inched towards the entrance of a room. Billy held them up at the door, with Pete practically climbing up his back. He slowly panned his light around the walls. There was a large table in the centre of the room with chairs scattered randomly around it. On the end wall, the tattered remains of a flag hung tenuously on nails. On the wall directly across from the door was a black chalkboard with some esoteric scrawling left on it.

"Billy...what's that?" Pete's voice was frozen in a monotone. His flashlight was directed on the soles of a pair of tall, leather boots sprawled on the floor and just visible from under the table. They crept around the end of the table, fighting panic and the overwhelming desire to flee.

"Oh God! Oh God! Oh God!" Billy recited like some sort of mantra. His terror mounted in lock step with the beam of his flashlight as it slowly made its way up the pant leg tucked into the boot. It felt just like that scene in the horror movies—the scene just before all hell breaks loose. Billy was overwhelmed with the urge to charge out of there and out of the valley, but some irresistible force held him captive. Pete clung to him with a death grip.

Pete let out a prolonged, shrill scream that reverberated around the walls. The uniformed skeleton lay sprawled on the floor. The skull stared back at the two interlopers both paralyzed with shock, fixated on the grisly sight. For several minutes, they stood silently staring, their brains madly scrambling to find an explanation for the scene before them.

"I've never even seen a body before...and that's not even a body, it's a skeleton," Pete stammered in disbelief.

"Me neither."

After the crescendo of sheer terror had drained every ounce of adrenalin from their bodies, the boys regained some composure.

"Billy, look at this," Pete said, as he shone his light around the end of the room beneath the tattered flag.

"Jesus, not another one," replied Billy staring at the clothed skeleton illuminated by Pete.

"And look at the hole in his forehead...Billy, I think these guys were murdered. We've got to tell the cops."

Billy, lost in thought, ignored his friend's comments and stared in fascination at the floor in front of him. "Pete...I know who this guy is."

"What are you talking about?"

"Look at the writing on the floor beside him," Billy replied. Beside the skeleton wearing a Confederate uniform was a clearly discernible message written in chalk:

Emily Susannah
I am so sorry I love you both
look in the pond for

The message trailed off uncompleted.

"This is Colonel William Reynolds of the Confederate army." Billy stood at attention and saluted. He felt a wave of respect and reverence for the fallen soldier.

Pete shook his head in bewilderment. "I don't know what you're talking about, but let's get out of here and tell somebody."

"Pete...you've got to promise me one thing," Billy asked with a pronounced intensity, "you can't tell anyone yet. I have a job to do. I'll explain later."

"This is getting weirder all the time...I just want to get out of here," Pete said as he headed towards the door.

Billy followed but suddenly stopped short. "Pete, wait a second." He returned to the colonel's side. The significance of the last broken sentence of the scrawled message suddenly became clear to him. With the toe of his shoe, he erased the last line of the chalk message—"look in the pond for."

Chapter 17

The Break-in,
Rosedale, Toronto—July 1964

Chuck stood impatiently in the phone booth at the precise time of the planned call. A businessman, lined up outside of the booth, rapped on the glass doors when he saw that Chuck was making no attempt to use the phone. One glare from Chuck dissuaded him from pursuing the matter. Chuck had the distinct look of an ex-convict—which he was—and the personality of a deranged lunatic.

The phone finally rang, several minutes past the prescribed time. "Chuck, this is Frank Mackay."

"Yeah, I know who you are. Who else is going to be calling this phone booth? You're late."

Frank Mackay hesitated to calm himself. As much as he wanted to, he could not afford to offend his Canadian operative. "We discussed the situation at the meeting yesterday. It was unanimous that we take more aggressive action," Mackay said.

"So what's that mean?"

"It means that you have to get into the old girl's house and see what you can find or what she can tell you. She's not going to be around much longer." Chuck went silent, thinking about what was just asked of him. "Chuck...you still there?"

"Yeah, I'm still here...and I'll get in the house...but it's gonna cost ya."

"Good man," Mackay replied, "and what about the kid?"

"I've been watching him, and I'm sure he knows something…I'm not through with him yet."

♦ ♦ ♦

Paintie felt a cold draft coming from the downstairs parlour, and as she entered the room she could see the sheers covering the bay window billowing gracefully in the breeze. An open window was a bit disconcerting, since normally she was the only person in the house besides Miss Emily. But she could have forgotten, she thought. As she closed the open window, her explanation became much less plausible. The broken pane of glass sent a cold chill of fear through her body.

She had little time to contemplate the situation as a cloth-covered hand the size of a baseball glove covered her nose and mouth. Her struggle slowly waned, and she slipped into unconsciousness as the foul smell of chloroform permeated her nostrils.

Emily's hearing had a very limited range, and normally people would be at the foot of her bed before they were audible to her. But what she lacked in hearing she made up for with a well-developed sixth sense that could pick up a not-so-friendly visitor. She was like a dog that could always discern friend or foe from behind a door. And today she sensed an unwelcome visitor.

"Paintie, is that you?" She paused but there was only silence. "Bert, is that you? There was still no answer. Emily struggled to raise her bedridden body from the mattress. "I demand that you identify yourself!"

"Hello, Emily." She recognized the voice from the threatening phone call. Her hands scrambled for the bedside telephone. "The phone won't work with a broken cord, Emily." The intruder in a calm but terrorizing voice seemed to take great pleasure in her rising panic.

"What do you want with me?" she demanded.

"I want to know where I can find the little gift that your father left you, Emily...you know what I am talking about."

Like her mother, Emily came from stern stuff and was not easily intimidated. She could make up for over-whelming odds against her with an iron bar for a backbone. "My father did give me gift, and I would like to show it to you." Her panic was now gone—replaced by a confident smirk. The intruder's look of self-satisfaction quickly turned to horror as she pulled a palm-sized, .25 calibre Browning pistol out from under the covers. She fired it in the direction of the voice, and the intruder fell back holding his right arm. Two more quick rounds sent him fleeing down the hallway, stumbling down the stairs and into a dead run out onto the street. Chuck had let his guard down around the wrong person. He had known that she was bedridden and blind but underestimated the vigour that a one-hundred-and-four year old Southern belle could muster.

Chapter 18

The Confession, Rosedale—July 1964

"Look, Billy, Aunt Emily and Paintie have gone through a horrendous experience, and we will have to be very gentle with them," Bert cautioned his son on their way to 99 Castle Frank Road.

"What happened?" Billy asked.

"Some low down, despicable coward broke into their house, tied up Paintie, and started rifling through Aunt Emily's bedroom, probably looking for jewellery."

No he wasn't, Billy thought.

"Aunt Emily told police that she slept through the whole thing, which is a godsend. It would have scared her half to death if she had known he was in her room." Billy vacillated between fear and anger. Fear because he knew that the whole situation had escalated now and he had managed to get himself right in the middle of it and anger at that creep-workie he knew was somehow involved. But today he had a duty to perform, and he intended to do it regardless of the consequences.

"It's just Billy and Bert, Aunt Emily," Bert announced, assuming that she would be wary of strangers. "We're really sorry about what you and Paintie had to go through with that intruder...they'll get the guy."

"Hello Billy, hello Bert," she replied, with no sign of distress over the incident. "Somehow I do not think that he will be back. And how was your week, Billy?" Bert was amazed at her equanimity.

"It...it was really good, Aunt Emily," Billy seemed to stumble on his words. There was an awkward silence as both Emily and Bert assumed that he would expand on that. "I...I have something to tell you," Billy said with great diffidence.

"Well, go ahead, Billy," she replied. Bert looked askance at his son—his curiosity piqued.

Billy hesitated again. "Your father...I found your father," he blurted out.

"Billy! What?" Bert's jaw dropped open in shock.

"He was dead, Aunt Emily—him and another guy—in a secret hideaway on the farm."

"You will have to excuse us, Aunt Emily. I don't know what has come over Billy."

"No! I have to finish," Billy pleaded, tears running down his cheeks.

"Please let him finish, Bert!" she asked emotionally.

"Pete and I think that they were murdered...and he had his uniform on." Billy was openly bawling now. "He left a note for you, Aunt Emily...he wrote it on the floor...it said...it said...'Emily…Susannah...I am so sorry...I love you both.'" Billy buried his head into the bed, and Emily ran her hand through his hair as they both wept. Bert surveyed the scene in a state of shell-shocked disbelief. It took several minutes to gather his wits.

"Thank you, Billy...thank you so much." Tears of joy streamed down her face. With both hands on Billy's shoulders, Bert gently guided him out of the room—this was not a time for anger. The profound effect that Billy had on the old lady transcended whatever mischief that he had been up to. He was proud of Billy.

Billy and his dad sat in the Pontiac, parked in a school-yard parking lot as Billy recounted every detail of his story— every detail except one: the cryptic message that he had erased. "Billy, we are going down to the police station now and you must repeat everything that you said to me, okay?"

"Okay, Dad."

Chapter 19
Billy's Peril

Toronto Telegram
Tuesday, July 7th, 1964
BOYS FIND TWO SKELETONS

Last week, two Don Mills boys discovered a secret room with two skeletons in it at the Dixie Golf and Country Club. The room was built underground off an old stable, but its purpose is still unknown. Police believe that one of the skeletons was that of Colonel William Reynolds, who had owned the Dixie Farm in the late 1800s and had disappeared in 1875. The boys were obviously trespassing, but police do not intend to press....

♦ ♦ ♦

With his right arm in a sling, Chuck had to use his left hand to put change into the slot and turn the rotary dialler on the pay phone. The phone kept slipping from between his right shoulder and his ear. Chuck was frustrated and in pain. People passing by on the sidewalk gave a wide berth to the guy cursing, kicking, and swearing in the phone booth. By the time his collect call was accepted by Frank Mackay in Georgia, he was in a very ugly mood.

"No more of your bright ideas, Mackay...that crazy old broad winged me in the arm and then parted my hair with another one."

"Why, she's a good Georgia girl, Chuck. I should have warned you," Mackay replied, a touch amused.

"Damn right ya shoulda!"

"Okay, Chuck, calm down. We're sending you up some money as well as some qualified help. Where do we go from here?"

"The old girl is out of the question...they'll be arresting everything that moves on her property, including the squirrels. But that kid knows something. I watched him visit her alone a couple of times, and now he miraculously discovers her old man's body...no coincidence."

"He discovered Colonel Reynolds' body?" Mackay asked incredulously.

"That's right...haven't you read the papers?"

"We're not in Canada, Chuck. We'll have to see that the colonel gets a good Rebel funeral."

"To hell with the colonel!" Chuck was getting flustered. "He's just a pile of bones. I'm going after the kid, his buddy, and maybe even his girlfriend."

"Chuck—nobody gets hurt, okay?" Mackay asked. He worried about his loose cannon operative.

"We'll see."

Chapter 20

Grounded II, Don Mills—July 1964

Billy laid out the towel meticulously on the back lawn, making sure that there was no cut grass underneath it. He was serving the second week of an extended two-week sentence. Every day he would phone his buddy Pete—who spent most days in his bedroom reading comics—to commiserate. Every day, Pete would emphatically tell Billy that he would never follow him into the valley again for as long as he lived. Billy knew that this threat would last right up to the day of Pete's release and then it would be promptly forgotten, which was good because Billy was already planning their next mission.

"Doing time, Billy?" Sally asked as she popped her head above his back gate.

"Yeah, I guess," he replied sullenly. There was no hiding it this time. Billy was now a bit of a celebrity in the neighbourhood, and Sally needed no coaxing to join him in his backyard compound.

"Everybody's talking about you and Pete. What was it like to see those skeletons?"

"It was really creepy...we were really scared." Billy pondered his answer for a second. "Well, not that scared." He puffed out his chest a little.

"What will you guys do next?" Sally pondered, "I wish my life was as exciting as yours." Just the mention of a possible next escapade sent Billy's spirits soaring from the doldrums of the life he was presently living.

"If I do everything right for the next couple of days, then Mom and Dad are going to let us have our campout this Saturday night," he said, suddenly perking up.

"You mean the one where you pretend that you are good little Boy Scouts sitting around the campfire?" Sally replied.

"What do ya mean?"

"I mean that after you pitch the tents, make the fire, and all that Boy Scout stuff, you just sit around the fire waiting for your parents' bedroom light to go out. And then you sneak out and do whatever it is that you do in the middle of the night."

"How'd you know that?" Billy demanded defensively.

"Because I can see perfectly from my bedroom window, that's how." Sally was enjoying being in the driver's seat.

Billy was looking a bit defeated now—he knew that she had the power if she felt like wielding it. "Promise you won't tell?" His puffed out chest sunk reluctantly.

"I promise," she replied, heading for the gate, "for now."

♦ ♦ ♦

The backyard campout was becoming a bit of a tradition with Billy and his friends, and it was one of the few extracurricular activities that most of their parents fully endorsed. It had that Norman Rockwell feel to it with tents, sleeping bags, campfires, and all the trappings that an ideal boyhood should have. Watching Billy and his friends embrace such a wholesome pursuit warmed Bert and Barb Parker's hearts. All was well with modern boyhood, they thought, settling into a contented slumber. The reality of modern boyhood set in about one-half hour after their bedroom light extinguished for the night.

There were three tents set up in Billy's backyard, with two guys to a tent. The agenda for the evening was set out long before darkness set in. Four of the campers had plans to spend the night touring the neighbourhood—touring the neighbourhood on borrowed transportation. A few streets over, Lenny Coutts, while doing his paper route, had watched a guy start up his Lambretta motor scooter, which he kept in the carport. This was fairly mundane operation to watch, except for one important thing—the Lambretta did not require an ignition key. All that Lenny and Dave Walters had to do was quietly wheel the motor scooter down the driveway, and they had their ride for the night. Driving the machine was kind of like on-the-job training or flying your first solo before anyone had explained the controls. But that did not faze them in the least.

The other pair—Wally Nelson and Brad Crowthers—had their hearts set on a neat little go-cart powered by a 3.5 horsepower Briggs and Stratton engine that belonged to Danny Smith and was also conveniently parked in a carport. The plan was for the foursome to meet in the schoolyard and set their night's itinerary from there.

Billy and Pete, as far as everyone knew, were going to the golf course to see about borrowing a golf cart for the night. It did not strike any of the guys as terribly unusual that they were bringing along a hacksaw and flashlights for the operation.

According to plan, just before sunup, the Lambretta, the go-cart, and the golf cart would be returned to their rightful owners and the six Boy Scouts would be back in the tents with nobody being the wiser.

Chapter 21

The Mill Pond,
Don Valley—July 1964

Billy and Pete hopped the back fence heading for the valley, unaware that they had company. As they made their way down the hillside, Billy glanced back and froze in his tracks. Ten yards behind them there was a silhouette following them down the hill. By now, Pete had seen it as well and was staring aghast at the approaching form.

"Hi Billy...hi Pete." Sally pranced down the hill as if this were just another routine daytime greeting.

"Sally, what're you doin' here?" Billy asked.

"I'm goin' with you guys. I wanna have some fun too."

"Sally, you can't, this is gonna be dangerous," Pete piped in, trying to scare her off.

"Then that's even better." She was not being deterred.

"No way, Sal...no way are you comin' with us," Billy said, drawing a line in the sand.

"Remember that promise I gave you the other day, Billy?"

Billy thought back, knowing where she was going. "Yeah, I remember."

"Then I might break it."

"That's not fair!"

"Then let's get going."

Billy gave a perplexed look at Pete, who threw up his hands and rolled his eyes in mock resignation. "Okay...let's go," they said in unison.

The golf course had a mystical atmosphere after midnight, and walking down it was a pleasant experience—especially since there was no one chasing them for a change. As the three strolled towards the barns, Billy explained the details of the operation. "I thought about it and I thought about it and then I finally understood...when Colonel Reynolds wrote 'look in the pond,' he meant the old mill pond...just up from the barns."

"Look in the pond for what?" Sally asked.

"For gold, Sal—Billy hasn't explained that part yet," Pete replied.

"Are you kidding me? Buried treasure!" Sally was incredulous.

"If it's in the pond, how are we supposed to get it?" Pete asked.

"I scouted it out. In the middle of the dam, there's a door where the water flows out. The door has this valve sort of thing made out of rusty metal, and I figured out how it works. There's this wheel with a bunch of gears, and when you turn it, this door starts to open up."

"This is crazy...are you guys for real?" Sally had severely underestimated the scope of their operation.

"So when you turn the wheel, the door opens, the water starts to flow out and the pond empties...it's simple."

"And then we just walk down and grab the treasure...you're a smart guy, Billy," replied Pete. "How come you're so dumb in school?"

"Only problem is there's a padlock on the wheel, but this hacksaw will fix that."

The old mill pond was about fifty yards wide and a couple of hundred long. What remained of the mill's foundation was still protruding from one shore and was connected to the dam. Each end of the dam was protected by a chain link fence topped with barbed wire. Clambering over a barbed wire fence took a little finesse, and a rookie could easily leave some clothes or skin behind, so Sally chose to wait for the pair on the shore. She watched as the shadows of Billy and Pete jogged along the top of the dam to the metal contraption in the centre.

The boys shone their lights on the torrent of water as it funnelled through the gate valve and crashed to the river below. Every part of the valve mechanism was badly rusted except for the shiny Yale lock that prevented the wheel from turning. Billy made several frantic and clumsy attempts at sawing the lock, but the blade just skipped across the metal. After five minutes of taking turns at running the hacksaw across the lock, the blade finally penetrated the hard metal and created a small but expanding trough.

Sally sat nervously on the shore, trying to convince herself that the noises she heard were strictly generated by her imagination. She was now regretting coming but did not have the courage to strike out for home on her own.

Finally the arm of the padlock separated into two pieces, and they slipped it out of its hole. Billy and Pete each grabbed a section of the wheel and pulled with all the force that eighty-pound bodies could generate, but nothing moved—the mechanism was seized.

Pete stood back and pondered the situation. "Billy, get on your back, and we'll both kick the wheel at the same time." As they each kicked at the spokes, the wheel made a tiny, initial movement, which grew with each successive blow, and finally they were able to crank open the valve by hand. As it opened, thousands of gallons of extra water roared through the dam and crashed down on the river, producing a racket that temporarily stunned the pair. The effects on the pond side became apparent immediately. Ducks and bullfrogs that had been sleeping peacefully in the bulrushes suddenly found themselves high and dry, and the cacophony of startled wildlife alarmed the boys, who quietly wondered if they had gone too far. But the immediate apparent success of the operation allayed any further doubting—the pond was draining. They shone their flashlights on the expanding, muddy bottom while Sally, now in a fitful state on the shore, watched in terror.

Chapter 22

Night Games, Don Mills—July 1964

A go-cart and a Lambretta motor scooter tearing through the streets of Don Mills after midnight tended to arouse a little suspicion, and the boys, being reasonably astute, were quite conscious of that fact. Fortunately, Don Mills was laid out in four quadrants, all interconnected by a series of parks and pathways that could be used in place of the roads and had the added benefit of not being easily navigable by police car.

The calls were coming into 52 Division fast and furiously from residents who backed onto the park and were not particularly pleased about being woken up by a mufflerless go-cart. The frustrated officers were always one step behind. Just as they responded to a call from one quadrant, the switchboard would light up with calls from an adjacent quadrant. So went the cat-and-mouse game into the early hours of the morning.

The cops at 52 Division were a touch brighter than Lenny and the boys ever gave them credit for, and it was not long before the boys in blue predicted where the Lambretta and go-cart would show up next. As the cocky foursome tore down a trail, hooting and hollering like they were invulnerable, the patrol car, with lights off, slowly slid into position across the path. All that juvenile hubris suddenly disappeared as the boys made a quick U-turn to avoid the car across their path and drove right into the headlights of an oncoming patrol car. The noose was starting to tighten, and that should have been the end of the night right there, but for a stroke of luck that the foursome did not deserve in the form of a side trail leading to a schoolyard. The approaching patrol car tore up the grass, attempting to cut off the escape route, and it became a foot race to see who could get to the entrance first. The Lambretta–go-cart combination just squeaked by the police car's front bumper and tore down the path with the patrol car right on their tail. At the entrance to the schoolyard were four posts standing like sentries, which they could fit between, and it was the end of the chase for the police.

Things were getting a little too hot for Lenny and the boys, so they high-tailed back to their quadrant to call it a night. When they got back into the neighbourhood, they killed their engines and proceeded to push their borrowed steeds back to their respective carports.

Things went smoothly for Wally and Brad returning the go-cart, but for Lenny and Dave, the night did not end well. Just prior to the boys showing up with the Lambretta, the owner had returned home and immediately noticed his machine missing. He just happened to be on the phone to the police when Lenny and Dave slid the scooter into the carport and managed to clip a garbage can in the process. Even before they could get the Lambretta onto its stand, the side door flew open and two-hundred pounds of enraged owner blocked their path. Any thought of escape quickly evaporated when the two patrol cars screeched into the driveway. Their night was over.

Chapter 23

Bullion on the Bottom—July 1964

The pond was slowly reverting to a river, revealing a featureless, mucky bottom on each side. Billy and Pete panned their flashlights across the mudflats, unsure of what they were looking for.

"Pete! Look at this," Billy said, focusing his light on a rectangular feature slowly taking shape as the residual muddy water drained off. About fifty feet from the dam, off to one side of the river, a stone vault was beginning to appear in the mud. Sally watched with rapt attention from the shore.

"Let's check it out," Pete replied. They scrambled down a set of metal rungs embedded into the dam and waded into the muck below. The mud sucked at their feet as they slogged their way towards the object, which was now sitting up a good six inches above the bottom. They hopped out of the muck and onto the ten-foot-square structure with the outlines of some sort of hatch in the middle.

"Billy, this thing's made out of metal," Pete said as he scuffed the surface with his shoe. "It looks like a manhole cover."

Billy dropped to his knees and began to clean the muck away with his hand. "Grab the hole here...let's see if we can open it." Along one side was a slot, meant for a pry bar.

There was no shortage of lifting power between the two, who were powered by the excitement of their find. The slab of rusty iron slowly levered open and dropped heavily onto the stones. Before them now lay a black hole.

The boys were more apprehensive this time. The last time that they had shone their lights into a black abyss, they were treated with the sight of a skeleton, and it was not something that they wanted to repeat. "Pete, we've got to do it, but I'm not sure that I want to know what's in there." Billy looked warily at the hole.

"That makes two of us. Let's close our eyes, turn on the lights, and then slowly open them. That way it shouldn't be as much of a shock." To Billy it seemed a bit like slowly immersing yourself in the cold water instead of just diving in—you still end up in the same place. But for lack of a better plan he agreed. Their eyes closed and the lights went on.

"Okay. Slowly open your eyes now," Pete instructed. They stood speechless, fixated on the hole as their light beams reflected back at them, revealing a brilliant yellow hue. They were staring at bars of gold. "H-o-l-y crap, Billy," Pete shook his head in astonishment. Billy leaned over and pulled a bar from the hole. It was stamped with the letters "CSA." He waved it above his head triumphantly with his light shining on it, trying to show Sally. The boys did a little a little victory jig around the vault, both wielding a gold bar in each hand.

They were so obsessed with their celebrating that neither heard Sally scream from the shore. Then the victory dance ended abruptly as a pair of headlights suddenly illuminated from the shore, and the boys froze in mid step. Their natural instincts screamed at them to head through the muck to the opposite shore, but Sally's yells for help brought them back to the reality of the situation. "Pete, we can't leave her. It's gotta be the workies." Their minds raced trying to come up with a viable solution to their predicament, but there was only one option.

"Why did we bring her?" Pete spit into the muck with disgust. "Let's go." They walked slowly through the muck and up the embankment where three shadowy figures were waiting for them.

"I didn't think that we'd have to chase you boys this time...not as long as we had your girlfriend." In the darkness they could not see who was doing the talking. "Throw them in the back of the van," the voice ordered. "Okay, boys, load up that bullion into the other van and let's get the hell outa here."

The door of the cube van slammed shut behind them, leaving them in darkness. They could see the silhouette of Sally huddled in the corner. "I'm sorry," Sally said remorsefully as the boys sprawled out on the floor beside her. "You guys could have gotten away without me."

"Don't worry about it, Sal," Billy replied, trying to console her.

"My old man's going to ground me for life this time," Pete said, pondering his dismal future.

"What will they do with us?" Sally asked.

"They'll take us to workie headquarters in the barn, yell and scream a lot, probably call the cops, and definitely call our parents," Billy answered.

"I'm really sorry," Sally repeated. "My parents will never believe it."

The three sat in silence awaiting their fate. Billy knew that he had pushed the envelope this time, and it would not just be a matter of serving out his punishment and then business as usual. Pete knew that his dad would make good on his warning of "One more time, and life was going to change; and not for the better."

"One of the guys out there was the same guy that we saw looking in your backyard," Sally said, breaking the silence. Billy did not give it a lot of thought; it made no difference who they were.

After a tortuous hour of waiting, they heard the driver's door open and the van's engine roar to life. The three rattled around the back as the van pounded through the potholes of the dirt road. It was obvious that their driver did not have a lot of concern for his human cargo. After several minutes of driving on a route that the boys knew too well, Billy and Pete expected the van to come to a halt in front of the barn compound. Instead, the vehicle tilted upward on the climb out of the valley, sending them all careening against the back door.

"He must be goin' straight to 52 Division," Billy speculated.

"Oh, great...this is gettin' better all the time," Pete replied.

"What's 52 Division?" Sally asked.

The boys managed a weak smile at her innocence. "The cop shop," they answered in unison. But after another fifteen minutes of driving, it became obvious that a visit to the local constabulary was not part of the agenda either—a drive that would have taken five minutes at the outside.

Chapter 24
Kidnapped—July 1964

Facing angry parents started looking like a much better option to the threesome than the hard reality of their current situation. It was becoming increasingly obvious to Billy that these were not golf course security employees and they may have stumbled into something much more ominous and fraught with danger. Finding buried treasure was the ultimate fantasy of most boys of Billy and Pete's age, but being held captive was not part of that fantasy.

"Billy, if I'm not home by morning, my parents will have a fit," Sally lectured, trying to hold back tears. The reality of their current situation was not something that she was ready to grasp.

"Sal...I don't think any of us will be home by morning. That creepy guy you saw has been following me for weeks now. He wants the gold that Colonel Reynolds hid after the Civil War and we found tonight. He must have seen me at Aunt Emily's...she's the colonel's daughter," Billy replied, trying to explain a complex story in a few sentences.

Sally grimaced in confusion. "I don't know what you are talking about, Billy Parker, but you have to get me home by morning!"

"Sal...I don't know the whole story either, but I know that those guys want what we found tonight, and we'd better just do what they say for now," Pete said, trying to calm her. They went silent again; Sally quietly crying and Billy beating himself up with pangs of guilt for dragging his friends into another one of his schemes.

The hours of intense emotion were exhausting, and eventually the hypnotic hum of the tires on pavement lulled the three to sleep. When the vehicle left the pavement for a gravel road, they awoke. Like a nightmare that does not go away upon wakening, the threesome silently surveyed their surroundings, looking desperately for any sign that it was all a bad dream.

For more than an hour, the van bounced down the trail, which seemed to get progressively worse as time went on. They could hear branches scraping along the sides and under frame of the truck, and there no longer seemed to be a straight piece of road as they swung from one corner right into the next. Finally the van rolled to a stop. Billy, Pete, and Sally huddled together with eyes fixed on the roll-up door at the back end. Through the walls, they could hear men's gruff voices that sounded similar to dogs barking at each other. A fist banging on the side of the truck sent the startled threesome scrambling for non-existent cover just as the rear door began to roll up.

"Morning, children...hope I didn't wake you guys up." One of the men smiled in on his three captives. He looked even uglier than Billy had remembered him, with three days' growth and the dishevelled appearance of someone who sleeps too little and rarely in a bed. "My name's Chuck...I'll be your tour guide today, so make your way down here."

Wary as caged cats, the threesome tentatively inched towards the open door, squinting as the sunlight hit their eyes. They silently surveyed their surrounding, which was nothing short of magnificent—a pine forest on the shore of a huge, blue lake, calm as a sheet of glass. The morning mist was slowly dissipating as the warm sun burned it off. The grandeur of the scene mitigated their predicament, at least temporarily.

Chuck whistled and called for his two cronies to come up from the beach. They were in the process of loading one of the vans onto a landing craft at the water's edge. "Gentlemen, let me introduce you to my three friends; this here is Billy, Pete, and Sally." The men nodded feigned pleasure at the introduction, enjoying the sarcastic civilities. "Billy and Pete here were good enough to lead us to the bullion—and Sally—well as they say, behind every successful man is a woman." Chuck and the boys shared a silly giggle.

"What are you going to do with us?" Sally barked at him.

"Why, you're a little fire cracker, aren't ya...I like that," Chuck answered. "You three get on that landing craft there...we're going for a little ride."

Chapter 25

On the Landing Craft—July 1964

As they boarded the landing craft, the dichotomy of being captives on this magnificent, northern lake on a beautiful July morning gave a surreal air to their predicament. It had the feel of a summer's day at camp, and it was quite easy for Billy, Pete, and Sally to forget the reality of their situation.

The landing craft chugged down half the lake, then took an inexplicable turn and headed into what appeared to be a dead end bay, but as they progressed further, a channel opened up. They set course through the channel and entered into another lake. After holding a heading through most of the lake, the barge made another abrupt change in course and again headed into a bay with no visible outlet. Again, just as it seemed that they would run aground, the mouth of a small river appeared, barely wide enough to accommodate them, and onward they went. The shoreline teemed with deer, beaver, eagles, and even the occasional moose, but nowhere was there any sign of civilization. Billy lost track of how many lakes and channels that they had run, and he knew for certain that they would have no chance of finding their way back unguided. As they entered into yet another lake, the landing craft set course for a point and this time did not deviate.

Billy looked at Sally, who was holding her head up like a trooper, and felt a wave of empathy for her. Up until that day, the most exciting experience in her life was playing British Bulldog in the schoolyard, and now she was caught up in a kidnapping. He glanced at his buddy Pete—always solid as a rock—sometimes more guts than brains, but a guy that you could always count on. Billy desperately wanted to lift their flagging spirits, to give them hope, however little. "Sal, Pete," he started hesitantly, "I got us into this, and I'm real sorry. I promise you guys I'll do everything I can to get us back to Don Mills. We'll never go into the valley again. You guys are my best friends." It was like a veil of gloom lifted off them. The three beaming faces clasped hands in the centre of their huddle. "Buddies?" Billy asked.

"Buddies forever," Sal and Pete replied.

Chapter 26
Loon Lake Lodge—July 1964

Signs of civilization began to appear as they approached the point. A large wharf extended from a beach with several small boats and a floatplane alongside, and further back into the woods there appeared to be a large lodge with several smaller outbuildings.

The sight of other people was comforting to the three-some, even if it was unlikely that their hosts would be any more hospitable than Chuck. The pilot of the landing craft backed off on the throttle and let it drift into the beach. When they made contact, the ramp was dropped and the van was driven off.

"Come on, children...follow me." Chuck took great pleasure flaunting his position of power and treating his captives with condescension. Pete muttered a few choice words under his breath, barely able to hide his displeasure. In an instant Chuck flew around, grabbed Pete by the T-shirt, and with a piston-like arm, dragged him within inches of his face. "What was that, kid?"

"I didn't say nothin'" Pete's feet were barely touching the ground. He trembled with fear but still stared back defiantly at Chuck.

"You watch what you say, you little bastard!"

"Let him go!" a voice boomed out at the top of the beach. A tall, unshaven, lumberjack-looking guy wearing a plaid shirt and tall leather boots shook his head in disgust. Chuck reluctantly dropped Pete back to his feet. "You must be Chuck," he said with no emotion.

"That's right," Chuck replied. Billy was surprised at the air of coolness between the two, who he assumed would have been familiar with each other. "And this must be Billy, Pete, and Sally. Very pleased to meet you three...my name is Peter." Their host seemed much more amicable to them than he did to Chuck.

They made their way to the old lodge, which was a beautiful, rustic log structure built in the style of a ranch house. "Welcome to our lodge," he continued. Peter's civility and precise articulation belied his appearance as a lumberjack. "It was built sixty years ago by an old Southern gentleman to use as hunting and fishing camp. The nearest civilization is fifty miles away in any direction...in fact, very few people even know that we are here."

Sally began to feel very comfortable with Peter, as if they were there on a tour. "When can we go home?" she asked innocently.

"I am afraid, my dear, that I cannot answer that at the moment. You will be very comfortable here, if you cooperate. Should you decide to leave us, there is virtually no chance of reaching civilization through the bush...which I should remind you, is teeming with bears and wolves."

"But why do you want us?" Pete asked.

"Because you know too much, that's why." Peter signalled a subordinate to come over. "Ivan will take you to your cabin. No more questions." Peter's tone was much colder.

Ivan was short, not much taller than Billy or Pete, and had a distinct foreign look with a bushy grey beard. The threesome followed him towards one of the outbuildings, which looked like a scaled-down version of the main lodge but with two distinct living quarters on each side. He signalled for them to enter one of the quarters, which on first appearance seemed like a typical cottage bunkhouse, except for the bars on the windows and the lack of a door handle. "You have everything you need here," Ivan finally spoke, slowly articulating each word with a strong foreign accent. "We will bring you food at the prescribed time." He fixated his cold, hollow eyes directly on Billy. "Do not try to escape."

Chapter 27
News Headlines—July 1964

Toronto Telegram
Monday—July 20th, 1964

Three Kids Disappear
Mystery in Don Mills

Three Don Mills twelve-year-olds, Billy Parker, Pete Mills, and Sally Olmstead, all friends, have been missing since Saturday night. Parker and Mills were last seen heading into the valley around midnight Saturday during a backyard campout. Sally Olmstead was safely in her bed at ten p.m. Saturday but nowhere to be found Sunday morning. Strangely, Billy Parker and Pete Mills were the same two boys who found the human remains in the valley two weeks ago. Even more strangely, an old mill pond in the valley was found drained Sunday morning, revealing a large, empty vault. Police do not know if these events have any relationship to the disappearances, but they now have cordoned off the barns and clubhouse at the golf course to try and get to the bottom of…

Emily Reynolds Dies

One of Toronto's oldest residents, Emily Reynolds, passed away Sunday afternoon at the age of one hundred and four. Mrs. Reynolds had been bedridden for several years, but her mind remained sharp. She had emigrated from Georgia to Canada after the Civil War as a young girl. Her father, Colonel William Reynolds, and his wife, Susannah, left the United States in 1870, refusing to live under "Yankee rule."

Coincidentally, police will no longer have the opportunity to speak with Mrs. Reynolds about the recent discovery of her father's body and other strange events that have been happening at her old farm, which is now the Dixie Country Club.

Chapter 28

Loon Lake Lodge, Algonquin Park—July 1964

Ivan summoned Chuck from his bedroom in the main lodge for a meeting with Peter. It was the first full night's sleep Chuck had enjoyed in a long time, and he was in no mood to end it. "Yeah, yeah, I'll be there," Chuck barked at Ivan, who pounded on the flimsy plank door. He slid out of bed and put his boots back on, which were the only articles of clothing that he had removed the night before, and staggered out the door. Ivan led the way through the great room of the lodge to an office at the far end.

Peter was seated behind a massive oak desk. Behind him hung a large red flag, which Chuck knew was not the Rebel banner, but he was not sophisticated enough to understand the significance of the hammer and sickle.

"Good morning, Chuck...I trust that you slept well."

"Yeah, I slept well, Peter...now let's cut the bullshit and get down to business. Give me my money, and I'll be getting outta here."

"You have no idea, do you, Chuck. Doesn't this flag behind me surprise you a little?" Peter peered across the desk at Chuck, not sure what to make of this strange, ignorant character before him.

"My deal was with Mackay. I kept my end of it. You got the gold, and now you keep your end of it—and screw the goddamn flag—it doesn't mean anything to me." Peter sat silently for a few seconds, covering his face with his hands and slowly shaking his head.

"Listen, Peter!" Chuck started in again with a vengeance.

"No! You listen, Chuck!" Peter roared cutting him off. "Frank Mackay does not exist. Do you know what his real name is?"

"What the hell are you talking about?" Chuck asked, somewhat taken aback.

"His real name is Dimitri Tretiak, and he works for me. I'm Petar Andropov, and we both work for the KGB. Those two guys that you came up here with...both KGB agents." Chuck had enough world smarts to know that the KGB was Russian. He sat in a puzzled silence. "Let me give you some history, Chuck," Petar said, much more calmly this time. "We in the KGB infiltrated the Brothers of the Gray Ghost and several other Confederate-inspired groups over ten years ago. As you may know—but I have my doubts—we are in a cold war with the United States. In the ex-Confederate States of America, there is still a lot of antipathy towards the USA, and we thought that we could take advantage of that—possibly foment a little unrest—anything to destabilize. Are you still with me, Chuck?" Chuck, just a petty crook was in way over his head now, and Petar knew it. "As we got more involved with these Confederate groups, we started hearing more and more about lost gold bullion. A few million in bullion would go a long way towards financing our operation, so we changed focus and that is where you came in."

"If you guys are Ruskies...how come you don't talk Ruskie?"

"Because, Chuck, it is KGB policy to always talk English while on operations...even among ourselves."

"So you can just pay me, and I'll be on my way," Chuck said, lacking the bravado.

"Would you like to know what we have planned, Chuck?" Petar asked rhetorically. "That kind of money would go a long way in financing an insurrection...and there is a certain amount of enthusiasm among certain groups in the South for an insurrection. After all...if you destabilize your enemy from within, it's just as effective as attacking him from the outside, which is what he expects."

"So why are you telling me?" Chuck asked, much more belligerently.

"Because you are not going to be with us much longer, Chuck." Chuck sat in stunned silence, contemplating his next move. He knew exactly what Petar meant.

"Why, you commie son of a bitch!" Chuck yelled, lunging at Petar. If nothing else, Chuck was not a coward and he would go out fighting. Two of Petar's henchmen quickly ran to their boss's aid and subdued Chuck.

"Take him outside...you know what to do with him!" Petar ordered.

"Not so fast, Petar," Chuck said, hanging off the two henchmen. "If you think you got all of the gold, you're very wrong. I planned for something like this and stashed half of it on the trip up here. You need me, Petar!" Chuck was sweating profusely as he waited for the verdict from Petar.

"Lock him up in the other cabin."

Chapter 29
Captives—July 1964

Billy, Pete, and Sally wandered around their cell like cats thrown into a cage for the first time—inspecting every inch of the place repeatedly, as if somehow they had missed something. The walls were made of thick, round logs with white cement chinking. There was a small roughed-in washroom in one corner and two sets of bunk beds. It was the kind of place that would be nice to spend a summer in—nice if there was the option of going out the front door.

"I don't see any way out of here...any ideas, Billy?" Pete asked.

"In the movies, somebody always has a file, but I don't even think a file would help us," Billy answered.

"Hey, look at this," Sally said, "Somebody else was a prisoner here too." The inscription "TSH 1960" was carved into a log. "I wonder how TSH got out."

"Or if he got out," Pete added. After a few more circles of the cabin, inspecting every nook and cranny, they each lay down on a bunk.

"Do you think that they are going to kill us?" Sally asked, as if this was just a routine question. Their whole situation was still a bit of a fantasy to her.

"Naw—they won't kill kids," Pete reassured her.

"Listen!" Billy cut them off. There was the clunking of heavy boots climbing the stairs and walking across the front verandah. They could hear some muffled expletives and the cabin door next to theirs open and slam shut. "Somebody else is a prisoner too." The threesome lay silently listening to their fellow prisoner stomp around the cell, going through the same routine that they had just completed. And then there was silence. "I'm going to try and contact whoever it is. I need something metal," Billy said as he proceeded to scour the room. The room was devoid of anything extraneous, and there was nothing metal to be found—except for the bunk beds.

"Help me with this," Pete asked from underneath one of the lower bunks. "There's a loose nut on this brace, and I think I can undo one end. Then if we bend it back and forth enough it'll break; I've done it in shop class." The steel brace got warm as they flexed it, then hot, and then soft, just before it cleanly sheared off.

Billy crawled under the bunk along the common wall between the two cells and began to chip away at a section of chinking. Once he had a hole large enough to get some leverage, it pried out quite easily. He slid the metal between the two logs and began to hammer away at the chinking on the opposite side and soon there was light as the concrete dropped to the floor.

"Hey kid...it's me...Chuck." Chuck's voice came through clear as a bell through the small opening.

"It's that creepy guy," Billy whispered to his partners. "What're you doing here? I thought you were one of them?" he asked Chuck.

"It's a long story, and I don't have time, so listen up. We've gotta get outta here. This place is run by the commies."

"Who are the commies?" Billy queried.

"Ever heard of the KGB?"

"Yeah...they're Russian spies," Billy answered. Billy's generation were well versed in cold war players.

"That's right, and they've infiltrated the Brothers of the Gray Ghost down in Georgia." Billy was now totally confused but let Chuck finish. "They want the gold to pay for a revolution—a revolution in the United States."

"Who are the Brothers of the Gray Ghost?"

"It doesn't matter, and the revolution don't matter either," Chuck answered. "What matters is that they are going to kill us, so start planning a way to get us out of here. Understand?"

Billy gulped. This part of the story he did not want to pass onto his friends. "Yeah...I understand."

Chapter 30
Plotting the Escape—July 1964

"Chuck's lying," Petar said to his henchmen as they sat in his office. "I talked with the guys driving the other van. They had all the gold...Chuck's van only had the kids. You know what to do. Wait till he's asleep...and use the Beretta with the silencer...don't want to wake up the children."

"Why don't we get rid of them at the same time?" one of the henchmen suggested.

Petar paused to consider the idea. "No...leave them...for now."

The excitement and tension of the previous twenty-four hours had the fortunate effect of overriding their hunger, but the sight of food left them famished. The three prisoners voraciously devoured their dinners like half-starved dogs.

"We can't get out through the walls, or the bars, or the roof...but maybe through the floor," Billy said, thinking out loud.

"We pry up some floorboards with our bar," Pete said, finishing his thought.

"And go where, into the woods to get eaten by wolves?" Sally rolled her eyes.

"We'll figure that out later...let's try it," Billy replied.

The floor was constructed of planks butted together and nailed down. They pulled out a bunk bed from the wall and started to chip away at the flooring. Slowly as they worked in shifts, the first plank started to loosen on the wall joist. When it became free at the wall, Billy would lift it and Pete would start to pry with the bar on the second joist, then the third until the plank was free from the floor. The second and third floorboards gave way much more easily with the first one out. With three floorboards out, there was enough room for an eighty-pound body to slip through, and Billy went head first into the hole up to his waist. "It's pitch black in here...I can't see anything...I need a light," he said, clambering out of the hole.

"The only light here is that thing on the ceiling," Pete answered, pointing to the lone bulb suspended from the ceiling.

As they pondered, Sally wandered into the washroom. "Try this," she said, displaying a small wall mirror.

Billy went back into the hole using the mirror to reflect light below the floor and scanned all four sides. He hauled himself out of the hole again, looking defeated. "It's no use. The whole cabin is sitting on a stone wall. There's no way out." They placed the flooring back, making sure that the nails lined up with their holes and pushed the bunk back to the wall.

The kids lay on their bunks in silence, each immersed in their own thoughts. Billy drifted between a semi-conscious state and the parallel universe that is sleep. The haunting, other-worldly call of a loon beckoned him from the other side. He walked up the oak-lined laneway of the Reynolds plantation towards the big house. Emily waved to him from the verandah. She looked radiant and stunningly beautiful—just like the painting that never failed to mesmerize him.

"Hello, Billy." He tried to reply to her but there was only silence from his lips.

"Everything is fine now, Billy. Thank you, Billy."

He knew that he was visiting a world where he could not stay and did not belong. He smiled and waved to her a last farewell as her image faded and their two worlds separated. Billy knew Aunt Emily had died.

Sally put the finishing touches on her plan as the other two slept.

Chapter 31

The Escape—July 1964

Ivan carried the tray of food up the trail to feed his captives. He clomped up the cabin steps, put the tray down, and began to open the deadbolts on the large plank door. As the door swung inward, he knelt to retrieve the tray but suddenly froze in his prone position. He bolted upright, kicking the tray over, and ran into the cabin in a frenzy. "Those little bastards," he stammered in his thick foreign accent as his gaze swung wildly around the empty cabin. He turned and ran out towards the main lodge.

The floorboards popped open, and the threesome jumped from their hiding place, agile as rabbits. "Head for the woods," Billy whispered. He ran to Chuck's cell, drew back the six deadbolts, and threw open the door. The room was empty.

Once they had reached the cover of the forest, Pete and Sally followed by Billy changed course and headed for the lake. They darted nimbly through the trees and reached the water's edge with adrenalin surging through their pounding hearts. "We've got to get to that plane," Pete said gasping for air. "It's going somewhere...I watched them load it this morning through a crack in the shutter."

"We can't cross the beach...they'll see us. We have to swim, and swim on your back with just your mouth out of the water," Sally instructed. It was quickly becoming apparent to the boys that they had the asset of a very analytical mind in Sally.

Petar was in his office giving last-minute flight plans to Hank, his KGB pilot. "You're loaded to gross with the gold, but it's all nicely strapped down. Keep under a thousand feet...we don't want any radar picking you up. Fly two-eight-zero to the lake. That should get you over Byng Inlet in an hour, but keep an eye on the crosswind. Put it down on Byng Inlet and wait. Your contact will rendezvous with you at 1500 hours Zulu."

"But how do I identify them?"

"Believe me...you'll know them when you see them...you with me so far?"

"Yeah, I'm with you...what about the body here?" he asked, gesturing towards a body bag containing Chuck.

"When you're ten minutes out, bank it hard over and give Chucky a boost out the door. Nobody will ever find him in that bush."

Just then the office door flew open and Ivan burst in. "The little bastards have escaped," he stammered.

"What?" Petar yelled.

"When I deliver food, cabin was empty."

"Get a couple of guys and the dogs...they won't get far in this bush," Petar instructed. "Chances are they will die out there, but if they run into a trapper or an Indian, we've got problems."

"Understand," Ivan replied.

About twenty-feet offshore, three turtles slid through the water heading for the wharf. They swam under the wharf and slid silently along one of the floatplane's pontoons. The aircraft was a single-engine, twelve-passenger Otter with all the seats removed for cargo. Nobody paid much attention to the dock as the search party was being assembled, and the threesome slipped unnoticed into the open cargo door.

Hank hauled his six-foot-two frame into the aircraft to make a last check of his cargo. He knew from bad experience what could happen if a load shifted in flight. Strapped down in the centre of the aircraft was a row of crates, which forced him to maneuver down the port side of the aircraft, bent into an uncomfortable hunch. If he had been able to fully stand up, he would have noticed the three bodies huddled alongside the crates on the starboard side. When he was satisfied all was secure, he made his way to the cockpit.

The two henchmen struggled along the wharf hauling the body in a burlap sack. "Bring him in through here," Hank instructed, motioning the two from the cockpit door. They heaved and struggled and complained about Chuck being overweight, but eventually they got him placed in the copilot's seat. Hank leaned over to unlatch the copilot's door to prepare for Chuck's evacuation.

Ivan struggled to hold back the two yelping hounds as they dragged him towards the water. At the water's edge, he was losing patience with his canine trackers after his second attempt to get them headed off into the bush. "Damn animals! Doze kids not swim home." He hauled back on the leashes with enough force to convince the hounds that a run through the woods would be in their best interests.

Hank completed his pre-flight checks as the Otter taxied downwind to get into position for takeoff. At the far end of the lake, he hit hard left rudder and she swung around into the wind. With the propeller at fine pitch, he slowly advanced the throttle to takeoff power, and the six-hundred-horsepower radial engine reached for the sky. Hank knew that they were over gross takeoff weight and he would need the whole lake to get airborne. The Otter roared and struggled like a roped stallion, trying to break free of the lake's grip. Both floats slowly rose out of the water as they began to win the battle, and soon they were skimming across the surface of the lake. He pulled back gently on the yoke, and they roared over top of the lodge with a hundred feet to spare. Ivan cursed the Otter as the big bird sent the dogs into frenzy.

At a thousand feet and a heading of two-hundred-and-eighty degrees, Hank cut the engine back to cruise power and adjusted the propeller pitch. It was time to deal with Chuck. With bush as far as the eye could see in every direction, disposing of a body where it would not be found was a pretty easy task. He gave Chuck a little nudge against the copilot's door to prepare him for his first skydiving lesson. Hank then threw the Otter into a forty-five-degree steep turn to starboard and gave Chuck another shove of encouragement against the open door.

After Ivan finished cursing out the Otter and resumed his search of the woods, a troubling thought began to gnaw at him. *What if the dogs were not as dumb as I thought?* "Those little bastards!" he howled at the heavens, as the gears in his rusty brain began to mesh and piece the story together. Ivan did a quick about face and headed off at full tilt in the direction of the lodge.

Chuck was not cooperating and was now stuck halfway out of the aircraft, jammed in between the door and fuselage. Getting rid of Chuck's body was getting a bit riskier now and was not going according to plan. Hank levelled out the aircraft and unbuckled his seat belt. Standing up with his left hand on the yoke and his right on the burlap sack, he again banked the aircraft hard to starboard.

"Hank...come in, Hank!" the radio blared, but Hank was in no position to answer. "Hank, we think that you have company onboard!"

Like a cork popping out of a bottle, Chuck suddenly broke free of his bonds and plummeted earthward. At the sudden release of pressure, Hank lost his balance and fell towards the copilot's door. He desperately tried to pull himself back from the brink of disaster, grabbing the yoke in his left hand, which had the unfortunate effect of banking the aircraft into a near-vertical position. Hank now too crashed through the door and joined Chuck plummeting earthward in his first skydiving experience.

Billy, Pete, and Sally were screaming hysterically in the cargo bay as the Otter rolled violently back to port with the loss of Hank. The aircraft was trimmed for straight and level flight, and the rolls from side to side slowly attenuated as the three hysterical passengers made their way to the cockpit. Pete was the first to arrive in the front end and turned an ashen white at the sight of an empty cockpit. The other two followed shortly afterwards, and all three stared aghast at their predicament.

"Let me in there!" Billy said, as he pushed Pete out of the way and jumped in the pilot's seat. "I used to fly in a Cessna with my dad, and I know what the controls do." Billy grappled with the yoke, severely over-controlling, and the Otter pitched and banked like a drunken porpoise, but he kept them out of the trees.

"Do you know how to land?" Pete screamed.

"You pull it back just before you get to the runway and then stop the engine...but I don't know anything about the engine," Billy replied.

"There's a lake straight ahead!" Sally yelled as a long narrow lake started to appear on the horizon.

"I'm going to try and land there...when I tell you, pull back all those handles," Billy instructed Pete, his copilot. "One of them has to stop the engine!"

Up and down like a roller coaster, they bounced through the sky, slowly losing altitude. The pontoons barely cleared the pines as they crossed the perimeter of the lake. Billy pushed the yoke forward, trying to force the aircraft down, and their air speed soared as the lake rushed up to meet them. Alarmed at their drastic rate of descent, Billy pulled back hard and they reared skyward. "Stop the engine," he yelled. Pete pulled back all the levers on the control stand and the engine RPM went to idle. They had now climbed back up one hundred feet above the lake, and the shore was fast approaching. Billy panicked and pushed the nose down again for their second demonstration of the porpoise routine, and as the lake threatened to swallow them, he pulled back, but a little too late this time. The Otter pancaked onto the surface of the lake and bounced skyward, but with less momentum as their air speed bled off. Billy had lost his grip on the yoke from the force of the initial impact, and the airplane was now flying itself as it headed towards the water for a third time.

After two more short skips, they had lost all aerodynamic lift, and a meeting with the shore was now inevitable. The Otter careened up the embankment and plowed through the bush as the three unfortunate passengers screamed in unison. The floats sheared off shortly after the initial impact, and then trees removed most of both wings before the naked fuselage came to rest. Just as quickly as the forest had opened up from their impact, the evergreens swallowed them up and closed up the door. From the lake, there was no trace that anything eventful had ever happened.

"Ho-ly crap...ho-ly crap!" Pete repeated over and over. Billy and Sally sat in stunned silence—eyes as wide as saucers.

"A plane crash...I've never been in any crash...I haven't even fallen off my bicycle!" Sally was in tears.

"That was the craziest ride I ever had...way worse than anything at the Exhibition!" exclaimed Billy.

Chapter 32

Survival in the Woods—July 1964

Petar stomped back and forth across his office floor while Ivan cowered in the doorway. "Our comrades called me on the radio. They're sitting in Byng Inlet waiting for the airplane. What the hell do I tell them?" he asked, not expecting an answer. "It should have been there an hour ago. Those kids have something to do with this...I just know it. The dogs aren't stupid like you, Ivan." Ivan cowered even lower. "If they tell you they went into the water...they went into the water!" Ivan silently cursed the threesome who had made him look so bad in front of his boss. He swore to get even. "Get another floatplane in here and fly every inch of that route until you find them. Understand?"

"Yes, boss...understand, boss," Ivan replied meekly.

Sally dabbed at a cut over Billy's eye using an onboard first-aid kit, while Pete went through the aircraft to see what would be of use to them. Using a fire axe, he whacked away at the wooden crates. "Look at this, Billy...they got our gold, and now we've got it back," Pete laughed as he displayed a gold bar to the two in the cockpit.

"Wish we could eat it," Billy lamented. Pete disappeared into the fuselage and returned to the front end with the pilot's lunch pail.

"Lunchtime," he said smiling. They split up the generous lunch that Hank had prepared for himself.

Billy and Sally climbed out of the still-intact fuselage to survey their new neighbourhood. They were buried in a pine bush a hundred or so feet from the shore and were covered by an impenetrable ceiling of boughs. Billy looked around in dismay. "Nobody will ever find us in here."

"Billy, the only people looking for us up here...we don't want to be found by," Sally replied. "Those guys want their gold...I don't think that they care much about us."

Sal—the girl next door—was really starting to impress Billy. While Pete and he would bungle their way through trouble and use their legs instead of their wits, Sally seemed to have the knack of analyzing a situation.

"Lookie here," Pete proudly announced from the plane. "A survival kit with a nice .22 rifle, just like mine at home and with lots of shells—and a fishing rod. We're going to do some huntin' and fishin'." He was beaming at his find.

As Cub Scouts, Billy and Pete had learned all sorts of survival-in-the-woods-type skills, but like most Cub Scouts, they never believed that their lives would ever depend on them. The scout masters would always dramatize the notion of survival in the woods. This made little sense to city kids who never spent any time in the woods, but that was what the Cubs were all about. All Billy and his friends were concerned with was getting their proficiency badges because there was a certain amount of status in having a shirt covered in badges. Now Billy and Pete were confronted with the necessity of using these skills and wishing that they had paid more attention.

Priority number one of the Lord Baden-Powell manual was shelter and heat, which meant a lean-to and fire. Pete, who was much more inclined to go fishing, reasoned that if the others looked after the shelter, he would use his hunting and fishing background to bring home dinner. Billy and Sally took the fire axe and began cutting poles and boughs from the abundant spruce and cedar to construct a lean-to, while Pete headed for the lake.

Pete, who had spent many hours angling with his dad, knew what type of bait was most attractive to bass, and this looked like a good bass lake. The fishing rod stored in the airplane was a stubby little unit with the basic coil-type reel and was meant as a last-resort means of survival. Pete knew that with a crayfish on the end of the line, anything would catch bass. He waded through the shallow water, slowly lifting up rocks, looking for one of those miniature lobsters just the right size.

The lean-to was now taking shape as they laid the spruce boughs on the pole frame and covered the floor with cedar. At the entrance, they constructed their fire pit and started on a supply of dead wood for fuel.

On his third cast, the end of Pete's rod gave that telltale quiver just before the big hit. The small-mouth bass wrenched the rod as it headed deep, and Pete let him run. This was a fish that could easily snap the line if Pete chose to fight him, and the only way to win the battle was to wear him down. The taut line tore for the surface as the small-mouth bass headed for the sky. In one glorious leap of defiance, this blinding flash of silver rocketed out of the water and then crashed back through the surface, heading for the bottom once again.

It was early evening, and the slabs of bass fillet sizzled on the hot rocks as the threesome relaxed in their wooden shelter. There was plenty of bass to go around, and they used makeshift wooden forks to devour it.

"There must have been a fight going on in the cockpit and both guys fell out. It's really weird," Billy pondered out loud.

"How long do you think that we can stay here?" Sally asked, "You know they are going to come looking for that gold."

"I don't know, but I kinda like it here," Pete answered. "Tomorrow I'm going to get us a partridge, and there's a huge blueberry patch over that hill. Come to think about it...I wouldn't mind staying here all summer."

"Yeah, but how do we get outta here...and where do we go? We don't even know where we are." Billy replied.

"There's a map in the plane...maybe we can figure it out," Sally said. "Do you think that we will ever get back to Don Mills? I'm starting to feel like Dorothy in the Wizard of Oz."

"Yeah, and Billy's the scarecrow 'cause he hasn't got a brain."

"Guess that makes you the cowardly lion, eh Mills?"

"Shut up, Parker,"

"Naw, you shut up, Mills."

"Both of you shut up...you're just like kids." Sally's condescension had the desired effect. The mildly humiliated boys went silent, and each claimed a corner of the lean-to to bed down for the night. Sleep came quickly for the exhausted threesome on a mattress of cedar boughs, with a couple of tarpaulins from the plane for bedding.

Chapter 33

Evading the KGB—July 1964

The DeHavilland Beaver floatplane taxied towards the shore, then cut its engine while doing a slow one-hundred-and-eighty-degree turn gliding neatly alongside the dock. Petar opened the copilot's door and greeted his visitor.

"Comrade Yuri, welcome to our humble camp."

"Doesn't look too humble to me, Petar. I heard from the embassy that you lost Hank and the Otter."

"That's right...and a whole lot of gold. He was flying a two-hundred-and-eighty-degree course to Byng Inlet, and he never got there. You guys are going to fly every day until you find him—or what's left of him," Petar instructed. "Ivan...get in." Ivan scrambled like the humble lackey he was.

"Roger, Petar, we'll find him."

"Oh...and Yuri...keep your eye out for three kids that we suspect were with him. Ivan will give you the whole ugly story."

◆ ◆ ◆

Morning came early for the threesome as the sun began to filter through the tree line and the mist drifted off the lake. Every living thing in this wilderness paradise seemed to waken at the same time. The woods were alive with an orchestra of songbirds and beasts looking for their break-fast. One by one they began to shake off their early-morning grogginess.

"That was the first time I ever slept outside," Sally stretched while stifling a yawn, "and I like it."

"If you don't count a tent, that was the first time outside for me too," Billy said.

"If I'm outside at night...I'm usually never sleeping...but I guess me too," Pete replied.

"Yeah, like camping out in the backyard," Billy added. "Sure wish we had just gone to sleep."

"Listen!" Sally put an arm on both her comrades. In the distance there was the dull roar of an engine, which grew progressively louder.

Pete leaped to his feet and started running to the shore. "It's a plane!"

"Pete...stop!" Billy yelled and took off after him. He caught up to him at the shore, where Pete was frantically waving at the sky before the plane had come into sight. Billy wrestled him back into the woods kicking and screaming and dragged him to the ground just as the air-craft roared down the middle of the lake. "You idiot, they don't want to rescue us, they wanna kill us!" he raged at his buddy.

Pete struggled and fought back until what Billy had said sunk in. His body went limp. "Maybe you're right."

There was still a tension between the two when Sally arrived to try and diffuse it. "You guys relax...we've got to make some plans. We can't stay here because sooner or later they're going to find us." Pete was feeling humiliated at his lack of thought, and Billy was feeling contrite for insulting his buddy.

"Maybe I'll show you guys how to fish. And I'll show you where the blueberry patch is, and then I'll go hunting," Pete said. He just wanted to get off on his own for awhile.

Billy did not have the knack for fishing that his friend had, and the only bites he got were rocks on the bottom. After a futile hour, he made a few more lacklustre casts and headed back to the camp. On his way back up the shore, he skirted the two sheared-off floats, which were about fifty feet from the main fuselage.

Sally headed back to camp from the blueberry patch. Her makeshift canvas bag was overflowing with fresh blueberries, and she had barely made a dent in the crop.

Chapter 34

The Raft—July 1964

Yuri banked the aircraft hard over and headed for the next lake off their starboard wing. He dropped some flap and put the Beaver into slow flight—as slow as he dared at this low altitude. "If Hank had engine trouble, he would have put her down on one of these lakes. There's just too many of them around here to miss. Otherwise, he's in the bush somewhere and it's going to be real hard to find because the trees close up around you," he said to Ivan, who was staring intently earthward.

◆ ◆ ◆

Sally heard the axe frantically whacking away at a log, somewhere near the shore. Billy did not even notice her arrive as he concentrated all his thoughts and efforts on the project at hand. It quickly became quite obvious what he was up to.

"Billy...you're a genius," she marvelled.

"They're dented...but there's no holes." Billy was beaming with pride. "We tie poles across the two pontoons...there's plenty of rope and straps in the plane...and we've got a great raft."

"Then we carve some paddles with the axe, and away we go...it's great," Sally said.

The Otter pontoons were fifteen feet long, but being hollow and aluminum, they were quite light. All through the morning and afternoon, Billy tied saplings across the pontoons and then started on a decking made of the crates from onboard the aircraft. The project became an obsession for Billy, and nothing would distract him, not even his gnawing hunger.

Sally made her way back to the broken aircraft and seated herself in the pilot's seat. The map from their brief flight was still clipped to the control column. She studiously examined it, occasionally glancing up at the small compass mounted at the top of the windshield.

Pete steadied the barrel of the .22 rifle against a birch tree as drew a bead on the largest of the three partridges beneath a small spruce. The rifle cracked, and the bird dropped to the ground without even a last twitch of life, while the other two took flight in that awkward style of a bird that did not seem designed to fly. The two survivors flapped furiously for fifty feet and then landed as if they were now somehow out of danger. Pete knew that the partridge was not nature's most intelligent animal and his chances of having two more in the bag were good.

◆ ◆ ◆

After four hours of flying at tree-top level up every lake that Hank could have conceivably landed on, Yuri and Ivan had seen nothing but water, trees, and more trees. It was not going to be a simple search, and now they needed to regroup and formulate a plan. Yuri lined up the Beaver on the final leg of his landing pattern back to the lodge while Petar stood impatiently waiting for the plane to glide up to the dock.

"What did you find?" Petar demanded as he swung open the aircraft door as the plane was still coming to a stop.

Ivan took a deep breath and exhaled. "We find nothing," he quietly replied.

"What!" Petar began his tirade, "you had enough time to cover every inch of this province, and you found nothing!"

"I was listening for his emergency locator transmitter; a crash would have set it off...but nothing," Yuri tried to explain.

Petar paused for a second. His anger seemed to fade. "You didn't hear anything because we took the ELT out. Hank had a habit of setting it off with hard landings, and we didn't want to attract the search-and-rescue boys," he paused again. "But tomorrow don't come back here unless you've found them!" Petar marched off the dock towards the lodge.

♦ ♦ ♦

Billy, Pete, and Sally lay around the campfire dining on partridge and blueberries. Despite their circumstances, life seemed quite idyllic and it was easy to forget that they were being hunted.

"I studied the map, and I think that we're on Big Deer Lake, miles from nowhere," Sally said, "but if I'm right, there's a river at the west end of the lake and it goes into a bigger river and then out to Georgian Bay."

"Maybe we should put a sail on that thing," Pete replied, giving little thought to Sally's navigational efforts.

"How far?" Billy asked.

"It's hard to measure it 'cause the river makes so many turns, but I guess about thirty miles to the bigger river and then another fifty to the bay."

"If we leave first thing in the morning, I bet we can do the thirty miles tomorrow, and then another day or two and we're at the bay and going home," Billy said confidently.

"We bring the gun and the fishing rod, and I'll make sure we eat. Tomorrow night, we're eatin' duck," replied Pete, equally confidently.

Chapter 35

Launching the Raft—July 1964

"Come Yuri...let's get out of here before Petar kill me," Ivan said, not completely joking.

"We're going to fly a sweep pattern back and forth between here and Georgian Bay until we have every piece of territory covered. You're the eyes, Ivan, because I've got my hands full flying." The Beaver coughed and sputtered to life, shattering the tranquility of the morning.

♦ ♦ ♦

The watercraft that the threesome launched from the shores of Big Deer Lake was a strange sight: part Huck Finn raft and part sleek catamaran. But it worked, and they were ecstatic.

"What do we call her," Billy asked while paddling on the port side. Pete had paddling duties on the starboard side.

"Let's call her the 'Billy Boat'...because you made her," Sally said. She was the skipper of the raft, steering with a long, hand-carved rudder strapped to the transom.

♦ ♦ ♦

Ivan and Yuri had only been airborne for a couple of minutes when Ivan did a double take at the scene below. "What the hell that?" His eyes bulged as he pressed his face against the aircraft window. "Go down...go down...look at end of that lake!"

♦ ♦ ♦

"You hear something?" Pete asked. He looked bug eyed at the far end of the lake. "Ho-ly crap!" A floatplane was roaring down directly at them.

"Get down!" Billy screamed. The threesome lay flat out on the raft as the floats sailed by, barely above their heads.

"Paddle hard! If we get to the river, he won't be able to get in there," Sally yelled as her crew paddled like windmills. She watched as the Beaver made a steep turn at the end of the lake and was now coming back head on.

"Where's the gun...I going to show those little bastards," Ivan said.

"We haven't got a gun, Ivan. All we can do is give them another haircut," his partner replied. The threesome hit the deck again as the Beaver roared overhead and this time landed a couple hundred yards down the lake.

"Pull...Pull! We have to get to the river!" Sally screamed. The water-borne Beaver swung around, and Yuri pushed the throttle to the firewall. It was now a foot race to the river's mouth.

Chapter 36

Brothers of the Gray Ghost, Sandersville, Georgia—July 1964

"The meeting will come to order," Frank Mackay said as he pounded the gavel down on the lectern. "All rise." The membership rose and en masse placed their right hands over their hearts. Their blood stirred as the banjo player followed by a guitar began the prelude to "Dixie." The collective voices raised the rafters of the old clubhouse, as they belted out the Confederate anthem. As usual, the beloved tune was ended with a resounding "Yee-hah!"

"Gentlemen," Mackay started to address the crowd. "We have a great deal of business to get through this afternoon, but I will cut right to the chase for news that I know you have all been waiting for." He paused while the membership quieted down. "At our last meeting, I and Brother Cyril told you of a certain Colonel William Reynolds of the Confederate army and our suspicions that he may have been involved in smuggling the Confederate treasury into Canada. We have investigated this lead thoroughly with our operative in Canada." He paused again for several seconds. "We have investigated thoroughly and have come up with nothing...absolutely no credible evidence that the gold was smuggled to Canada." There was a collective sigh followed by a rumble of discontent throughout the membership. "In the meantime, Colonel Reynolds' daughter has passed away...God rest her soul...we have lost our last contact with the colonel."

Before he could continue, a member cut him off. "Brother Mackay...several of us have researched Colonel Reynolds, and we are more convinced than ever that he was involved in smuggling the gold to Canada. The colonel ran a spy camp in Toronto during the war."

"Honourable member, please do not interrupt," Mackay stopped him short. "I will say it once more, and the issue is closed. There is absolutely no reason to believe that the gold is in Canada, and we will now pursue other leads!" The rumbling was no longer muted, and several members rose to voice their displeasure at the abrupt end that Mackay was trying to impose. "Order!...Order!" Mackay yelled, crashing his gavel down on the lectern.

Gravel was flying as some of the good old boys put the horsepower to their pickup trucks on the way out of the Brothers of the Gray Ghost parking lot. The meeting had ended on a hostile note with most members displeased with Mackay's dictatorial style, and some of them were down-right enraged. As per the usual routine after the meeting, some of the boys would wet their whistles and loosen their tongues over a few beers at the legion hall.

The cowboy boots stomped on the well-worn wooden floor of the Sandersville County branch of the American Legion as the three members made their way to a favourite table. The place had a permanent odour of stale beer and nicotine that was wafted out the doors and onto the side-walk by the overhead fans.

"What do think of that guy Mackay?" Jebb started out the bitch session. "He's getting a little too big for his britches."

"I'm not sure that I can believe the son of a bitch any-more...a few things make me real suspicious of him," Mike said.

"Funny you should say that, Mike...'cause I got something here you guys will be real interested in," Wally replied. He pulled some folded newspapers from his jacket. "I got a friend up there in Canada, and he sent me copies of a local paper, the *Toronto Telegram*. Said I might be interested, and he was so right." He passed a paper to Mike and one to Jebb.

"So what am I looking for?" Jebb asked.

"Read the article 'bout the bodies those two kids found...Colonel Reynolds no less. And the other one has an article bout the two kids going missing and an empty vault on the colonel's old farm and an obit for his daughter...the one Mackay was talking 'bout."

"Goddamn!" Mike marvelled as he read, "Mackay didn't say anything bout this."

"Yeah...they figure the colonel was murdered...empty vault...seems mighty fishy," Wally said. "Somebody knows something."

"Yeah, and we got to find out," Jebb answered.

"Mackay claims to be a born-and-bred Southerner. A good Confederate boy," Mike said. "Well, you ever hear him sing Dixie? The son of a bitch hums every second word because he doesn't know the words. What if...what if he were a Yankee...a Yankee plant looking for the gold?"

"I've heard enough. We need to take some action," Jebb said. "We need to hold a meeting with a few more of the boys that we can trust—not Mackay flunkies. You guys put a tail on Mackay—see where he hangs out...who he hangs out with. I'll try to get something on his background. Ain't no Yankee getting our gold."

Chapter 37
Narrow Escape—July 1964

On the lake, the Beaver was now picking up speed and quickly closing the gap with the raft as the lake began to narrow down into the river's mouth. Billy and Pete gasped for breath as they pulled on the makeshift paddles in a blur of arms and wood. Sally watched in horror as the propeller pulled closer and closer to the raft. Just as the race seemed lost, the Beaver engine shut down and gave up the chase.

"What the hell you do that for?" Ivan asked angrily.

"Ivan, this is an airplane, not a canoe," Yuri answered condescendingly. "We go any further down this river, and we won't be able to turn around. We'll go back to get a canoe...then we'll get them."

"Look at that little bastard," Ivan said angrily. Pete was standing on the stern of the raft cheerfully waving goodbye.

"Jesus, Pete...they hate us enough without you rubbin' it in," Billy said, shaking his head in amusement.

Back at the dock, Yuri and Ivan strapped a canoe to one of the Beaver's floats while Petar studied a map. "The river out of Big Deer Lake winds its way down to the Magnetawan River. There's nowhere else to go. You two chase them downstream, and me and the boys will wait for them at the Magnetawan. We'll slowly close the noose," Petar instructed. "The gold's in the bush somewhere, and those three are the only ones who know where...so don't kill them...yet."

The river narrowed to fifty feet across with a gentle current that was strong enough to dissuade Billy and Pete from doing any more paddling. Sally used the rudder paddle as a scull for any necessary course changes while Billy lay out on the deck and Pete trolled a fishing line. As it always seemed to go for the threesome, they went from sheer terror to tranquil bliss all within half an hour.

The raft was seaworthy but very slow and difficult to maneuver. Any obstructions in the river would definitely cause a problem, and portaging was out of the question.

"I am just dying for a hamburger," Billy said, lost in a reverie of hamburgers, french fries, and milkshakes.

"Don't even mention it," Sally replied. "I'm trying not to think about food."

"This time I'll get us a trout...there should be trout in this river...and maybe a duck...uh oh," Pete cut himself off in mid-sentence as he stared back down the river, "Plane again!" Half a mile down the river behind them, the Beaver banked and set course directly towards them. The river was too narrow for any low-level buzzing, and it passed overhead just above the tree line and then went into a steep bank, heading back towards the lake.

"There's a canoe tied to the plane...they're coming after us in a canoe. Billy, what are we going to do?!" Sally was in a semi-panic now, worn down from the tension of the last few days.

"Pete, paddle!" Billy yelled to his partner. He knew that trying to outrun the canoe would be futile in the long run. The streamlined canoe had little drag compared to their awkward craft and took much less energy to propel it. Billy and Pete were paddling at a rate that was not sustainable, but they had to buy some time and distance while they could.

After half an hour of following the meandering river, the boys were starting to tire, but resting would mean capture. Billy wracked his brains for an alternative. *We could pull into shore and try to escape on foot, but escape to where?* he thought. They would have no time to study the map and would most likely end up hopelessly lost. As he continued the monotonous, fatiguing stroke, he stared at the supplies that they had salvaged from the plane, which were now tied to the deck. "The rope!" he blurted out loud in a "eureka" moment. "I've got an idea. Don't ask questions, just paddle."

The river was no longer keeping its predictable and lazy pace. More often now it would narrow to a rapid, and the current would pick up and toss them out the bottom. Fortunately, their two-pontoon craft was very stable and never in danger of flipping. They soon found out that to maintain rudder control, they had to keep their speed above that of the current and could not let up paddling.

As they made their way down a two-hundred-yard section of straight, flat water, Billy could see two large rock outcroppings up ahead where the river disappeared from view. As they neared the drop off, the current picked up from the funnel effect of the rocks, and the possibility of running for shore was now gone. "Get down and hang on!" Billy yelled above the din of the fast water. They reached the precipice of the water hill with pounding hearts, praying for a safe landing into the flat water below. Like a roller coaster, the water swept them through a rock gorge, around a steep turn, and down into a pond. The pontoon raft rode out the flume like it was fastened to rails, and the threesome yelled and hollered from pure exhilaration and relief.

"Sal...steer into shore," Billy ordered when they hit the flat water. When they neared shore, Billy jumped out with one end of the hundred-foot rope. After a quick briefing, Sally and Pete headed for the opposite shore with the other end.

Chapter 38

Following Mackay, Sandersville, Georgia—July 1964

Wally and Mike were parked on the tree-lined Sandersville street, well down from Mackay's house. They stared intently at the front porch of the aging, red-brick house, looking for any sign of movement, but after several hours, their powers of attention were waning.

"We've watched all morning now. Doesn't the son of a bitch ever leave home?" Mike asked rhetorically. "Saturday morning and I'm out of the house quick as a scalded cat."

"He must have read your mind," Wally said pointing to the porch. Frank Mackay was in the process of locking his front door. He glanced warily up and down the street before hopping into a white Ford Econoline van. The boys slunk slowly down in their seats.

"He's heading the other way. Stay with him, Wally, but keep well back...he seems concerned about company." Wally pulled out after he let several cars pass. The Econoline wound around the neighbourhood streets in a convoluted pattern that made no sense for anyone with a destination in mind. Wally did his best to keep the van in sight and keep them out of sight, but Mackay was making it difficult.

"Goddamn...that guy shouldn't have a license," Wally complained as he punched the gas pedal on his Chevy Impala to keep up.

"Stay with him, stay with him!" Mike yelled as they fell several blocks back, stuck behind the proverbial Sunday driver. Wally had the Impala whining into overdrive as he passed the slower car illegally on the side street while they both showed their displeasure verbally and with hand gestures towards the shocked, timid driver. They screeched to a halt at a four-way stop, with the white van no longer in sight.

"Damn, Wally...pull over and park," Mike said, shaking his head with disapproval.

"Don't blame me...next time you can drive."

The boys looked like they were headed for a little toe-to-toe confrontation at the side of the road when a white Econoline van showed up in the rearview mirror, heading through the stop in the perpendicular direction.

"Why he's gone and done some more of that creative driving, and now he's headed out towards the highway," Wally said, putting the Impala in gear. This time Mackay seemed to have gotten all the diversionary driving out of his system and headed directly to the interstate, which he remained on for thirty minutes and then turned onto a secondary rural road. Traffic was pretty much non-existent in this part of the country, so Wally and Mike were forced to keep the Impala well back and could only hope to get occasional glimpses of the white van. Chances of Mackay spotting them were good, and chances of them losing him were equally good. They headed deeper and deeper into the hill country, and the road dipped, climbed, and spiralled like a roller coaster.

"Pull over, Wally," Mike ordered. As they descended down a steep grade, he had caught a glimpse of the white back end of the van headed down a forest trail. Wally nosed the Impala into the trail, which was little more than a cow path.

"What the hell would he be doing way back here?" Wally asked. "Unless he's deer hunting, there ain't no reason to be here."

"Yeah, hunting out of season too—but he can't have gone far through this crap. Let's grab the guns and walk in." The trail started to climb up a wooded hillside, and from the ruts left in the mud, it was obvious that Mackay had difficulty coaxing the van up the slope. Mike, walking about ten feet ahead, signalled to Wally to catch up with him and to keep quiet. At the peak of the hill, the van was parked in a clearing and Mackay was now outside of the van setting up some equipment.

"That's a short-wave antenna he's putting on top of the van," Mike whispered, "and he's running the cabling inside. I do believe that he's got himself a transmitter in there. What do you say we get a little closer and listen in?"

♦ ♦ ♦

Petar sat restlessly in his lodge office listening to the static on the short-wave, frequency-scrambling radio. He was losing patience for a scheduled call that was now ten minutes late, and he had boats to prepare for a launch into the Magnetawan River.

"Far North from Deep South...come in, Far North," the radio crackled to life.

"This is Far North...you're late, Deep South."

"Maybe Far North would like to come down here and set up for me next time," Mackay retorted, a touch perturbed. "Give me an update on the bullion situation."

"As we speak, Ivan and Yuri are on the tail of the three

kids going down a river. Me and the boys are setting up an ambush where it connects to a bigger river. We'll get them there if they get by Ivan."

"Where's the bullion?"

Petar hesitated to calm himself. "If we knew where the bullion was, we wouldn't be chasing kids. Those little bastards are the only ones that know. When we get them, we will bring them back to camp at Loon Lake." The thin walls of the van easily transmitted the voice booming from the radio's speaker. Wally and Mike looked at each other, aghast at what they had just heard.

Mackay and Petar exchanged a few more sarcastic comments before ending the conversation. Mackay shut the radio down and began coiling the cable back up to the antenna. He stepped out of the back of the van and was greeted with two twelve-gauge barrels on either side of his head.

"Howdy, Mackay...Wally and me was just out huntin'...huntin' for Yanks."

♦ ♦ ♦

Jebb sat slouched on his barstool, listening intently to the story being recounted by Wally and Mike. "And he admitted to being part of a Yank conspiracy," Wally said, with a touch of pride in their successful mission.

"That makes sense because he has no history in the South," Jebb replied.

"I found Loon Lake up in Canada. It's a couple of hundred miles north of Toronto in the middle of nowhere," Mike added.

Jebb paused to ponder for a few seconds. "Boys, we're going on a huntin' trip to Canada, and Mackay is coming with us; we may need him."

Chapter 39

The Trap on the River—July 1964

"Here they come, Billy!" Pete yelled across the river as the bow of the canoe came into sight three-hundred yards down the river. The threesome scrambled down the embankment to the pond below. Sally and Pete launched the pontoon boat and picked up Billy on the opposite shore.

"When they get close to the chute, start to yell, and while they're looking at us, they won't even notice the trap," Billy instructed.

Ivan and Yuri were pulling hard, and the cedar strip canoe cut through the water like a knife. "Hey Ivan," Yuri called back to Ivan, who was paddling from the stern position, "there's some fast water coming up."

"Nothing canoe can't handle," Ivan replied confidently.

The pontoon boat was another hundred yards down the river beyond the chute and now well within sight. Pete, doing what Pete did best, rose from the deck to taunt them: "Hey idiots! Come and get us!"

Yuri and Ivan were now fixated upon their prey and paid little attention to the water ahead of them.

"Ha ha...you're ours now, you little vermin!" Ivan was practically smacking his lips in delight. He was much less delighted when he saw what lay across the section of fast water quickly approaching. "Back paddle!" he screamed to his bowman, but it was too late—the current had them and the shore was not an option. The bow of the canoe plowed into the rope that was strung across the rapids. The line stretched, then held and the boat began to yaw sideways just before it slid up the curved bow of the canoe and snapped back to catch Yuri across the chest. Yuri fought to get underneath the rope, but the canoe had now swung across the current and began to swamp. Both Yuri and Ivan were now hanging from the rope while the submerged canoe headed downstream without them. The two struggled futilely to keep their heads above water but soon gave up the fight and joined the canoe heading downstream. Billy and his fellow saboteurs were now well down the river, but not too far ahead to have missed the spectacle.

With the immediate threat of capture by Ivan and Yuri at least temporarily gone, the threesome knew that they had to cover some territory before nightfall. Their energy levels were now very low from lack of food, and after several hours, the boys were only making desultory attempts at paddling and just concentrated on keeping their ship off the rocks. Sally studied the map intently.

"Do you think those guys are really Russian KGB?" Billy asked lackadaisically.

"Who cares what they are. They want us because we know where the gold is." Pete replied. "So why don't we just tell 'em, and maybe they'll leave us alone?"

"That isn't the way it ever works in the movies. If you know too much...they kill you."

"Stop talking like that," Sally interrupted, "besides...I think we have another problem,"

"What now?" Billy stretched himself out on the deck of the raft and stared up at the blue sky.

"I think I know where we are on the river, and we're not far from coming into another river called the Magnetawan."

"Fantastic!" Pete said.

"Not really. Those guys aren't stupid, and they know where we'll be coming out. I bet you they're just waiting for us." Sally's analytical brain was running like a Swiss watch. "We have to get out of this boat before we get to the big river."

"Aw, come on, Sal...I like it just fine right here," Billy protested. The thought of trudging through the bush on an empty stomach was not appealing.

"Billy, there are only two of them chasing us. What do you think the others are doing?" Sally was visibly losing her patience. "Okay, Billy Parker...have it your way. But remember...we're here because we followed you."

Billy took a deep breath and exhaled like a deflated balloon. He glanced over at Pete to see if he could muster some support, but to no avail. Pete threw up his hands in mock resignation. "She's probably right, Billy."

The decision of when and where to abandon ship was quickly being made for them as the temperament of the river started to change. The water became more shallow and ran faster as the raft bucked and dove over the submerged rocks. A couple of hundred yards downstream, the river appeared to boil as the whitewater threw up a misty shroud. "Head for that pool!" Billy yelled at the skipper. Off to their starboard side was one of the few remaining eddy pools before all hell broke loose. Sally held the rudder hard over as the boys pulled for all they were worth. The raft slid nicely into the calm water and ran into shore.

"We have to flip it over," Sally instructed after they had unloaded the few supplies that they had salvaged from the plane.

"Flip it over…what for?" Pete complained, not anxious to exert any more energy than was necessary.

But Billy started to see her logic. "She's right, Pete. We want them to find it upside down." They struggled to lift one pontoon and then shoved the upturned boat back into the current and watched painfully as their faithful ship bashed against the rocks and slowly came apart in the whitewater. There was a sorrowful silence as the last vestiges of the raft disappeared downstream—like they had lost a friend.

"She was a good boat," Sally lamented.

"The best," Pete concurred.

"Pete…Sal…let's get going. If we follow the river, we won't get lost, but we have to stay out of sight…walk about fifty yards up from the bank."

Fortunately for the threesome and for Yuri and Ivan— the days were long in July. It was early evening when Ivan and his comrade made the whitewater—their progress severely hindered by lack of a second paddle. There was no question of shooting any rapids this time as they portaged their canoe around the rough water.

"Look Ivan!" Yuri said, pointing to a half-submerged pontoon jammed between two boulders.

"Goddamn!" Ivan stammered shaking his head, "if those little bastards drowned, Petar going to kill me."

◆ ◆ ◆

Between hunger and fatigue, things were starting to look bleak for the threesome. The endless bush broken up by the odd clearing started to look all the same—like they were making no progress. Another night in the woods would not be so idyllic this time—with no food or energy to build a shelter.

"You guys see what I see?" Billy asked, as if he were seeing a mirage. Twenty yards ahead a small log cabin had appeared in the bush.

"Let's go!" Pete broke into a run followed by his partners. They surveyed the small, round-log structure that had a granite chimney and shuttered windows—as if they had found paradise. "This is somebody's fishin' camp. I've been to lots of them with my dad."

Billy was busy swinging the fire axe at the padlock on the slab door. A couple of well-aimed whacks, and it fell to pieces on the ground. They cautiously entered the cabin, their eyes adjusting to the little light let in by the open door. The cabin consisted of one large room and a loft—with a floor-to-ceiling granite fireplace on one wall and a steep staircase on the opposite side. Every piece of wall seemed to be taken up with trophy fish, fishing rods, hats, raincoats, and the requisite white tail buck staring over the room. Everything was hung by nails driven into the logs. Along the back wall was the kitchen, with a countertop running the length of the room and a sink with a hand-operated pump. Beneath the counter was shelving covered by a blue-and-white-checked cloth to add a touch of civility.

"Look what I've found!" Billy said, pulling up the cloth cover to display rows of cans. The shelves were lined with pork and beans, sardines, corn, peas, and all sorts of weird and wonderful canned foodstuffs. The other two let out a simultaneous "Wow" as they stared with infatuation. To the three of them at that moment, there was nothing more precious in the world than food.

"What are we waitin' for?" Pete exclaimed, grabbing a can opener. There was no time for etiquette as the cans were opened and the contents quickly devoured. Food had never tasted this good.

♦ ♦ ♦

"Another mile and we'll be at the Magnetawan," Ivan said, while he grudgingly paddled the canoe by himself. Ivan and Yuri glided by the fishing camp, hidden seventy yards back in the bush, completely unaware of its existence.

Petar and his two henchmen waited just downstream of the confluence of the Magnetawan and Big Deer rivers— their launch tied along the shore. The sun was going down, and there was still no sign of Ivan and Yuri or the kids.

"Hey, boss, what's that?" one of the henchmen asked, pointing out to a half-submerged pontoon heading downstream.

Petar scanned it with his binoculars. "If that's what I think it is, you had better start looking for bodies. Ivan and Yuri better have a good explanation."

Chapter 40
The Fishing Cabin—July 1964

The old cabin took on a magical ambience after dark, lit up by the soft flickering light of the fire crackling in the fireplace. The place had ghosts—ghosts of bygone fishermen and hundreds of after-dinner conversations by the fireside. Billy sunk into a big old armchair while Sally and Pete took up opposite ends of a sofa. They lounged back contentedly in front of the fire—free from the incessant hunger pangs for the first time in days.

"That was the best food that I've ever eaten," Sally said euphorically, "and at home I won't even eat pork and beans."

"And I ate a can of peas," Pete marvelled. "My mom wouldn't believe it."

"This whole thing seems like a dream," Billy started to philosophize while gazing into the fire. "I went from finding golf balls to running from Russian KGB guys. Doesn't it seem weird to you guys?"

"Billy, if you just stuck to lookin' for golf balls then we wouldn't be in this trouble. My old man says that your middle name is trouble. I wonder what he'll do to me this time?" Pete gazed into the fire, slowly shaking his head at the thought.

"Come on, Pete...you get into enough trouble all by yourself...you don't need me."

"Yeah, with friends like you who needs enemies?"

"You guys think it's weird...what about me. The scariest thing that I've ever done was teasing Millers' dog, and he was even tied up." Billy and Pete roared in laughter. Sally let them calm down before she continued: "You know the strangest thing is...I think I actually like this. I mean, it scares me more than I've ever been scared before...but in the last few days...or week...or whatever it's been...I've had more fun and excitement than in my whole life. I never understood why you guys liked getting chased around the valley so much...now I do."

The boys were quiet now and strangely pensive, which was completely out of character for either twelve-year-old.

"You know, I never thought about it before," Billy started in, "but everything else seems so boring...like school and homework and hanging around the house. When I'm in the valley, I'm always getting into trouble, and I just love going there because it's so much fun."

"Yeah, me too...my dad says I should get my thrills from sports...but it's not the same," Pete said. "I really don't like organized stuff."

Each of them seemed to be content to drift off into their own thoughts as the fire burned down and the evening mellowed. There was the odd perfunctory comment, but soon even this ceased, and they fell into a deep, pleasant slumber.

♦ ♦ ♦

Darkness had fallen when Ivan and Yuri pulled the canoe up alongside the launch. Petar and his boys, who had fallen asleep from the boredom of the evening, were startled out of their reverie by the clunking of the canoe against the launch. The two henchmen jumped into action, and the canoeists found themselves staring down the barrels of two Beretta automatics.

"Put the guns down, you trigger-happy idiots." Petar had little respect for the goons. "Where have you guys been?"

"We had a little accident a few miles back...got caught in some whitewater...really bad stuff...and the canoe flipped." Ivan wasn't about to mention they had fallen into a trap.

Petar was not a sympathetic guy, and he shook his head in feigned disgust. "So where are they?"

Yuri wisely chose to remain silent and let Ivan take the heat. "Well ah...they...they...may have drowned."

"That's what I was afraid of. So now how do we locate the bullion!" he raved, not expecting an answer. Ivan attempted a reply, but Petar signalled to him to shut up while he thought. "I'm not so sure they've drowned. Those kids are smarter than we've ever given them credit for," he said with grudging respect. "Pitch the tents...we're not going anywhere."

Chapter 41

Lake Oconee, Georgia—July 1964

The amphibious Grumman Goose airplane proudly sported the Confederate battle flag on her tail. Above the flag were the letters "CAF," designating this plane as part of the Confederate Air Force. She was being loaded up at the dock on Lake Oconee before the long flight north. There was plenty of freight capacity in the eight-seat aircraft since there was only going to be four passengers and a pilot making the trip. All the hunting rifles and fishing rods were laid out in plain sight, to make them nice and obvious for Customs to see. All the illegal firearms were broken down and hidden in secret compartments all over the plane, along with enough ammunition to start a small war.

Jebb, Mike, and Wally, all decked out in their finest "camo" attire, went over the last-minute preparations for the so-called hunting trip. This was technically correct except that the game was gold bullion. Frank Mackay sat quietly in the plane, handcuffed to his seat.

"Here comes Butch...the finest pilot in the Confederate Air Force," Jebb said, looking down the dock. Butch, rugged and tall, was the epitome of the Hollywood pilot. Decked out in a flying suit and aviator glasses, he came swaggering up the dock.

"Mornin' gentlemen," Butch greeted them with his fine Southern drawl. "Great day to go flying."

"That it is, Butch...that it is," Jebb replied. "Let's go over the flight plan one more time."

"Okay boys," Butch began, "weather looks CAVOK all the way to the border and beyond. First stop is Columbus International to refuel; then we head for Sault Ste. Marie, Canada. We put her down on the water and clear Customs at Sault Ste. Marie and refuel again. Wally stays on the plane with Mackay while we check into some fleabag motel for the night. Next day, we set course for this here Loon Lake where Mackay says they have their camp."

"Couldn't have said it any better myself," Jebb said. "When we hit Canada, we'll be winging it, so to speak. All we know is that the Yanks are up there chasing three kids...three kids who know where the bullion is. So we got to get to 'em first...any questions?" They each indicated in the negative. "Then let's get her into the air."

Chapter 42
In Disguise—July 1964

As he opened his eyes the following morning, Billy had to take a long, hard look at his surroundings until it finally sunk in that he was not in his bedroom at home. This was the way it happened every morning since their escapade had begun—like a dream that had turned into reality. He had to review the events of the past few days to convince himself that what he saw was real and not a figment of his imagination. He glanced over at the couch where Sally was still happily in dream land, but the end where Pete had settled in for the night was empty. A little alarmed at the absence of his buddy, he jumped out of his chair and headed for the door. The alarm was quickly turning to semi-panic as his gaze panned the immediate vicinity of the cabin and there was still no sign of Pete. The sound of a door slamming from behind the cabin calmed his spiralling tension. Quick as a startled deer, Billy rounded the back corner of the building and barely avoided a head-on collision with his partner heading the other way.

"You gotta see what I found," Pete exclaimed. He led Billy to a shed fifty yards behind the cabin, which had obviously been opened using an axe for the key. "No more paddling for us." He proudly displayed the contents of the shed, which included a cedar-strip boat and outboard motor.

"Holy smokes!" Billy said as he handled the motor like it was some kind of icon. "Do you know how to work this?"

"It's an Evinrude outboard, just like my dad's...and five gallons of gas. When my dad and I go fishing, I do all the driving. We're going to have a nice easy ride outta here."

"Yeah, but what if they're waiting for us at the big river? We'll drive right into them."

Pete thought about the dilemma for a second. "Let's go ask Sal. She'll come up with a plan." By now the boys were happy to defer the "brain work" to Sally, who seemed to have a knack for getting them out of tight spots.

Sally was beginning to take pride in her new role as the brains of the operation. Her superior imagination, which had served her so well in school, now had a very practical use. The new plan did not take long to devise. "Okay Pete, put the life jacket on first," she instructed. He pulled the bulky orange vest over his head. "Now put on this rain slicker." Pete slid his head and arms into the dark green rubber slicker, which could have doubled as a tent. "Now the hat." He pulled the fedora covered in fishing lures down to his ears. Billy giggled in delight as she began to smear charcoal from the previous night's fire all over his face.

"Shut up, Billy," Pete attempted a weak reprimand to his buddy, but found it hard to hide his enjoyment of the whole procedure as well.

"Perfect...you look just like Joe Fisherman...as long as you stay far enough from shore," Sally said, admiring her work. She was right. Pete now appeared about twice his size and from a distance could easily be mistaken for a half-shaved old angler.

♦ ♦ ♦

Petar and the boys had broken camp first thing in the morning. The mist was still coming off the river when he sent Ivan and Yuri back to the lodge to get the tracking dogs. Waiting for their return, he and his two henchmen sat around a campfire. "Trust me...they'll be hiking through the bush...the bloodhounds will pick them up in no time. That busted-up pontoon boat was just a ploy," Petar said to no one in particular and more to reassure himself.

"Boss...do you hear that?" one of the henchmen said, looking out over the river. The sound of an outboard engine was coming through the mist, and shortly thereafter a sixteen-foot, cedar-strip boat began to materialize. The henchman picked up his rifle and aimed it in the direction of the craft.

"Put that goddamn thing down!" Petar ordered. "You can't just take a shot at every fisherman that goes by...you'll have the Mounties all over us, you idiot." Petar smiled and waved in his most neighbourly fashion. The old bugger at the helm of the fishing boat raised his arm to return the greeting and then resettled himself in the seat, with his back towards shore, as he slowly chugged out of sight down the river and around the bend.

"The coast is clear. You can come out now," said a triumphant Pete to his two stowaways. Billy and Sally dragged themselves out from under the deck.

♦ ♦ ♦

The dogs were yelping and straining against their leashes—raring to go into action. "Give them scent from the bedding, and let's get outta here," Petar instructed. The dogs seemed to know instinctively who their prey was and were not much interested in the pillows and sheets that Ivan was shoving in their muzzles. "We'll follow the shore of the river until they pick up their trail." The search party hit the bush like a cattle stampede, dragged along by the hounds.

After two hours of tramping through the woods with nothing to show for it, the party walked into the fishing camp. The dogs went into a frenzy with the fresh scent of their prey everywhere, and Petar started to reluctantly piece the story together with the available evidence. The broken padlocks on the cabin and shed, the track from the keel of the boat leading from the shed towards the water, and the dog's insistence of following the trail to the river's edge did not make the obvious any easier to take. He knew that they had been fooled again. "You guys paddled right by here...and I waved to them going right under my nose," Petar huffed in disgust, not knowing who to be angry with.

"What's wrong with doze kids...no sense of fair play," Ivan said, trying to mitigate their gullibility. "We can go after them with the launch, boss."

"Sure, Ivan...and what do we do when we run out of gas...swim?" Petar rolled his eyes in disgust and wandered off to think and be clear of anymore fatuous comments. "They have a four-hour head start on us, and they should be running out of gas right about now...assuming that they only had five gallons. If they paddle and drift with the current, it will be the middle of the night at the earliest before they hit the bay...more likely around sunup. We'll get out of here now, and I'll arrange a little greeting party for them," Petar thought out loud.

Chapter 43
Magnetawan River—July 1964

The old Evinrude outboard pushed them along at a respectable eight knots with Pete proudly at the helm. Following the river was quite simple since it was wide and quite predictable and, save for the odd log, had few unpleasant surprises. They passed under an old railway trestle, but beyond that, there were no signs of civilization anywhere.

After three uneventful hours, the outboard began to surge uncontrollably as if it were just clinging to life. The threesome, who had been lulled into a pleasant sense of security, were now jolted back to reality.

"What's happening, Pete?" Billy asked.

"Out of gas." After one last death rattle, the engine went silent. "Looks like we're rowing."

Using a life preserver as a pillow, Sally was relaxing across one of the bench seats. She reluctantly dragged herself vertical. With a yawn and a smile, she surveyed their surroundings. "You know, I was just thinking about my mom and dad. They must be worried sick. I wish I could somehow let them know I'm okay...okay at least for now," she lamented. "You guys think about your parents?"

"Yeah...I think about them all the time...but not 'cause they're worried," Pete replied.

"I never really thought about them being worried," Billy pitched in, "cause usually they just seem mad at me for messin' up...but maybe it's 'cause they're worried."

"Until now I've never done much to make them mad," Sally said, "so it's kinda new to me."

Pete smiled at her innocence. "Don't worry, Sal. After awhile you get used to it, but I do feel kinda bad if they are worried."

Even with the engine tilted, the big, old cedar strip boat rowed like a log, and most of their progress downstream came with the gentle current. After several more hours, it was fast becoming obvious to the threesome that they had to decide between a night on the water or another night camped out in the bush.

♦ ♦ ♦

Everybody was feeling pretty ragged as Butch taxied the Grumman Goose up to the customs dock at Sault Ste. Marie. After ten hours in the air, the drone of the twin, four-hundred-and-fifty horsepower, radial engines had implanted a permanent hum in their ears. The Goose did a neat one-hundred-and-eighty-degree turn and drifted smartly up to the wharf. "Butch...you and I will get out and do the talking," Jebb instructed, "the rest of you guys stay here with Mackay. Chances are the customs guy will want to say hello, so do the South proud with your hospitality...and keep the .45 in Mackay's back." Butch and Jebb started down the dock as the crisp uniformed Customs agent headed their way.

"Evening, gentlemen—welcome to Canada—and to what do we owe this pleasure?"

"Evening, officer...I'm the pilot of this little bird," Butch replied. "We've just flown up from Georgia by way of Columbus."

"Why, you've come a long way...sure hope that you had an uneventful flight."

"Long and boring, sir," Jebb said. "We've come to do some hunting and fishing and just generally enjoy your beautiful country." The customs officer smiled with approval.

"Well, come on inside and fill out some paperwork, declare your firearms...that sort of thing...oh, and you'll need fishing and hunting licenses. You can leave the plane at the dock, and I can recommend some good accommodation for the night."

"I've heard about that great Canadian hospitality, and it's definitely true," Jebb gushed.

"And I've never met a Southern boy that I couldn't trust," the officer replied. Jebb and Butch flashed each other a relieved smile.

Chapter 44

A Direction-Finding Steer—July 1964

"True North...this is Deep South...come in, True North," the radio cackled in Petar's office.

What the hell is he calling for? Petar thought to himself. *He's days away from the scheduled time.*

"Go ahead, Deep South," Petar replied suspiciously.

Mackay grunted as Mike poked him in the ribs with the gun as a gentle reminder. "Just checking in on the treasure hunt...have you got those kids yet...and how are the northern lights this time of year?"

Petar urgently signalled to Ivan. "Get a DF steer on their bearing next time he transmits...and get signal strength," he ordered before replying to Mackay. "What kids would that be, Deep South? I don't follow your question."

"Don't answer him yet," Jebb ordered Mackay. "You guys told me that they were chasing some kids who knew where the gold was?" He glared at Mike and Wally.

"Heard it with my own ears, Jebb," Mike replied, feeling attacked.

"Me too, Jebb," Wally pitched in.

"Ask him again," Jebb commanded Mackay.

Mackay was sweating now, knowing that Petar suspected something was up and was playing dumb. "You know...the kids!"

"I think that there is some confusion, Deep South. I did mention some kids, but they had nothing to do with the bullion," Petar replied.

"He's a lyin' bastard," Jebb huffed. "Tell him you're signing off."

"Deep South signing off."

"Roger Deep South."

Mackay was flushed and visibly nervous, knowing that he was in a very perilous position.

"You Yanks even lie to each other," Jebb started in on Mackay. "We're going to pay your friends an uninvited visit...they think we're in Georgia so they won't be expecting us."

♦ ♦ ♦

Petar put the microphone down and looked over at Ivan, who was tweaking a direction finder. "You get a bearing?"

"Looks like three-hundred degrees from north-west...and strong signal...maybe a couple hundred miles at the most," Ivan replied.

Petar wandered over to a map on the wall and traced out three-hundred degrees from their position. "They're right on our doorstep...probably in Sault Ste. Marie."

"Why you ask me to get a steer, boss...you never do that before?" Ivan queried.

"Because he mentioned the northern lights...that means he's in some sort of trouble." Petar pondered in silence for a few seconds. "I have a strong suspicion that we are going to have uninvited guests."

Chapter 45
Georgian Bay—July 1964

The sun was descending behind the pines, leaving a beautiful red hue on the sky and on the river behind them. It was a wonderful but ominous sight to the threesome because it meant that darkness would soon fall as they drifted into the unknown. Most of the activity in the boat consisted of the occasional pull on an oar by Pete to keep them straight while the other two were comfortably flaked out across the bench seats.

"Let's stay out here for the night," Sally said, while pondering the dark walls of the forest closing in on them from each shore.

"That sounds good to me," Billy replied.

"Make that three," Pete said.

"Once we get out to the bay, there has to be some people around, or even a town." Sally was trying to sound optimistic.

"We should go right to the police and report those guys," Billy added.

"Who's ever gonna believe us...the KGB...gold bullion...they'll think we're nuts," Pete replied.

"Not if we lead them to that crashed airplane," Sally offered.

"Yeah, if we can even find it again," Billy said.

Sally let out a short giggle, pondering a humorous thought. "You know when you get back to school every September and you have to write those stupid 'what did you do on your summer vacation' essays?" Pete and Billy started to chuckle, getting her drift.

"I might even get a decent mark for a change," Pete said.

"Probably not...teacher will just think you made it up," Billy stifled that idea.

A rising full moon took the edge off the darkness and glistened on the river, creating a magical, mesmerizing ambience. As they floated along with the current, the conversation trailed off and the three weary travellers slowly drifted off to sleep.

It might have been three hours later or it could have been twenty minutes—Billy had no idea how long they had slept. He looked up at the sky, which was so bathed in moonlight that no stars were visible, while his two shipmates were still curled up on their makeshift beds. His vision was partially obscured by the gunwales of the boat, but as he started to haul himself upright, it was soon apparent that something had changed in their environment. The walls of trees were now gone. Billy sprang up from the hard bench seat and looked back at the mouth of the river, which was a quarter of a mile behind them and growing in distance. They were now well into a large bay, with no shore visible on the far side.

"Pete...Sal...wake up!" Sally, who was curled up in a bed of life preservers under the front deck, mumbled something incomprehensible and rolled over. "Pete, get up!" Billy concentrated on rousing his buddy, who was within shaking distance on the floor of the boat.

"What do ya want?" came the irritated reply.

"We made it...we're in the bay!"

The news took a few seconds to sink in, and suddenly like a man possessed, Pete bolted upright. "Ho-l-y crap!" he uttered as he scanned the horizon in amazement. "Sal...you gotta see this!" Pete scrambled to the bow to wake her up.

Still groggy and rubbing her eyes, Sally crawled out from under the deck and did a three-hundred-and-sixty-degree sweep of the horizon. "Hurrah! Hurrah! We're going home!" All three knew from studying the aircraft map that a small village was due south along the coast.

The boys each grabbed an oar and began rowing with a renewed vigour while Sally sat on the deck looking for the first sign of light along the coast. They were a mile offshore but making good time as the boys rowed with the energy of a horse heading back to the barn.

"You know, it's kinda scary out here. At least on the river the shore was always in reach...but I'm not sure that I could even swim to shore now," she said.

"Don't worry, Sal, nothin's going to stop us now," Billy reassured her.

"We sure showed those old Russians," Pete started in with his typical bravado. "Just wait till I tell the guys back home...why—"

"Billy...what's that?" Sally asked, barely above a whisper, which was drowned out by Pete's monologue. The boys rowed facing the stern and could not see the turbulent water heading directly for them fifty yards away.

"I bet we'll even be in the papers...maybe the *Telegram*—"

"Billy! What is it?" Sally screamed pointing directly ahead. This time she caught their attention, and the boys did a quick about-face to see a wake of bubbling water heading right on to their bow. Sally jumped horrified off the deck and back into the boat. All three stood huddled together in a state of shock, trying to make sense of what was approaching them. There was a collective gasp of terror as the wake swept underneath their hull and the moonlight revealed a huge, black object sliding silently under the dark waters. This time the collective gasp turned to a blood-curdling, hair-raising scream as the boat shimmied in the turbulence and the threesome toppled to the floor.

Fifty yards away, the bubbling waters began to boil and geyser-like waves emanated from below the surface. They silently held each other, transfixed on a huge black object ascending from the depths. The conning tower rose and rose until the long, black hull of the submarine broke the surface, and then all was quiet. They stood in stunned silence for several minutes until the clanging of metal on metal broke their spell and the silhouette of a man appeared at the top of the conning tower. The penetrating beam of a spotlight swept across the water until it hit the small boat and temporarily blinded the awestruck threesome, who threw up their arms in defense.

"You...in the small boat...I command you to report here immediately!" a foreign-accented voice called through a megaphone. "Do not delay!" There was no hesitation among the traumatized threesome and absolutely no desire to flee as they rowed to the sub. The cedar strip boat banged into the sub's hull, and the three scrambled aboard.

"Welcome aboard, children...I hope that we did not frighten you too much," the boat's captain greeted the threesome from the conning tower. He was quite sincere in his wishes since he had children of the same age back home and was very empathetic to their situation. "I am Captain Nemski, but you may call me Ilya. Petar told me that you were coming...we caught you at the mouth of the river with night vision binoculars."

"Captain Nemski...we just wanna go home." Sally tore at his heart strings with her plaintive pleas.

"Don't worry, my dear...we will not harm you."

"We'll tell you where the lousy old gold is...we never cared about it...just let us go home," Billy pleaded.

Chapter 46

Loon Lake Lodge, Algonquin Park—July 1964

Petar dozed uncomfortably on a cot in his office, slipping in and out of a restless sleep. Even when he was fortunate enough to catch a few winks of sleep, he would be tormented by dreams of capture and his fate as a foreign spy. He was tired of life in the bush in a hostile country and longed for the day when his relief would come and he could return to a peaceful, plebeian life in his hometown of Leningrad. He was weary of constantly playing his role as the dedicated, emotionless patriot who put the motherland ahead of everything, including his own life. Petar was trained that to show emotion was to show weakness, and the weak are defeated.

"Far North...this is Neptune...come in, Far North." Petar ignored the radio call as his subconscious incorporated it into one of his dreams. "Far North, come in!" Petar bolted upright as his consciousness took control and processed the incoming message.

"This is Far North...the northern lights are out tonight...the northern lights are out tonight...do you copy, Neptune?"

There was a brief pause from Neptune. "Neptune copies...mission accomplished, Far North."

"Excellent...will rendezvous at 2400 hours, Neptune."

Petar threw the mike down and let out a yelp of relief as he charged out of his office.

♦ ♦ ♦

Jebb, Mike, and Butch finished up their breakfast in the dining room of the White Pines motel. It was a typical northern restaurant with the knotty pine panelling adorned with six-point bucks, lake trout, and all manner of unfortunate wildlife hanging off the walls. The breakfast of greasy fried eggs, sausages, toast, and home fries suited the Southern boys to a T. "I think I could get used to living here," Butch said. "It kind of reminds me of the South except it's a damn sight colder."

"I bet ya that Mackay and Wally in the plane are saying the same thing right about now," Mike replied.

Jebb smirked a little at the thought. "Somebody had to stay onboard with Mackay, and Wally drew the short straw. Let's get on with the plan." Jebb pulled out a tattered map and laid it out on the table. "We fly pretty much due east to this here Loon Lake...in Algonkin...Algon-something park," he stumbled over the pronunciation. "Mackay says their camp is on the north shore...and he's in no position to lie to us at the moment. We land out of sight on the southeast side and then hit the bush and take 'em by surprise...any questions?"

"Yeah...how many are we talking about?" Butch asked.

"Mackay says five, maybe six...but we got surprise and we got the weapons. Besides...it was two to one at Bull Run and we still whipped 'em."

"Well, amen to that," Mike said with a satisfied drawl.

The Southerners bade farewell to the customs officers, and the Goose was refuelled and back in the air by mid-morning. For the next hour and a half, all was quiet in the cabin as they marvelled at the endless expanse of green bush and blue lakes unfolding beneath them. Up front, Butch and Jebb struggled to navigate—trying to identify one lake from the hundreds visible to them was like finding the proverbial needle in a haystack. Back in the States, Butch could always drop down and read the town name from a water tower if his navigation aids failed him, but here it was all seat-of-the-pants, dead-reckoning flying. "Goddamn...I haven't flown like this since I was a rookie pilot...but if my training hasn't failed me, that should be our lake straight ahead." When he figured that they were within gliding distance of the south shore, Butch pulled the power for a dead-stick landing. With the props windmilling, the Goose swished over the treetops on the lakeshore and silently touched down.

Jebb shook his head in amazement. "Damn...you're good."

"The best, partner," Butch was not big on modesty.

Chapter 47

The Raid,
Loon Lake Lodge—July 1964

With face paint, full camo gear, and M16s at the ready, the four Southerners and their hostage trudged through the bush, heading for the camp on the north shore. For Jebb, this was a picnic compared to clawing his way through the jungle during a stint in Vietnam. The others grunted and cursed as they tripped over juniper bushes and the underbrush tore at their clothes. After stern looks from Jebb, they kept any disgruntled feelings down to a few similar expletives uttered under their breath. He wished he had his old platoon with him instead of these "play soldier on Saturday afternoon" guys.

Trails through the bush and the odd empty liquor bottle indicated they were nearing some sort of human habitation. Jebb signalled for the others to hold back while he crept onward until the outlines of a log cabin took shape about one-hundred yards ahead of him. It was déjà vu for Jebb, with all the same fear and exhilaration of creeping up on a Viet Cong encampment. As per their plan, he signalled for two of the others to sweep across to the far side of the cabin while Wally stayed back with a gun on Mackay, who would be their bargaining chip, should they need it.

At fifty yards out, there was still no sign of any activity, and Jebb signalled Butch and Mike to split up for the final rush to the cabin. At his signal, they took off running, closing the distance from three sides with guns at their shoulders. As they reached the cabin, all was still eerily quiet—at least until they pounded across the front porch and kicked in the front door. Inside the old lodge, they proceeded to make match sticks out of every door as they stormed each room ready to fire off their weapons. It was soon very apparent that nobody was home, and fearing an ambush, they charged back outside and tore around every inch of the camp looking for somebody to shoot. All to no avail—the place was deserted.

♦ ♦ ♦

At the same time, but now quite a distance from the camp, the Beaver floatplane was beached on the north shore of Byng Inlet while its Russian crew either cast fishing lines into the bay or relaxed on the shore sipping vodka. For Petar and the boys, it was a pleasant way to spend the afternoon, even if it was all just a façade for any wayward boaters that happened to pass by. It was just your typical good old boys' well-lubricated fishing party. Petar was feeling pretty good about life as he scanned the bay with binoculars in between slugs of the bottle. "It's hard to believe that a Russian submarine is just lying on the bottom out there, isn't it."

"Sure glad it's them and not me," Ivan replied, shaking his head. "When they drop me off one year ago, I think I was going to die from claustrophobia in dat thing."

"Better get used to the idea, Ivan...come midnight, we're going aboard again." Ivan shuddered at the thought.

♦ ♦ ♦

Jebb, Butch, Larry, and Mike made themselves right at home in Petar's old office, which was now stripped down to the old tattered furniture and a few maps on the wall. It looked a bit like a locker room after a victory as each one of them had their own peculiar way of slouching into a comfortable position on the available chairs and couches. Nobody came right out and said it, but they were all feeling pretty smug after taking the camp in their precision military operation. Everyone except for Jebb, who knew what the real thing felt like—to him this was a joke.

Jebb ignored the bravado circulating around the room and stared at a beaten-up wall map. "Mike...you said something about chasin' those kids down a river...and an ambush at another river. You know...when you were listenin' to Mackay on the radio."

"Yeah, that's right. Chasin' em down a river that came out at a larger river."

Jebb hauled his six-foot frame out of the chair and headed for the map. "Well lookie here...there's a red X right on this Big Deer Lake. A river goes out of the west end," Jebb followed the river with his finger, "and it comes out at this bigger river." He stopped to ponder. "It looks to be about fifty miles west of here. Butch...ya think that you can find this shit-hole of a lake?"

"I can find anything," Butch replied with his usual modesty.

"Good, then tomorrow, boys, we are taking a little trip to Big Deer Lake."

♦ ♦ ♦

Petar scanned the bay with his night-vision binoculars. To the naked eye, there was nothing but a black void on the horizon on this moonless night, but his glasses could pick up the contours of the opposite shore and anything in between. Exactly at 2400 hours, the conning tower silently broke the surface one mile offshore and eerily rose above the bay like some sort of sea creature. "Everybody in the Zodiac...let's go," he commanded.

"Welcome aboard, Comrade Petar," Ilya greeted his first guest down the ladder.

"Great to be aboard a ship of the motherland," Petar answered, giving the captain a Russian bear hug. "Take me to see my three young friends." The others followed him down the ladder with Ivan looking pale and phobic, the last to arrive.

Ilya led Petar down the narrow passage of the cramped submarine. The sub was small by any navy's standards and was only designed to operate out of a mother ship, dropping off and picking up personnel in clandestine operations. Ilya threw open a curtain that gave a modicum of privacy to three small, stacked bunks fastened to the hull of the craft. Billy, Pete, and Sally reluctantly began to stir from their slumber.

"Greetings, my friends...we meet again." Petar was genuinely pleased to see the threesome who he had developed a grudging respect for. They slipped from their bunks and lined up in front of him. "I must compliment you on your abilities...you are very worthy adversaries."

"Thanks," Billy diffidently mumbled, not entirely sure what Petar meant.

"They would make great young pioneers for the motherland, wouldn't you say, Petar?"

"They certainly would...they would be a credit to any nation. Whose idea was it to slip by us in the fishing boat?"

"I...I guess it was mine," Sally answered shyly.

Petar smiled in admiration. "You are a very smart young lady." Sally blushed coyly. "Now...if you would be so good to tell us where our Otter ended up." The threesome looked among themselves, confused. "I mean the airplane that you were so briefly aboard."

"Oh, the airplane," Pete started in. "Well, Billy flew it and we crashed."

"Slow down...slow down...first things first. What happened to the pilot?" Petar cut in.

"He must have fallen out...the plane started to go crazy and then it settled down a bit, and when we went to the cockpit, it was empty," Billy explained.

Petar looked at Ilya in amazement. "Must have left with Chuck."

"Who's Chuck?"

"I'll explain later. Now can you show us where the plane is now?"

"Sure," Sally answered enthusiastically. She hoped that the information would set them free. "I'll show you on the map that we found on the plane."

They continued the debriefing gathered around the only small table available on the sub. Sally pored over the map, planting an X where the Otter lay on the north shore of Big Deer Lake. Billy and Pete happily recounted all the details of their journey to date, as if they were talking with a group of buddies. The fact that they were not among friends had completely disappeared in the false camaraderie.

"Just by the point on the north shore of Big Deer Lake," Petar said to Ilya after the threesome had returned to their bunks. "Tomorrow morning we will fly in and load up the

Beaver. It should take several trips because that plane won't take the load."

"Good, because the mother ship is due by here tomorrow night...she's going to the lakehead to pick up a load of grain. I have to get this sub docked for re-supply."

"They will be very pleased when they see the additional cargo that we bring aboard," Petar added.

"What about Dimitri...sorry…I meant Mackay?"

"He's in some sort of trouble, but I don't know what. It doesn't surprise me with that group of crazies."

"And what do we do with the children?"

"For now, take them with us to the mother ship...we'll decide after that."

Chapter 48

Standoff in the Bush—July 1964

By the time Jebb and the boys slugged their way back through the bush to the Grumman Goose and got her back into the air, the morning was half spent. After a short thirty minute flight due west, Big Deer Lake began to appear on the horizon and Butch started a slow descent for a surveillance run up the lake. "Looks like we have company," Butch called to Jebb over the din of the engines. "There...on the north side." He pointed to a floatplane tied off, parallel to the shore.

Jebb fixed the binoculars on the aircraft as they swung by at one thousand feet. "Let's put her down. There's a few guys wandering around the plane...might just be fishermen, but we gotta be ready for anything."

Petar, Ilya, and the rest of the crew watched with concern as the Goose turned onto final approach for Big Deer Lake. Two floatplanes landing on the same lake in this part of the country was a rare occurrence.

Butch greased it onto the surface of the lake and let her settle into the water. He swung the plane around to starboard and taxied at an idle towards the floatplane on the shore.

"Okay boys, keep the guns down, but keep 'em ready," Jebb ordered. "Put her into that little clearing over there, Butch." Jebb pointed to a small piece of beach about fifty yards from the Beaver floatplane.

Petar, Ilya, Yuri, and Ivan stood silently fixated on the awkward appearance of the amphibious aircraft that was starting to spoil their day. Things had been going well as they loaded the bullion onto the Beaver, and up until that point, the Russian KGB were having an enjoyable afternoon. The Grumman Goose shut its engine down and glided silently onto the beach.

"Okay you guys, stay well back. Keep the guns out of sight...but ready. I'm doing all the talking...if I need you; you'll know it. We're just here on a fishing trip!" Petar turned to wipe the beads of sweat off his forehead and regain his composure. He was the picture of calm as he started to saunter towards the shore.

"We don't know who these guys are...they just might be boys out on a fishing trip and we don't want to alarm anybody," Jebb instructed. "You guys stay back here and keep the guns out of sight. I'll do the talking." Jebb climbed out of the cockpit door, trying to look casual and non-threatening.

As they closed the gap between them, Jebb and Petar smiled amicably as if they were greeting old friends. Any sign of tension was well disguised by both of them.

"Howdy pal...we never expect to meet anybody way out here when we're fishing," Jebb opened the dialogue.

"Either do we," Petar replied, sticking out his hand. "Name's Peter...from Toronto...where you guys from?"

"You can probably tell from the accent that we're Americans, from the South, that is...from the Deep South...Georgia, to be exact...name's Jebb."

"Well, welcome to Canada," Petar replied, cringing inside. His suspicions were confirmed. These were the Southern boys that Dimitri had infiltrated, and he knew what they were after. "I've always been fond of Americans from the Southern states...find them much friendlier than Americans from the northern states." Petar played to Jebb's secessionist beliefs.

"That's because we are friendlier. And we're not American. We're from the Confederate States of America." Petar began whistling a rough version of Dixie, to the delight of Jebb. "For a Canadian, you do a fine rendition of Dixie. I always knew that you Canucks were partial to the South."

"That we are, Jebb. You guys should have won that war."

"That war ain't lost yet, partner. Let's just say we took a one-hundred-year hiatus. We'll finish what Lee started."

Petar was relaxing a bit now. He could see that he was slowly gaining the confidence of Jebb. "Well, we were just on our way out...but maybe we could plan to meet up a little later and share some Jack Daniels...talk about your unfinished war a little more."

"That is a damn good idea...you guys are real hospitable—" Jebb cut himself short. He grimaced as he stared at the ground directly to the left of Petar, who looked to his left and spotted what now had every bit of Jebb's attention. To his horror, a gold bar that must have been dropped lay gleaming in the sunshine with the letters CSA clearly stamped in the metal. In a flash, Jebb made for the sidearm hidden under his camo jacket with Petar just one step behind him reaching for the pistol in his shoulder holster. As they watched the events transpire between their two leaders, the Southerners and the Russians scrambled for their rifles. The sound of AK47s and M16s being cocked echoed through the bush. Then all fell silent in a classic standoff. Each Southerner had a Russian in his sights, and each Russian had a Southerner lined up, and no one dared pull the trigger, knowing full well that the first shot would spark a mutually destructive massacre. Pulses raced and sweat dripped from the brows of all the potential combatants. Each passing second amplified the tension, which was heading to crescendo where all hell was going to break loose. The next move belonged to Petar and Jebb, and they both knew it.

"I'm going to put my gun down very slowly, and I will instruct my men to do the same. Please follow our lead, and no one will get hurt," Petar slowly and carefully enunciated each word so that there would be no misunderstanding. His slowly lowered the barrel of his side arm. "Ilya, Yuri, Ivan...calmly lower your rifles." His three comrades complied.

"Boys...lower those guns real slow," Jebb ordered. All barrels were now at least temporarily pointed in a safe direction, but one quick movement would set things off, and the tension was still palpable.

"Now I am going to put my gun on the ground and ask one of my colleagues to do the same. I would like some time to confer with him...we will remain in sight," Petar cautiously advised.

"That gold belongs to the Confederacy...it belongs to us. You'd better start talking about giving it back to us," Jebb replied. "Go ahead...real slow."

"Ilya...put your gun on the ground and meet in front of that pine tree," Petar motioned to a tall pine fifty yards from the confrontation. Both unarmed men walked slowly away from the group.

"Who the hell are these guys?" asked a clearly alarmed Ilya as they reached the pine.

"They are part of that group that we infiltrated down in the Southern states. There're still fighting the Civil War," Petar answered, "and they want the gold."

"So they are not particularly fond of the United States of America."

"That is correct...you heard him...he wants to continue the war...leave the union. We infiltrated them to see what they were all about; to see how serious they were, but we got preoccupied with the gold."

"So it appears that we have a bit of a common interest."

"As they say, the enemy of my enemy is my friend," Petar quoted. "Our enemy is the United States of America, and our purpose being here is to cause them as much disruption as possible."

"So we are looking at the solution. We play to our common interests," Ilya advised.

"Exactly...so we give them the gold...who cares...they're sort of on our side anyway."

"I doubt that they are communist, Petar."

"Probably not...but if they use the gold to finance terrorist operations, they do our work for us."

"Pardon me if I sound disrespectful. But those guys do not look like they could organize a parade," Ilya said sarcastically.

"You are probably correct, Ilya, but in some ways that will make our job easier." Petar and Ilya returned to the group.

"Okay let's hear it...what's the decision?" Jebb demanded.

"We have decided—" Petar cut himself off when he noticed a handcuffed Dimitri become visible from behind the group of Southerners. "Greetings Comrade Dimitri. How are you?" He asked in Russian.

"Very well," Dimtri replied in Russian, "and yourself?"

"Just excellent," a smiling Petar answered.

"What the hell language they talking, Jebb?" Mike was becoming alarmed. "Yanks talk English...must be code, Jebb!" The alarm was contagious among the Southerners, and the gun barrels started to come up again. Petar knew that he must diffuse the situation before panic ensued.

"Easy, easy, gentlemen! Let's get something straight right away...we're not Yanks, we're Russians. KGB to be exact."

"What the hell you talking about...and make it fast!" Jebb waved the barrel of his weapon like a baton.

"Let me explain," Dimitri cut in. "You know me as Frank Mackay, but I am really Dimitri Olganov of the Russian KGB." The Southern boys stared at him aghast. "We Russians are a peaceful people, but the government of the United States is intent on overthrowing us...just like they did to you one hundred years ago. Ten years ago, I joined your group because we felt that we had a common cause...an enemy that would not leave us alone." Jebb and the boys started to soften up a touch. "I had to come into your group under false pretenses because of all the propaganda that the United States was feeding you."

"So you're a bunch of commies," Wally piped in defiantly.

"Shut up, Wally...let him talk," Jebb slapped him down.

"Look...forget economic systems...we are just like you...we want to be left alone, but they won't let us," Petar said, playing to their commonalities. "The gold is yours...but you need our help."

"Us Southern boys don't need anybody's help," Jebb replied, showing his stubborn, Southern pride.

"Agreed...you have shown that one Southerner is as good as ten Yanks," Petar stroked the Southern pride. "But everyone can use help. We can turn that gold into cold, hard, US currency...and at the going rate. And with all that cash and the resources that we have available to us, we can help you carry out some very effective operations...if you know what I mean."

"This is all too goddamn weird," Jebb said, shaking his head in bewilderment, "Now it's our turn to talk...leave your guns on the ground." He carefully laid his gun down and cautiously headed back to confer with his group.

"This has got to be some sort of trick, Jebb. I wouldn't trust those guys as far as I can throw 'em," Mike said.

"Neither do I," Jebb replied, "but I think they're Russians 'cause I heard some Russian in Vietnam when we captured this commie...was there to advise the Viet Cong even though the official line denied the Ruskies were there."

"Even if they're not legit, we have a problem," Butch started in. "If our Grumman could carry that load of gold, which it can't, we'd never get it back into the States. They'd nail us at Customs. We need cold hard cash."

"Bunch of commie bastards if you ask me," Wally sneered.

"We're not askin' you, Wally...and if they're commies or not doesn't matter. The guy may be right...we have a common cause," Jebb replied. "Take the cuffs off Mackay…or Dimitri…or whatever the hell his name is. It would be a goodwill gesture." Jebb headed back to the Russian enclave. "Okay, we're willing to talk...but the gold is ours, and it doesn't leave our sight."

Petar nodded his head, "Agreed."

"And what about those kids we've been hearing about...they know too much...they could blow this whole thing wide open," Jebb said.

"They also know enough to have us arrested as spies. Right now they are our captives."

"You can't let em go," Jebb emphasized.

"We have no intention of letting them go. At the moment we just don't know what to do with them." Neither side had the stomach to speculate about an obvious answer to the problem, so the conversation was dropped. Petar held out his hand as a peace offering. Jebb reluctantly reciprocated.

Chapter 49

Meeting the Parents, Don Mills—July 1964

The doorbell rang just as Bert and Barb Parker were sitting down to their ritual gin and tonic before dinner. Ever since Billy had disappeared, the one-or-two-drink cocktail hour had transformed into a three-or-four-drink crutch. They both looked haggard from lack of sleep and the ever-present, gnawing thought that their son was not returning. The gin offered a short ceasefire with reality. "I'll get it," Bert said, reluctantly rising from his chair.

"Good evening, sir, Bert Parker, I assume?" The tall, neatly groomed gentleman at the door had a distinct military bearing, despite being dressed in a suit.

"That's correct."

"I am Sergeant Bryce of the Royal Canadian Mounted Police. I have some information about your son...may I come in?"

For an instant, Bert Parker felt that wallop of dread— the same dread that wartime mothers felt when the military came to the door. "Please do." As they entered the living room, Barb Parker quickly downed her fresh drink, fearing the worst after overhearing the front-door conversation.

"Sergeant, this is my wife, Barb."

"Pleased to meet you, ma'am." She held out a limp hand to the sergeant but did not reply.

"Can I get you a drink, Sergeant?"

"I am afraid not while I'm on duty, but thank you anyway. I have some news about your son, Billy." The sergeant noticed both Parkers immediately tensed up. "Not bad news...we believe that he is still alive." Relief made the Parkers looked like two deflated balloons. "We were given this note, written by a Sally Olmstead, who I believe you know." They both nodded as he handed the note to Bert Parker.

"Please read it aloud, Bert," Barb Parker asked.

To who it may concern,

We are very sorry to break into your cabin and eat some of your food, but we were starving. When we get back, we will pay you for what we took. We are running from the Russians. They want the gold. It is too long a story to tell right now. We're really sorry.

Yours truly,

Sally, Billy, and Pete

"Russians...gold...what is all this about, Sergeant?" asked a perplexed Bert Parker.

"The Russians and the gold part, we don't know, but let me give you some background. First of all, we have verified that the writing is Sally Olmstead's. We have spoken with her parents. About two hundred miles north of here, there is a river called the Big Deer...in an area known as Magnetawan."

"I am familiar with it," Bert Parker said.

"Well, on this river is a fishing camp...very iso-lated...you can only access it by boat. A couple of days ago, the guys who own the camp went in to do some fishing. They found it broken into...someone had spent some time there, and it appears to have been Billy, Sally, and Pete Mills. They left this note."

"Bert, what in God's name would they have been doing up there?" Barb Parker asked, not really expecting a satisfactory answer.

"There is a little more," the Mountie continued. "The fishermen reported that one of their boats was stolen along with a five-horse motor."

"Our Billy wouldn't have done that," said Barb Parker, coming to the defense of her son. "Well, maybe if he had to," she added, realizing that it was a ridiculous point under the circumstances.

"We found the boat floating in Georgian Bay about fifty miles downstream. The engine was out of gas and the oars were out, but otherwise it was in fine shape."

"Do you believe that they were in it, Sergeant?" asked Bert Parker.

"Yes we do, but we have taken prints just to verify it. I will need something around the house here that would have Billy's fingerprints on it."

"Help yourself to his bedroom." Bert Parker gestured down the hall. "Where do we go from here?"

"We think that they may have gone ashore, so we are conducting a land search."

"What about the gold and the Russians?" Barb Parker asked.

"All that we can surmise is that it is some sort of fantasy that they conjured up, but at the moment nothing seems to make much sense."

Chapter 50

On the Mother Ship, Lake Huron—July 1964

In the submerged submarine, night, day, and time were no longer relevant concepts to Billy, Sally, and Pete. There was only boredom, stifling heat, and claustrophobia, so when the threesome lying in their bunks felt the behemoth of steel come to life, it was like a breath of fresh air. Suddenly the place was alive. Clunks and clanks reverberated through the hull, motors whirred, and the sound of rushing water was ubiquitous.

"This is just like the movies," Pete said, "I saw this war movie about U-boats and it sounded just like this."

"I saw it too," Billy replied, "It was really neat...but not so neat when they started bombing them underwater."

"I hate war movies, and I hate this submarine," Sally now had little patience for boyhood fantasies. "Don't you guys ever think about what's going to happen to us?" She had that look of disdain that put an immediate damper on their enthusiasm.

"I guess I don't like to think about it much...things were great when we were on the river...but they're not so great now," Billy reluctantly agreed with her.

"Yeah, but think about it...I'd never been in a plane before and we actually flew one, and now we're in a submarine," Pete said, trying to be upbeat. "How neat is that?"

"Pete...this isn't Disneyland...and we're prisoners."

"She's right, Pete," Billy replied, "We gotta think of a way to escape...and not get caught this time."

"Did you feel that?" Pete said. "I think we're going up." They could feel a deceleration in their horizontal movement and now it felt more like an elevator. As the sub ascended, there was a series of loud bangs on the hull. The whole vessel shuddered, and a frightening surge of adrenalin coursed through the three captives. The sub felt rigid now, and it had lost that soft, floating sensation. From outside of the sub's hull came a cacophony of motors and rushing water that made conversation impossible. The threesome huddled together in fear, trying to make sense of their environment. And then all went quiet except for the sound of footsteps heading towards them down the sub's narrow passageway.

"Okay children, we're home in the mother ship," Petar said as he shoved his head through the curtain wall. "Follow me." The thought of release from their submerged prison sent a palpable surge of relief through Billy, Pete, and Sally. They followed their captor up the conning tower ladder into a huge metal cavern where the sub was now parked, high and dry. The threesome looked around in silent amazement as they inspected this submarine garage.

"Where are we?" Billy was the first to inquire.

"You're in the hold of the Polish freighter *Krakow*. She is especially designed to dock a sub through the bottom of the hull," Petar responded with a touch of pride in his voice.

"This is like James Bond." Pete looked around in awe of his surroundings. Petar frowned at the reference to James Bond, knowing that the Russians did not fare well in those films.

"I thought that you guys were Russians...and this is a Polish boat," Sally queried.

"Follow me." Petar smiled at her astuteness but did not offer an explanation. They followed through what seemed like an endless maze of ladders, catwalks, and bulkhead doors until they emerged on deck. All three of them winced as their eyes readjusted to the bright sunshine. From on deck, the ship was an impressive sight. She was close to the size of three football fields with an enormous four-story structure at the stern containing all the living quarters and the pilothouse on the top deck. "If you feel like escaping again, feel free to jump overboard," Petar smiled sarcastically. It was a good fifty feet down to the surface of the water, and the shore was only barely visible in one direction. Billy, Pete, and Sally gave a collective frown, not impressed with his offer. "No takers eh? Then follow me." He led them to a small cabin on a lower deck at the stern of the ship. It was a huge improvement over the submarine with good-sized bunks, a small washroom, and a porthole. "You will remain locked in here until we get to the lakehead. Perhaps after we depart the lakehead, you will get some deck time." Petar had a good look at the threesome, and it struck him for the first time how dishevelled they looked. "I will send someone to get you a fresh set of clothing when we get to the dock. I don't want any more trouble from you three...do you understand?"

"Yes, we understand," Sally replied as the other two nodded in agreement, "but what's the lakehead?"

"The lakehead is a town at the top of Lake Superior known as Fort William/Port Arthur. Don't you study geography in Canada?" Petar shook his head condescendingly as he left the cabin, "Such an inferior system."

The captives wandered their small cabin like animals in a zoo—scouring every inch of the place as if they could somehow find a miraculous escape route.

"I'm sure gettin' sick of being locked up," Pete opined.

"Me too." Billy predictably agreed with him. "If we manage to escape again, we sure better not get caught. I don't think that guy was kidding." He wandered over to the porthole and unscrewed the latches of the oblong window. "Sure won't fit through here...and even if we could, we'd land right on the propellers."

Sally winced at the thought, but her imagination was piqued. She lay down on one of the bunks and silently began to formulate a plan.

Chapter 51

KGB-Johnny Reb Agreement, Lake Huron—July 1964

The vodka bottle circulated around the arborite lunch room table. The Russians, Petar and Ilya, were much more accomplished at the downing of vodka than their Southern counterparts, but Jebb and Mike were holding their own. The Polish sailors would wander by to get a look at their guests and be amused by their grimaces as they glugged the vodka.

"That's damn fine stuff, Petar...almost as good as Jack Daniels," Jebb smiled at his Russian counterpart, "but not quite."

"To each his own, my friend...skol," Petar replied, raising his glass in a toast. The others responded in kind.

"I never did see anything quite like that submarine garage you guys got downstairs." Mike was still marvelling at the clandestine docking of the sub. "How's that thing work?"

Ilya beamed at his impressed guest. "That is top secret, but I will tell you anyway. The ship only has to slow down by a few knots. We line up underneath her and aim for a target that they lower along with a hitch. We just have to touch the hitch with our bow and we are locked in. Then we start to de-ballast while they winch us into the open bay doors. The bay is already flooded when they close it up and begin to pump out the water...simple no?"

"Goddamn brilliant, I'd say," Mike replied.

"If you open up the cargo hold above the sub, all you will see is grain,"

"Okay, tell me why we are in a Polish ship?" Jebb questioned.

"Because, my friend," Petar began to answer him, "when we bring a Russian freighter in here, the American and Canadian governments watch us like hawks. They are not as concerned with the Poles even though they are our allies. So we use this little outfit to drop off and pick up our KGB men."

"I think that we have the beginnings of a great friendship here." Jebb was feeling a vodka-supplemented camaraderie. "Let's talk about our operation...what can you do for us?"

"That depends on what you have in mind," Petar replied.

"You ever heard of a guy called Sherman?" Jebb asked.

"A Yankee general not very popular in the South, I believe." Petar played stupid, even though he had a thorough knowledge of American history as part of his KGB training.

Jebb spat on the floor in contempt. "He's a Yankee pig general that burned his way through the South...and they went and made some kind of hero's museum out of his house in a little place called Lancaster, Ohio. Well, I'll tell you what we are going to do...we are going to flatten that shithole with explosives right at the anniversary of Sherman's march to the sea." Jebb was puffed up with bravado. "Ever been to Gettysburg?"

"Never," Petar replied.

"Well, the Yanks have got every inch of the goddamn place covered with monuments. All a Yank had to do was show up for roll call and he got a monument...damn disgusting...and they outnumbered us two to one."

"What do you plan to do?" Petar asked calmly.

"One night we are going to plant plastic explosives on 'em and drop 'em to the ground."

"Very ambitious and commendable, I must say," Petar replied, "I think that we can help you on these endeavours and possibly more. First of all, when we arrive at the lakehead, we will meet an agent who will have a suitcase full of crisp American money...millions in exchange for the gold. You should be able to get the money back to the South quite easily." Jebb smiled at the thought. "We know from experience that you need the proper financing to be successful in this business. We might be communists, but we know the value of a dollar."

"Let's get something straight. We ain't communists, and we never will be," Jebb snarled.

"This isn't about communism or capitalism. This about ridding ourselves of an oppressor," Petar replied, regretting his reference to communism. "The millions that you have will buy materials—and most of all, it will buy people." Jebb seemed assuaged. "And we have the expertise and the contacts at your disposal."

Jebb sloppily poured a glug of vodka into everyone's glass. "Here's to beatin' the Yanks, boys." They all banged glasses in a show of solidarity.

"We'll beat those Yankee bastards...just you wait and see," Mike mumbled in drunken bravado.

"Maybe you had better show us to our rooms now," Jebb said, with a quick wink to Petar. "And tomorrow I want to meet those kids."

Petar signalled for a Polish sailor to come over. "Just follow this sailor, gentlemen. I trust that you will find your accommodation satisfactory."

"G'night boys," Jebb stumbled out of his chair. Petar and Ilya smiled as the two Southerners left the room draped over each other for support.

"So what do you think?" Ilya asked Petar while pouring him another glass of vodka. He had a slight smirk on his face, knowing quite well what the answer would be.

"Blowing up a house and a couple of monuments," Petar replied, shaking his head condescendingly. "That's their idea of a revolution?"

"Maybe they'll write nasty letters to the newspaper as well," Ilya added. The two shared a short, controlled laugh.

"We may be able to arrange something...a touch more catastrophic...without their knowledge," Petar said, enjoying their ridicule. "But we will certainly give them the credit." This time the two shared a good belly laugh.

Chapter 52

The Plan,
Lake Superior—July 1964

The freighter *Krakow* had passed through Sault Ste. Marie during the night and was now steaming full bore up Lake Superior on course for the lakehead. The morning weather, drizzle and fog, matched Jebb's head as he struggled to be sociable. Petar, on the other hand, was the perky picture of health, showing no effects from the copious amounts of downed vodka. Petar and Jebb headed for the cabin of their still-sleeping captives.

"Wake up, children," he commanded, while giving the door a cursory knock before unlocking the bolts. It was an abrupt awakening for Billy, Pete, and Sally, from the prisoner's escape of sleep to the morning reality of facing their captor. They reluctantly rolled from their bunks. "Jebb, meet Billy the mischievous, Sally the brains, and Pete the rabble rouser." The threesome were not amused by Petar's characterizations, which were surprisingly prescient.

"Good morning, good morning, and how are we all this fine morning?" The presence of youth was rejuvenating for Jebb's aching head. He slowly circled the three as if he were inspecting cattle. "My name is Jebb, and I'm from the great Confederate States of America. Does that mean anything to you?"

"No sir," Pete and Sally responded almost in unison. But bells were going off in Billy's memory. The hours that he had spent with Aunt Emily as she recounted tales of the Deep South; the Confederate States of America was how she referred to her country. The animosity towards the northern states, the Yanks—it was all coming back.

"How about you, son...we haven't heard from Billy the mischievous."

"The Confederate States of America fought the Yanks in the War of Northern Aggression," Billy blurted out.

"Go on, son...go on." Jebb was astounded.

"Sherman was a coward that burned up the Southern plantations. He even burned the deeds so that they couldn't get their plantations back."

"Well son, you are one smart lad." Jebb's condescension was now gone. "What else do you know?"

"The gold we found belonged to Colonel Reynolds. He had a big plantation in Sandersville, Georgia."

"Colonel Reynolds was the caretaker of the gold. His intention was to use it to finance the South's ultimate victory...and that is where we come in," Jebb corrected.

Billy knew that he was on a roll and needed a finale to really impress this man. "The South shall rise again!" he exclaimed with fervour.

"Damn, Petar...I like this kid...why, I like 'em all."

Petar was taken aback by the erudition of his young captive and not altogether enthusiastic about it. "Yes, they have potential," he reluctantly allowed. "It is time that we had breakfast."

"Well, you make sure that these youngsters eat a good breakfast too."

Petar forced a smile as they departed the cabin. Sympathy for his young captives was not what he needed, and he knew that Billy had scored a coup.

"Billy...that was great. Where did you learn all that stuff?" Sally was visibly impressed.

"How come you never say anything smart in school?" Pete shook his head in astonishment.

With a satisfied smile, Billy puffed out his chest. "I learned it from Aunt Emily...the old lady from the South...she taught me lots of stuff."

"That guy likes us...but Petar doesn't," Sally said, "and Petar is the boss, so we have to make a plan to get out of here."

"He's a jerk," Pete scoffed in his usual subtle manner.

"Sal...there is no way out of here. And even if we get out of here, how do we get off the ship?" Billy answered her.

"Aren't you guys Cub Scouts?"

"Yeah we are...why?"

"Because you must know something about making signals."

"I know semaphore," Pete said proudly.

Billy was amused. "Sure...we just stick flags out the window." The boys shared a giggle.

"We use light." Sally had little time for humour when the analytical gears of her brain began meshing. The juvenile silliness abruptly stopped as Billy and Pete realized that she might once again be on to something.

Billy's eyes lit up. "Morse code...Morse code, Sal."

Chapter 53
The *Krakow* and the Coast Guard, Lake Superior—July 1964

The *Krakow* heaved and tossed its way up Lake Superior for the next twelve hours, fighting the strong northwest winds. With their cabin located in the stern, the three captives had a gentle ride and were spared seasickness, but the shuddering of the hull with each pounding wave kept the adrenalin levels high. Around midnight, the battle was won and she slipped into the calm waters of the harbour at the lakehead as the threesome slept.

As the sun came up the next day, loading of the freighter was well underway. All the hatches were opened up, and a stream of grain was filling up each hold. No one ashore took notice of the shallow number-four hold. Petar used his usual urbane manner to charm the customs men and left for a trip to downtown, ostensibly to purchase some clothing. On his return he struggled with several bags of goods, a struggle that was exacerbated by the brief case purposely not visible. The Southern boys stayed out of sight to avoid any chance that they may have to explain what two Americans were doing onboard a Polish ship. They had that distinctive look and dress that screamed American.

Time spent in port was money for a freighter; and for a freighter that doubled as a spy ship, time in port was dangerous. There was a great wave of relief at 2200 hours as the

Polish captain, along with Petar and Ilya on the bridge, throttled up and left the lakehead in their wake.

Captain Kwasniewski was somewhat less than enamoured with his Russian passengers, knowing full well that he was captain in title only. The Russians called the shots— even on a Polish ship. He was never comfortable having his ship seconded and retrofitted for use in clandestine KGB operations. His dedication to communism was lukewarm at best, and the thought of being arrested as a Russian spy boiled his Polish blood.

"What is the ETA for Sault Ste. Marie, Captain?" Petar asked his Polish counterpart.

"By this time tomorrow, we will have cleared the locks, and at approximately 0300, your sub will be back in the water," Captain Kwasniewski replied in very tenuous, halting Russian. He resented having to address them in their language.

"Excellent. Together we Russians with our Polish allies will defeat the Americans." Petar sensed a definite lack of enthusiasm from the captain. "We beat the Germans together, didn't we, Captain?"

"German bastards," Kwasniewski muttered. He did not like Russians, but he hated the Germans. Kwasniewski was spared any false camaraderie with the Russians as the first officer entered the bridge to take the night watch.

"Let's go to bed, Ilya. Captain...we will see you back here first thing in the morning...and stay out of the vodka," Petar said, partially in jest. Kwasniewski replied with a Polish expletive unintelligible to the Russians.

By 0600, Lake Superior was at her tempestuous best with minimal visibility in the drizzle and fog. The first officer looked dishevelled after a trying night. Two hours into his watch, the autopilot had quit, forcing him to hand steer the ship while concentrating on the radar screen. He was more than happy to hand off the ship back to Kwasniewski.

"We have someone approaching us ten miles off the port bow, Captain." He pointed the vessel out to Kwasniewski on the radar screen.

"So we do...so we do...thank you, First Officer, you are relieved of duty. Go to bed."

Captain Kwasniewski started to grow concerned as the blip on the radar screen was closing on them and making no apparent effort to change course. He was the stand-on vessel and was obligated to hold his course. *What if they have no radar?* he thought to himself. Visibility was down to a quarter mile, and by the time they saw each other, collision avoidance would be unlikely. When they showed two miles and still closing on the radar screen, Kwasniewski prepared to pull back the throttle and make a course change. Before he made his move, the radio crackled to life.

"Freighter *Krakow*, this is Canadian Coast Guard vessel *St. Laurent*. Come in *Krakow*."

"This is *Krakow*, come in *St. Laurent*."

"Are you enjoying the weather, sir? Must be better in Poland."

"Polish weather is always better. *St. Laurent*...please state your business," Kwasniewski replied. His knuckles whitened as they put a strangle hold on the wheel. Now that he had been drafted into the spy ranks, any government vessel was cause for concern.

Coast Guard Captain Joe Evans was a bit taken aback by the cold response to his attempt at small talk. "Last night we received several reports of an SOS coming from one of your cabins...from the shore at the lakehead and from a passing boat."

"That is ridiculous, sir...there was no SOS from this ship," Kwasniewski replied. Petar and Ilya entered the bridge in time to catch the last transmission.

"I repeat...we received several calls about an SOS from your ship."

"Polish sailors do not use Morse code sir...I repeat...it was not from our ship."

Evans was getting hot now. The condescending tone of this captain was rubbing him the wrong way. "*Krakow*...we would like to come aboard...drop your boarding gangway."

Petar rolled his eyes in horror as he watched the conversation deteriorate. "Kwasniewski...they cannot come aboard under any circumstances...did you hear me...under no circumstances!" he ordered.

"*St. Laurent*...do not attempt to board. This is a sovereign vessel of Poland. It is against maritime law," Kwasniewski replied.

Evans was now fit to be tied. "*Krakow*...the Coast Guard has the right to board any vessel in Canadian waters. Drop your boarding ramp!"

By now, Alex, the first officer aboard the *St. Laurent*, was also getting a bit concerned about the acrimonious state of affairs between the two captains. "Joe, it's too rough to board safely anyway. Let him go. We'll get him at the Sault."

Joe took a few deep breaths and lowered the mike for a few seconds to cool down. He knew that Alex was right. "*Krakow*...this is the *St. Laurent*...we will be breaking off this conversation now." Joe paused again for a few seconds. "We'll see you in Sault St. Marie."

Petar wrapped his face in his hands and shook his head in anger and disgust. If he had arrived on the bridge a few seconds earlier, he could have easily talked them out of this situation. Instead Kwasniewski had talked them into an international incident, which was about to completely change their plans. He stomped off the bridge with Ilya following close behind.

"Goddamn Russians," Captain Kwasniewski muttered under his breath. He knew that there was going to be hell to pay for himself.

"Ilya...collect everything sensitive and load it on the sub," Petar ordered as they marched down the hall to the cafeteria, "and get those three little SOS-ing bastards onboard the sub immediately." As they entered the cafeteria, Jebb and Mike were putting the finishing touches on a huge Polish breakfast.

"Good morning, gentlemen," Jebb welcomed them as he rubbed his satisfied belly. "How are we this fine morning?"

"Not good," Petar replied, "I'll make a long story short. We are going to get boarded by the authorities at Sault St. Marie. You guys cannot be found onboard."

"What in the hell is going on?" Jebb demanded.

"I haven't got time to explain. Collect your stuff...and the money, of course, and get onboard the sub. You're going for a ride to Agawa Bay. We will radio your pilot to pick you up there." The Southern boys, visibly alarmed, were heading for the door. "And Jebb," Petar added. The boys stopped in their tracks. "Next time that we will meet...it will be in Dixie."

"Dixie it is, partner," Jebb answered.

Ilya made a move for the door to carry out his orders, but Petar put a hand on his arm to stop him. "Ilya...you are going to scuttle the sub in Agawa Bay. You will have to return to the ship in the Zodiac."

"Yes, Petar." Ilya made another move for the door, and Petar again held him up.

"One last thing."

"Yes, Petar."

"When you scuttle the sub...those kids go down with it."

Ilya was horrified. "I cannot do that, Petar."

"That is an order, Ilya. Do you plan to disobey it?"

Ilya remained silent for several seconds, writhing in agony. "No, Petar," he replied meekly.

Chapter 54
Scuttling the Submarine—July 1964

"Back in this hole again," Pete lamented, looking around at his surroundings on the sub. Ilya had led the threesome back to their tiny enclosure in the bow of the sub. He was very subdued and evasive with his captives. There seemed to be a pall of sadness hanging over him.

"Something bad is going on." Sally could sense the gloom. "He's hiding something."

"Bet you it's something to do with all the SOS we sent out," Billy said. "Could have done it all night if the light didn't burn out."

By now the whir of pumps and clanging of metal seemed commonplace to them as the sub returned to the depths. They could tell when she was free of the mother ship and floating again—it felt soft.

The trip to Agawa Bay was short, maybe thirty minutes. They slipped into the bay just below the surface at one thirty in the afternoon. Ilya scouted the remote bay with the periscope, and through misty eyes, he could see that it was deserted. He knew that he must act quickly. Otherwise the pangs of guilt and sheer terror that wracked his body would soon overwhelm him.

The sub surfaced, and Jebb, Mike, and Ilya scrambled up the conning tower to board the outboard-powered

Zodiac. Unknown to the others, Ilya had opened ballasting valves before departing the sub.

As they drifted into the bay, the sub was slowly slipping into the depths. Jebb looked around in mounting horror. "Where are they?" Ilya looked away, sobbing quietly. "I said, where are they?" Jebb screamed at him.

"It must be done," Ilya replied in barely a whisper.

"What must be done! Why you cruel son of a bitch!" Jebb pulled his service revolver and placed it at Ilya's temple. "You get your ass back on there and get them out!" Ilya scrambled like he was given a sudden reprieve. He leaped over the side of the Zodiac and swam like a man possessed to the slowly disappearing conning tower. They watched aghast as he disappeared into the sub.

Time stood still for the horrified onlookers as the sub made her last gasps of life, now with four occupants onboard. With a foot of freeboard left, Sally came popping out of the hatch like a cork from a bottle. She screamed hysterically, thrashing about in the water in a blind panic. They dragged her onboard the Zodiac just as water began to pour into the hatch cover. The head of Pete barely broke the surface as he struggled against the torrents of water trying to drag him back into the sub. He broke free, and the vessel slowly disappeared into the depths.

All was eerily calm and quiet now. Thirty seconds after the last sighting of the sub, there was barely a ripple on the water. The lake had swallowed her up without a trace. All eyes were fixated on the spot where the sub had disappeared—everyone silent and aghast in their mounting horror.

"Please, Billy...please," Sally prayed out loud. Pete had the gunwales of the boat in a death grip, wanting desperately to save his buddy but not knowing how. Each passing second tripled his anxiety.

And then from the depths came bubbles—few and small at first. As they ascended, they grew in size and were soon followed by a dark struggling form. It was Billy—thrashing for his life. All air had been expelled from his lungs as he fought against the irrepressible urge to inhale that fateful breath of water. Ten feet below the surface, Billy's struggles began to subside as his oxygen-starved body began to give up the fight. His buddy could take it no longer. Screaming Billy's name, Pete dove headlong into the dark waters and swam desperately for his now-disappearing friend. He grabbed Billy by the collar and headed for the light with everything he had. Billy was just running on spirit now, and his buddy's valiant attempt to save him gave him a last surge of energy. Two kicks later and they broke the surface. Billy let out a roar of life that no one onboard that day would soon forget as he expelled the water from his lungs. They pulled him onboard and he coughed, hacked, thrashed, and screamed as he lay on the bottom of the boat puking. In an instant, Sally and Pete were all over him. Jebb and Mike watched in astonishment as the three kids embraced, in an emphatic, joyful hug that seemed to meld them into one being as they rolled about on the Zodiac floor. There was a bond between them that only those who faced death together could know.

Mike quietly watched the scene as tears welled up in his eyes "Never seen spirit like this before in my life."

"Me neither," Jebb replied incredulously as he fought his quivering upper lip. "These kids are coming with us...they're going to Dixie."

Ilya had gone down with his ship and died an honourable captain. His last ounce of life had been spent pushing Billy out of the hatch. Ilya would now rest forever in the depths of Agawa Bay.

Chapter 55

Petar Abandons Ship—July 1964

Petar scrambled around his cabin, carelessly stuffing his few belongings into a waterproof sack. He left donning the survival suit to the last, to avoid overheating. Out of his cabin porthole, the lights of Batchawana Bay appeared to be about ten miles southeast, but it was difficult for him to tell. In any case, it was time to go—they would soon be abeam Pancake Point. He made his way on deck, trying not to be seen if at all possible. Kwasniewski would not be pleased if he knew that the Russian was bailing out on him just before there was some tough explaining to do with the authorities at Sault Ste. Marie. He looked out at the darkening shore for any sign of his contact. A small low-wattage beam soon illuminated and flashed the agreed-upon code. Petar started to climb the deck rail, trying to ignore the abyss below him. In the darkness there was little sign of the water, but he expected a drop of at least fifty feet into the frothing bow wave deflecting off the hull.

The plummet through the darkness felt surreal and much longer than he had expected, but he knew fear tends to expand time. He hit the surface and disappeared twenty feet into the strangely calm and eerie black depths. The flotation from his suit assisted his ascent, and he broke the surface into a chaos of boiling, turbulent water. He swam in a blind panic, trying to clear the hull and the fast-approaching stern. The props would show no mercy, sucking everything within twenty feet into their meat grinders. The stern slipped by, and he rested, using the flotation from his suit to support him. He could see the light on the shore still flashing.

Dimitri could hear something thrashing in the calm waters along the rocky shore. He scanned the surface with his light and illuminated an orange creature stumbling up the beach as it struggled to gain footing on the rocky bottom. "Comrade...good of you to drop by."

Petar smiled, very relieved that his little ordeal was over. "No vodka...what kind of welcome is this?"

Dimitri passed his countryman a bottle of the national pastime. Their car was a short walk away through the bush and the main highway another ten miles by gravel road.

Now warm, safe, and mildly intoxicated with the vodka, Petar was thoroughly enjoying the ride. "So Dimitri...I mean Frank...how did you get along with pilot Butch and that other hillbilly while I was gone?"

"I always get along with people, Petar...they trust me implicitly." They both smiled. "What happens now with our Polish spy ship...and what about Ilya, Ivan, and the others?"

"Ivan and the boys will make their way to Ottawa, and the embassy will quietly shuttle them out of the country. We don't need them anymore. Ilya speaks fluent Polish and has all the right documentation. He will be fine. As far as Captain Kwasniewski and his crew are concerned...they are on their own."

"But what if they talk?"

"Then let them talk if they are so foolish," Petar answered lackadaisically. "Their families are still in Poland,

and there is no Russian or any evidence of Russians anywhere on that ship. Kwasniewski can try to blame Russia, but he will just look like he is trying to save his own skin. He has no proof."

"But the gold, Petar, what about the gold—and we gave them millions in US currency."

"The gold, my dear Frank, has gone down with the submarine and only Ilya has the coordinates. We will pick it up later...oh and the millions—" a great smile broke out on Petar's face. He struggled to contain a rising hilarity. "All counterfeit, my dear friend...all counterfeit." The two Russian bears had a hearty laugh.

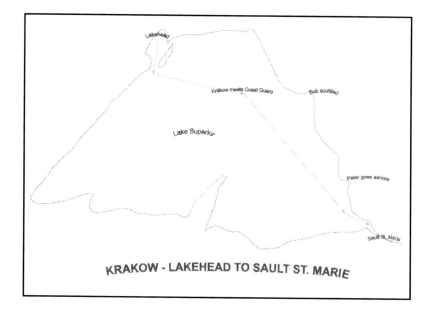

KRAKOW - LAKEHEAD TO SAULT ST. MARIE

Chapter 56

RCMP Headquarters, Ottawa—August 1964

Back at RCMP headquarters in Ottawa, Sergeant Bryce chewed on his egg salad sandwich while reading the police reports from the previous week. He had several investigations ongoing, but the only one that really interested him was those three missing kids. He was convinced that the land search would have either turned up the kids or some sign of them, but even the dogs could not pick up a scent. Now the trail had gone cold.

RCMP File # 440-8462

August 4th—RCMP/Coast Guard board Polish Freighter

The Polish freighter Krakow, coming from the lakehead with a load of grain, was boarded at Sault Ste. Marie at 2200. The Coast Guard had asked for RCMP presence during the boarding because of the potential for an international incident. The previous night, the Coast Guard had three independent reports of a distress (SOS) signal coming from one of the freighter's cabins. The Coast Guard had approached the ship at sea out of concern for her and her crew, but they were immediately rebuffed by her captain. They became suspicious at the captain's extreme reluctance to allow them aboard. Due to the rough conditions, boarding would have been too hazardous. At Sault Ste. Marie, the RCMP and Coast Guard interviewed the captain and did a cursory search of the ship. The captain displayed contempt for his interviewers but was mildly cooperative and nothing untoward was ascertained from the interview. The search of the cabin and ship revealed nothing. As per procedure with all Soviet bloc ships, all refuse left ashore was searched. The only thing of mild interest in the garbage was three sets of what appeared to be children's clothing but certainly nothing to warrant detaining the ship any further. It is now en route to the St. Lawrence.

Bryce was outraged at what he had just read. "Mild interest, are they nuts?" He thought, *What's wrong with this outfit? Doesn't the right hand talk to the left hand?*

Inspector Leblanc held the receiver away from his ear after giving up trying to get a word in with an animated Sergeant Bryce "We've got to stop that ship, Inspector...those kids might be onboard!"

Finally Leblanc had enough. "Look, Bryce, we can't stop an international ship because there were some clothes in the garbage. You want to start a war with Poland? If you're so damn convinced that they were the kids' clothes, then you have to prove it." The line went dead. Bryce was already heading for Toronto.

♦ ♦ ♦

Sergeant Bryce had three sets of clothing laid out nicely in three separate piles. The articles included three pairs of jeans, two t-shirts and a sweat shirt with some school initials across the front. Each piece was filthy with various cuts and tears. Bryce had invited the Parkers, the Olmsteads, and the Mills for an important meeting down at 52 Division, the local police station.

"Let me stress...if you happen to recognize some of these articles of clothing, it does not mean that they have come to any harm." Bryce might as well have saved his breath. Agnes Olmstead had already recognized Sally's school sweatshirt and fell weeping onto her husband's shoulder. Barb Parker was frantically turning the t-shirts inside out looking for the little name tag she sewed into Billy's clothes because Billy had a habit of somehow losing them. She found it and fell sobbing into her husband's arms. The Mills clan had a similar reaction. Bryce made another feeble attempt at reassuring the families, but nobody listened and the place resembled a funeral parlour as they filed out the door.

♦ ♦ ♦

"Inspector, I have made a positive identification...stop that ship!" Bryce was immediately on the phone with the inspector after his unplanned wake.

"Sergeant, I have bad news for you. We have been tracking the ship, and she entered international waters this morning."

"So send the navy...they kidnapped three kids!"

"You don't get it, do you, Sergeant," the inspector replied, shaking his head in exasperation, "that's called piracy."

"Piracy! *They're* the goddamn pirates!"

The inspector had his fill again. "We will pursue this issue through diplomatic channels. That will be all, Sergeant."

Chapter 57

Butler Plantation, Sandersville, Georgia—August 1964

"Okay kid, this is where you will stay," Jebb said as he led Billy up the worn wooden steps of the clapboard building. "You know what this was, kid?" Billy shook his head. "Over one hundred years ago, this was slave quarters. Slave quarters on my great-great-granddaddy's plantation, which I now own. One of the few Sherman missed."

Billy looked around the big old bunkhouse. It felt like a museum. It was tidy enough, but the sparse furnishings, the table and the chairs, and the few remaining bunks were not made for comfort or to be pleasing to the eye. Even the electric lights seemed to be somehow out of place and time. "Slaves actually lived here," he said as he wandered around awestruck.

"That's right, son, maybe twenty slaves of the Butler plantation...one of Sandersville's finest."

"Sandersville," Billy recalled the name, "are we near the Reynolds plantation?"

"Just a couple of miles down the road. You seem to know a lot about the Reynolds plantation."

"Yeah...one of my friends used to live there."

"One of your friends, eh?" Jebb rolled his eyes and stifled a giggle. "The Reynolds plantation was destroyed a long time ago, kid."

"What about Pete and Sally...when can I see them?"

"Sally's staying in the top floor of the big house, and your buddy is locked up in another slave quarters. We had to separate you three because you all have a reputation for causing trouble, and I don't need no trouble. Remember those Russian guys?"

"I'm tryin' not to," Billy answered defiantly.

"Well, in a couple of days they will be here, on business. They wanted to get rid of you kids...but that ain't going to happen as long as I'm here."

"What are you going to do with us?"

"At the moment I don't know...but I can guarantee you one thing. If any of you tries to escape, I can't help you any-more...understand?"

"Understand."

"Good. In the meantime, you've got lots of books here to read."

"I hate reading."

"Well, you better learn to like it. G'night kid." Billy heard the deadbolts sliding into place outside the door—just as they had done one hundred years earlier with the slaves.

As night fell, Billy struggled to curb his imagination. He wished Jebb had not told him about the history of the place because that just added fuel to the fire burning in the back of his thoughts. The place was creepy enough without the thought of the poor, abused slaves that had lived their miserable lives here. He agonized through chapters of an old, tattered copy of *David Copperfield,* but every creak of the floorboards sent shivers through his body. He was in a state of fatigue from little sleep in the past few nights, and at the same time his imagination kept him in a state of hyper vigilance. Finally, in an act of courage, he decided demons be damned, he was going to sleep, and he turned out the bedside lamp.

Billy could hear the plaintive, mournful singing, like gospel music that he had once heard. "Wade in the water, wade in the water, children." Over and over again, the same lyrics were repeated. But he was somewhere in that zone between sleep and wakefulness, not sure if it was a dream or reality.

Sunlight came streaming through the cracks in the shuttered windows. Night had ended. Billy sat upright in his bunk, relieved but fatigued from a fitful sleep. The singing, the images of slaves that raced through his head all night long—were they real or a dream? But the images were strangely comforting—as if he were among friends.

Billy wandered over to an old, rusted wood stove that sat against the end wall. He opened and shut the cast iron door. The sound of the creaking and clanging of the metal was familiar. Sometime in the netherworld of the previous night he felt certain that he could hear the cast iron door being opened and closed.

Chapter 58

Prisoners—August 1964

Billy could hear the deadbolts on the outside of the door being slid back and the two-by-six plank that was meant to discourage anyone from taking a run at the door being lifted out of its brackets. Jebb was in a fine mood that morning as he delivered breakfast to his captive. "Morning kid...sleep well?"

"Naw, not really."

"Well I got some food for ya and something else that you have to learn to use. Ever hear of a thunder mug?"

"Naw." Billy looked curiously at the pitcher of water and bedpan that Jebb was hauling in.

"Neither had your friends...but you'll get the hang of it. Your friend Pete there...he hates readin' as much as you do, but Sally, she's doin' real well...likes to read, crotchet...all that stuff."

"Jebb...do you believe in ghosts?"

Jebb was taken aback with the question. An instant and involuntary memory harkened him back to when he was a kid and this same slave quarters was his personal fort. He had attempted to spend the night there once and ran out in horror sometime after midnight. "No such thing as ghosts, Billy."

"Have you ever heard a song called 'Wade in the Water,' Jebb?"

Jebb was stunned a second time. "'Wade in the Water' is what they call a Negro spiritual song. How'd you know about that?"

"Thought I dreamed about it last night," Billy replied.

"Do you know why they sang it, Billy?" Jebb did not wait for an answer. "It was a sort of code. If a slave escaped, we'd put the dogs after him." Jebb did not differentiate between him and his ancestors, as if their deeds were his. "They soon found out that if they ran through swamps and rivers, the dogs would lose their scent. Few of 'em even made it to the North."

"Didn't people feel bad about keeping the slaves prisoner?" Billy asked innocently.

"I'll be back later in the afternoon," Jebb answered, ignoring the question, "bring you some comic books."

"Can you make it Archie?"

"Yah, Archie it is, kid." Jebb made a quick exit. He fumbled awkwardly getting the deadbolts and plank barricade in place. What started as a quick walk back to the big house ended in a flat-out run.

Billy started thinking about the previous night and what Jebb had told him. He was a prisoner just like the slaves. What if they were trying to help him? If they were, then the old wood stove had something to do with it.

Chapter 59

Sergeant Bryce thought he had his breakthrough in the case of the missing kids, and as far as he was concerned, the force had let it slip through their fingers—all for the sake of not offending the Poles. It had been one week, and he had nothing positive to tell the grieving parents, who were now even more convinced that their children had met an ignominious end. When the inspector summoned him to his office, Bryce was somewhat less than amicable.

"Sit down, Sergeant." Bryce took a chair but did not reply. His displeasure was obvious. "I have some news about that ship."

"Go ahead, Inspector." Bryce was tempted to respond with something sarcastic but he thought better of it.

"After we suggested Polish ships may not be welcome in our waters anymore, the Poles agreed to let us interview that Captain Kwasniewski...with conditions of course."

"What conditions would those be?"

"They insisted that a government official be in the room with him...kind of a censor."

"So what's the guy going to say...that he kidnapped three kids?" Bryce's frustration was just below the surface.

"Do you mind if I finish, Sergeant?"

"Please continue."

219

"We asked him if any Russians were onboard or if the ship had contact with any Russians. Of course we knew the answer. Both the government guy and the captain were emphatic that they didn't know what we were talking about...surprise, surprise. We explained to him what we found in the ship's garbage...even showed him. He seemed a bit taken aback along with the government guy. And then he said something quite strange. He said that the kids left with the Southern guys...that he had nothing to do with it."

"So he actually admitted that they were onboard."

"He did, but the translator had a different version...claimed that he didn't know what we were talking about."

"So how did you know what he said?"

"Because we sent Corporal Nowacsynski—fluent in Polish—and we renamed him Carter."

"What happened after that?"

"Nothing...the government guy barked at the captain in Polish and they ended the interview."

"Hope he enjoys Siberia."

The inspector smiled. "That's all I can do for you, Sergeant...one more piece to the puzzle."

♦ ♦ ♦

Bryce sat at his desk writing down everything that he knew to date, trying to find a link. Three kids from the same neighbourhood disappear. Two of them had found the bodies of dead Confederate soldiers in what was supposedly a Civil War spy camp. They find an empty vault in a drained pond. The kids turn up in Northern Ontario running from Russians trying to get at some gold. Somehow they end up on a Polish freighter and then leave with some Southern guys.

"Charlie, this is Sergeant Bryce from the RCMP. Remember us?" Bryce said calling up the RCMP contact with Canada Customs.

"Sergeant Dudley Do Right from the Rocky and Bullwinkle show. Of course I remember you."

"Listen, Charlie, I need a favour. I need the names of everyone from the Southern States that checked in with you guys in the last month, from the lakehead to Parry Sound."

Chapter 60
Solitary Confinement—August 1964

Into his second interminable day locked up, Billy was going stir crazy. He had never spent that much time alone in his life, and he was not good at it. He heard the singing again on his second night, but he now found it strangely comforting—as if he were not alone. And the old rusted stove rattled again.

The slave quarters reminded Billy of the POW barrack in "The Great Escape," a movie that he had seen with his dad the year before. The prisoners in the movie had built a trap door under the stove leading to an escape tunnel, and with the movie in mind, Billy spent hours going over every inch of the stove and surrounding floor. But there was nothing. No tell tale cuts in the floor planking, and even if there was a trap door there, he was not nearly strong enough to budge the stove.

In the heat of the afternoon, the only living things that seemed to have any energy were the cicadas with their endless chirping. The old slave quarters was like an oven and offered little relief from the oppressive sun and humidity. Pete lay on his bunk rereading a comic book and at regular intervals would get up to peer through cracks in the boarded up window. He would stare at the building across from his where he watched them lock up Billy. He got a little solace thinking that maybe Billy was staring right back at him. Both boys were not faring well. Being locked up alone was the absolute worst punishment for a twelve-year-old kid busting with energy.

Sally was better equipped to survive solitary. Reading, writing, and crocheting were natural pastimes for her, and she was making out quite well in her third-floor cell. Jebb even let her slide up the big, old window, since a drop of thirty feet pretty much discouraged any attempts to leave that way. She hung out the window looking at the two buildings in the back field—giving the occasional wave in the hopes that one of her buddies might see her.

Billy slowly and meticulously went around the room, tapping and pushing each wall plank, not even sure what he was looking for. But time was one thing that he had lots of, and any activity tended to alleviate the boredom. He was halfway along the stove wall when he realized that there were differences. Compared to the other three walls, this wall sounded hollow. Billy instantly perked up and shook off his lethargy. He carefully redid the whole experiment to prove to himself that this was not his imagination. Sure enough, three walls offered a dull thud and the fourth seemed to echo. He took one of the thin metal slats from the springs of his bed and slid it through cracks in the planking. On three walls, the piece of metal would stop dead against something solid while on the stove wall, he could insert it at least one foot before it halted. Billy was elated. His discovery pulled him out of the doldrums of solitary confinement.

Chapter 61

Sergeant's Search, RCMP Headquarters, Ottawa—August 1964

Sergeant Bryce reviewed the list he had received from the Canada Customs guys. "Goddamn bureaucrats," he mumbled to himself. He had requested a list of only visitors from the Southern states between the lakehead and Parry Sound in the past month, and he had received a list of everyone who had crossed the border. The list was long, and the job was laborious and boring. Bryce did what he always did with tedious jobs—he enlisted his secretary, Helen, into service.

There were hundreds of names, most who were day visitors from towns close to the border, but fortunately very few hailed from the Southern states. They plodded through the names and home states, selecting out those from the South and then chiselling the list down further into groups of all male visitors.

"Sergeant," Helen called from her desk, "where's Sandersville, GA?"

"That would be Sandersville, Georgia, Helen."

"Here's one you may be interested in. Five guys from Sandersville in a plane called a Goose. Not a good name for a plane if I do say so."

Bryce thought back to the report he had read after the ground search had been abandoned. One of the guys reported a low flying Grumman Goose in the area—maybe just to add some detail to a report that was desperately short of pertinent details. "Let me see that one."

Bryce went over the scant Customs details: all from Sandersville area, on a fishing trip, some registered small arms declared onboard. It piqued his interest. "Helen, get the Macon detachment of the FBI on the phone. Give them the call numbers of that plane and see what they know about the owner."

Helen rolled her eyes in mock disgust. Bryce was always doing that to her—as if she had the number of the Macon FBI right at her fingertips. "Yes, Sergeant," she replied with a hint of mockery in her voice.

An hour later, after being bounced around half a dozen telephone exchanges, Helen was on the phone to Detective Callaway of the Macon FBI detachment. "Please hold the phone for a second detective," Helen said, covering the receiver, "Sergeant Bryce...you had better pick up the phone on line one."

Bryce grabbed the phone. "This is Sergeant Bryce, RCMP."

"Sergeant, this is Detective Callaway, FBI...how y'all today?"

"Just fine, detective, sorry to bother you with our request."

"No problem at all...funny you should be asking about that airplane. What's your interest in it?"

"We have an investigation going concerning three missing kids. It's a real long story, but we think that whoever was on that plane might have a link to these kids."

Detective Callaway smiled at the coincidence. "I say 'funny,' Sergeant, because we're looking into the owners of that plane as we speak. It's registered to a group called 'The

Brothers of the Gray Ghost'...mostly guys that play Johnny Reb on the weekend...generally harmless."

"These guys got any interest in some gold?" Bryce asked.

"You seem to know more about them than I do, Sergeant. They are notorious for digging holes all over Dixie, lookin' for that supposed lost Confederate gold."

Sergeant Bryce was now all ears. "Please carry on, Detective. This is getting very interesting."

"Well, I said most of 'em were harmless but not all of 'em. There's a small faction still fightin' the Civil War, and now it seems that they are into counterfeiting. We traced some counterfeit thousand dollar bills to one of 'em...a guy named Jebb Butler."

"Detective, I would certainly like to pay you guys a visit and maybe talk to this Butler guy...if that would be okay with you."

"That would be our pleasure, Sergeant. As a matter of fact...if you can get down here today, we have a little raid planned on Jebb's house first thing tomorrow morning."

"I'll be there," Bryce replied.

Chapter 62
Southern Hospitality—August 1964

The 1955 Ford F150 pickup rattled up the rutted laneway to the old Butler plantation, country music blaring and the rebel flag flying. The guys in the cab, both sporting the good old boy's uniform of blue jeans, T-shirts, and cowboy boots with the heels half worn off, were knocking back a beer and finishing off a Players non filter. These were the descendants of Johnny Reb, the pride of every Southern town and the bane of every Yankee.

Jebb, Mike, Larry, and Butch were sprawled out on the front verandah of the big house, enjoying the cool air of the early evening. There was a chuckle of amusement as the Ford slid to a stop like it was sliding into home plate. The driver and his sidekick riding shotgun swaggered out of the truck.

"Well, I'll be goddamned," Jebb said with amusement, "look who we got here."

"Those bastards look more Southern than us," Butch smiled with approval.

"Evening, boys...name's Pete and this here is Frank," Petar addressed them, with a touch of pride.

Mike and Larry circled the two ex-Russians making a mock show of some sort of celebrity gawking. "Ain't no Ruskie in these boys."

"Just in time for a good Southern feed...now that you're one of us." Jebb issued the invitation. With great camaraderie, the group stomped into the old plantation home.

To say that the Butler plantation was on the decline would have been charitable or sarcastic. The place had been sliding since the Civil War had left the family and succeeding generations destitute. The genteel side had been bred out of the Butler progeny, but the spirit was still very much intact and very evident in Jebb. He had a fierce pride in where he had come from, and the family plantation was his bastion.

Five of them sat around the big old oak table in the back kitchen while Mike cooked with a massive skillet on a wood stove. The conversation was light and amicable until Jebb changed the tone.

"You know that submarine captain of yours?" Jebb stared directly at Petar, frowning. "He tried to drown those three kids. What kind of man would kill children?" Petar exchanged a quick, furtive glance with Dimitri.

"I am very shocked. I never would have dreamed that Ilya would be capable of that." Petar stared down at the table, slowly shaking his head.

"Well he was, and he paid for it. He's on the bottom, and the kids are locked up right here on this plantation." Petar continued to stare at the table. His look of shock was not visible to the others, while the pallor drained from Dimitri's face.

"I am so relieved," Petar stumbled, "so relieved to hear that. Ilya got what he deserved." Dimitri looked appalled at his boss. "So let's get on with business shall we?"

"On with business." Jebb nodded approval.

"The letter was delivered to the *Washington Post*...anonymously, yesterday," Petar said. "They of course will ignore it or maybe give it to the FBI...but for now it will be seen as the work of some quack."

"They won't ignore it when the fireworks start to fly," Butch smiled cockily. Petar nodded in agreement.

"Frank, give them the details," Petar instructed Dimitri.

"As you know, some of the money you guys supplied us financed some very competent operatives. Tonight, plastic explosives will be placed around some of the major Yank monuments at Gettysburg...all on a timer. Our man in Ohio has been scouting the Sherman museum. Security is next to nothing there. When the place closed this evening, he left a little treat in an upstairs closet...a few pounds of plastic. The house and the monuments should all come down at the same time...if our timers are set right."

"Nobody gets hurt?" Jebb asked.

"Very unlikely...nobody is around in the middle of the night."

"Good. We're not fightin' civilians...we're fightin' Washington, and this will shake 'em up...and maybe wake up a few people in the South too."

"Gentlemen...let us have a toast," Butch said. He had a few beers under his belt and was feeling downright patriotic. "The South shall rise again!" The call resounded through the room as they all clunked beer cans.

Chapter 63
A Taste of Freedom—August 1964

Billy spent the rest of the afternoon prying at the planks on the stove wall, trying to find one that came easily. He decided there must have been one board that the slaves had used for an entrance, and it was not long before his fire poker found it. All the planks on the wall were fastened vertically and disappeared below the floor line and above the roof line so there was little chance of prying them off. But one of them slid neatly up, just enough to be taken out. With what little light he had, Billy could make out this secret room, just large enough for a skinny man to disappear into. And sure enough, there was a trap door to freedom in the floor. He marvelled at the ingenuity of the slaves. The false wall was impossible to detect because there was no reference to the outside walls and no way of telling that the inside dimensions were a little shorter than the outside dimensions.

After a fairly inebriated Mike delivered his evening meal, Billy waited until darkness fell to make his move. He figured that his first trip to freedom would strictly be a reconnaissance mission to scout out where they were holding his partners and formulate some sort of plan. Like his predecessors one hundred years earlier, he slid through the trap door, removed a couple of rocks along the foundation, and he was breathing free air.

One hundred yards away, he could see the big house all lit up and, from a distance, looking quite grand. The silence of the night was shattered by a roar of laughter that seemed to come at regular intervals as if there were some sort of comedy show going on. Billy slipped across to the other clapboard barrack that looked very similar to his.

"Pete, you in there?" Billy whispered, tapping on the boarded-up window. He could hear somebody scramble across the floor and shadow the little bit of light coming from the window.

"Billy! How'd you get out?"

"I'll tell you later, keep your voice down."

"Get me out of here...I'm going nuts."

"I can't right now. There's too many of them around still, and they keep going outside to have a leak. I have to find Sal."

"She's in the house on the third floor...that Jebb guy told me."

"I'm going to try to contact her. I'll come back and get you out when they're all asleep. Then we have to figure a way to get her out."

"Okay, but hurry up...I don't think that I can stand this place much longer."

Pete watched through the cracks as Billy skirted the tree line and headed for the old mansion. He ran in short bursts with the agility and silence of a deer. After years of practice in the Don Valley, if there was one thing Billy excelled at it, it was stealth. He approached the mansion by the side, careful to avoid all the commotion blasting from the back kitchen. Through the leaves of a huge old sycamore tree, he could see Sally's silhouette in the third-floor bedroom.

Billy's other forte was climbing. He could scramble vertically up a tree, a tower, or a railway trestle with the ease of a monkey. The old sycamore tree did not remotely pose a challenge to him with its massive limbs spreading out with a breadth almost equal to the height of the tree. Billy slipped by the first two floors of the house, which were mostly dark except for some diffused light coming from the back kitchen. Within seconds, he was hanging off a massive limb within seven feet of Sally's window, which was open but covered by curtains.

Immersed in her crocheting, the annoying twitter from the window barely registered in Sally's consciousness. She had managed to tune out the roars of laughter coming from below and was quite happily ensconced in her own little world. But the twittering persisted, and she went over to close the window. As she pulled down the wooden frame, she was startled by the sight of a veiled figure through the curtains. Billy finally had her attention, and he desperately made the signal for silence, afraid that she may blurt something out in her surprise. The sight of her crazy partner hanging out of the tree was strangely hilarious to her. Who else but Billy would find a way to her window despite the overwhelming odds against him. She smiled and had to stifle her laughter. Their conversation was a series of confusing hand signals. Like a game of charades, Billy would point to his wrist to try and indicate time and Sally would respond like a clock using her arms as the hands. Finally they were on the same page—Billy would return somewhere between two and three in the morning to rescue her. They both smiled and Billy made his way down the tree.

Chapter 64
RCMP Meets FBI, Atlanta, Georgia—August 1964

American Airlines flight 706 to Atlanta touched down at 1900 hours. The Georgia heat and humidity assaulted Sergeant Bryce's senses as made his way down the aircraft stairs. With carry-on bag in hand, he slowly walked across the ramp to the terminal, following the rest of the horde. As the crowd diffused into the building, he was able to pick up the pace heading for the "Arrivals" area. Bryce surveyed the greeting throng and wondered if Detective Callaway of the FBI would be there to greet him or if he had sent an underling.

A cop can always recognize a cop, Bryce thought, and picking out the FBI man was simple. The guy with the crew cut and blazer still on to hide the shoulder holster despite the heat was an easy giveaway. The FBI man in turn nodded a greeting to Bryce, which Bryce found amusing. He wondered how cops ever managed to be successful at undercover work.

"Sergeant Bryce, I presume...welcome to America, sir. I'm Detective Callaway of the FBI."

"Thank you, Detective," Bryce replied, "I'm afraid you and I have 'cop' written all over us." Callaway chuckled.

Sergeant Bryce opened the door to the unmarked FBI car and reeled at the blast of hot air from inside the car.

Callaway was amused at the Canadian's reaction to the heat. "You may not want to get in just yet, and maybe take off that jacket. You Canucks aren't used to this, are y'all?"

"That's for darn sure, Detective." After a short delay, the two cops hopped in the Dodge Polaris and headed down the interstate towards Macon.

"So tell me what you know about these boys, Sergeant," Callaway asked as he hauled on his cigarette.

"Where do I start?" Bryce asked, taking a deep breath and slowly exhaling as he shook his head. "This thing has gone in so many directions I don't know if I'm coming or going. Your boys showed up in Canada in a Grumman Goose supposedly on a fishing trip. Around the same time, three kids disappear from a suburb of Toronto...and this part you'll never believe. We get evidence that the kids were on a Polish freighter and the Polish captain mentions some Southern boys who were also onboard."

"You're right, Sergeant...that is starting to sound like the weirdest tale that I ever did hear."

"It gets stranger," Bryce reassured him. "We find a note from the kids, and it mentions gold...and wait till you hear this. The note also mentions some Russians chasing them because of the gold."

"Strange things happen in the land of the midnight sun," Callaway replied, misquoting Robert Service, "and all I've got is some counterfeit money being passed by Jebb Butler and his boys...doesn't hold a candle to your story."

"Believe me...I'd much prefer a simple armed robbery," Bryce said.

"I do have something of interest...that may or may not be related," Callaway continued.

"What's that?"

"The *Washington Post* passed a letter on to us that appears to have come from the Brothers of the Gray Ghost. Probably just a crank...but it mentions some terrorist act about to happen, so we're taking it quite seriously."

"This just gets better all the time," Bryce added sarcastically.

"We should know more after tomorrow morning...we're raiding Jebb Butler's place at the crack of dawn."

Chapter 65
Assassination Plot—August 1964

The party was winding down, and the boys were slurring their words in various states of inebriation, with the exception of Petar and Dimitri. The two Russians had participated in the numerous toasts but had managed to do very little actual drinking. Petar looked over at Dimitri and gave him a surreptitious nod. "Gentlemen, thanks for a great evening...but I'm a bit tuckered out...think I'll call it a night. What about you, Frank?"

"That makes two of us...great hospitality, boys," Dimitri replied.

"I think we'll all turn in now," Jebb spoke for them all. "Big day comin' up tomorrow."

"Ya got that right, pal," Butch said. "How about 'nother toast?"

"No more toastin' fer tonight, Butch," Jebb directed.

"Frank and I are goin' to grab a breath of that sweet Georgia air before we turn in," Petar announced.

Pete looked through the crack in the planks in horror as he watched Billy climbing down the tree just as the rear door opened up and Petar and Dimitri walked out. Billy was negotiating the last massive branch of the huge sycamore when he heard voices speaking a foreign language approaching from around the corner. He scrambled back up the tree and lay flat out, clinging to a branch that mostly obscured his body.

"Don't call me Petar, and speak English, Frank," Petar said, stressing the "Frank." "We must obey KGB policy, especially while we're in this country."

"Sorry, Peter," Dimitri replied, a bit diminished.

They continued around the side of the house and took a seat on a bench directly below Billy, who barely dared to take a breath. Pete watched helplessly, his heart pounding as he vicariously experienced his buddy's predicament.

"Ilya is gone...and the kids are here." Petar spit into the ground with disgust. "We'll deal with them later."

"Okay, Peter...you can tell me the plan now. I have a need to know," Dimitri said with a touch of sarcasm.

"That you do, old boy...that you do," Petar replied, showing the British roots of his English. "That letter that went to the *Washington Post*...it didn't say exactly what Jebb thinks it did. I modified it a touch."

"You mean you tricked him?" Dimitri asked with mock horror.

"You could say that. There is no longer any mention that the explosions will take place in the north...just a general reference to an act of terror. And I made sure that these boys will get full credit for it."

"So what about bombing the house and the monuments?"

"Isn't going to happen...the operatives and all that stuff. Just a lie."

"So when nothing explodes, we're going to have some explaining to do tomorrow." Dimitri was confused.

"We have bigger fish to fry, as they say in English," Petar replied.

"And what would that be?"

"This fall there is going to be a presidential election. President Johnson, dear President Kennedy's successor, is obviously running for the Democrats."

"Kennedy should have known better than to screw with the KGB," Dimitri said. He paused for a second in thought. "You're not going to do what I'm thinking?"

"Not exactly, old boy...but close," Petar knew exactly what he was thinking. "Kennedy was trying to push through the Civil Rights Act until his unfortunate demise. Now Johnson is left to carry the ball. Guess how popular that makes him in the South?"

"I would think about as popular as we Russians are with the Americans."

"Exactly, so he needs some sort of peace offering with the Southerners, and his wife, Lady Bird, is a born and bred Southerner." About a mile to the south of them they could hear and partially see a freight train moving behind the trees. "See that freight," Petar continued, "it's on the Norfolk–Southern line between Macon and Savannah."

"I thought we were talking about Lyndon Johnson?" Dimitri was confused.

"We are. That is the last train through until seven o'clock tomorrow morning. Johnson has sent his wife on a goodwill mission through the South...try to drum up support. She is travelling by train...called the Lady Bird Special."

"I would bet you that it is coming through at seven o'clock tomorrow."

"You're catching on, Frank, old boy. In a few hours, you and I are heading out there with plastic explosive and a delay detonator."

Dimitri put his head into his hands, partly impressed and partly astounded by the audacity of the mission. "Carry on."

Petar was all business now. "We plant plastic under the tracks with the delay detonator on the rail. When the locomotive hits the detonator, he should be travelling at sixty miles per hour. Four seconds later, when Lady Bird's private car is over the plastic, it's set to go off."

"The president's wife is assassinated," Dimitri continued the plot, "the *Washington Post* releases the letter predicting the act of terror by a Southern secessionist group, and everyone in the North is outraged at the South."

"Exactly, my dear Frank, exactly. Can you image the turmoil that this act will throw the United States into? The North furious with the South...the South reacting with fury at the North. We'll start the war all over again."

Dimitri smiled, contemplating the enormity of the act. "Two more questions Peter. What happens with us...and what about those kids?"

"At seven tomorrow morning, we will be in the air for Cuba. There is a plane standing by at a private strip. And the kids—" Petar paused for a second. "In the truck, there is a Berretta with a silencer. After we return from planting the explosive, we'll pay each one a visit. One bullet should do it...should have been done a long time ago."

Billy was barely able to contain his terror. His fingers clamped into the bark of the sycamore with a death grip. Even Dimitri flinched slightly at the thought. Murdering children was well beyond his limit of sacrifice for the motherland. He wondered about his comrade, who had ice water running through his veins. "When the authorities raid this place, which they will surely do...Jebb and the boys will have to explain the bodies of three kids, among other things."

Petar smiled. He found the thought amusing. "Let's go to bed, comrade." Dimitri nodded, still shaken. "Better still, let's go say goodnight to Master Billy."

From his perch, Billy watched in horror as the two Russians headed for his lockup. He knew what would happen next. They would find him missing, and Pete and Sally would pay the price with a bullet. Billy prepared to jump from the tree screaming like a banshee. Maybe they would be satisfied with just him, at least for the moment.

"What the hell is all that racket?" Dimitri exclaimed looking over at the slave quarters holding Pete. It sounded like a barroom brawl was going on as Pete screamed and pounded the walls. They rushed over and unlocked the slab door. Pete lay on the floor screaming and pounding at the floorboards. The two figures looming over him looked down with disgust at this figure writhing before them. Performing an epileptic seizure usually worked well in the schoolyard for Pete, but he elicited no sympathy or amusement from his Russian audience.

Fearing that the act was wearing a bit thin, Pete slowly regained control over his badly over-acting body and lay panting on the floor. "I'll be okay now," Pete gulped for air, praying that he had bought enough time. "Can you help me up?" Petar and Dimitri brushed by his outstretched hand and marched out.

They slid the deadbolts back and removed the plank from the door to Billy's cell. Petar flipped the light switch by the side of the door. Billy lay fast asleep on his cot.

Chapter 66
The Plot Begins—August 1964

The big house was quiet now. Only three people were awake: Petar, Dimitri, and Sally. Except for the occasional snort and incomprehensible blubbering, the others were in an alcohol-induced, semi-paralytic state. The old Victorian clock on the downstairs mantel gonged out its haunting two o'clock call.

Sally left the blinds open but the window closed. She could hear the eerie squeaks emitted from bats leaving their home in the attic, and the thought of a flying mouse circling her room sent a tidal wave of shivers through her body. She reviewed her charades conversation with Billy, hoping and praying that she understood his message correctly. He was coming for her sometime in the middle of the night and would somehow rescue her from the third floor cell. Sally tried not to think about the logistics of the rescue, knowing full well that it would somehow involve the old sycamore tree. She thought she heard muffled footsteps from the floor below her. Her heightened state of consciousness picked up every barely audible activity in the house and supplemented them with imagined sounds. But this was real. The creaky old mansion was not kind to anyone making a clandestine exit. In their stocking feet, Petar and Dimitri slid their way along the floor and down the staircase.

Billy felt a surge of fear as he watched the screen door slowly open in the dim illumination from the porch light. The small slit in the boards only offered a narrow field of vision for one eye, but his fixated stare for the last three hours had paid off. Petar and Dimitri, with packs on their backs and shoulder holsters, were headed in his direction.

He had heard it clearly—they were going to pay him a visit with the silenced Beretta after their mission, not before. But what if he had heard wrong. What if the plan changed—his mind raced with unthinkable scenarios sending his heart pounding. His panic grew exponentially with each passing second, waiting for the door to be unlocked.

Petar and Dimitri could talk freely now, well clear of the house with just a mile of fields and small bush between them and the railway tracks. The half moon and clear skies made navigating easy.

"Just think, Peter...one hundred years ago the retreating rebels blew up these same tracks...for similar reasons to ours. They didn't want the Yanks to use them," Dimitri mused.

"You know a lot about this Civil War stuff, don't you," Petar replied.

"Hanging around with these Southern boys, you learn very quickly."

"Well, we want the Yanks to use them...but to use them while we're blowing them up," Petar chuckled. "Just a couple of Johnny Rebs."

They made their way across the last of the fields and through a thin stand of trees to the railway embankment. Petar had studied this section of track from railway maps and knew the exact speed that a train was required to be travelling at this point. He knew that an engineer carrying the president's wife would be completely vigilant to the rule book, and track speed along that tangent section was sixty miles per hour. At that speed, the train would cover eighty-eight feet in one second. Including the couplers, each car was around eighty feet long, so he set the delay for four seconds. The explosives would detonate somewhere in the length of the fifth car. The presidential car carrying Lady Bird Johnson would be a mangled mess of steel.

Chapter 67
Freeing Sally—August 1964

After the worst ninety seconds of his life, Billy realized that his time had not yet come and he sprang into action. He pulled the plank from the wall that served as a doorway into the concealed room and fed the length of it through the trap door and under the floor. Eight feet of plank did not feed easily through a two-foot opening, and he wasted valuable minutes struggling to maneuver it. Billy dragged the plank through the stones of the foundation and sprinted over to free his buddy Pete. He pulled back the deadbolts, removed the plank barricade, and swung the door open. There stood his partner beaming from ear to ear. The exhilaration of new-found freedom and the anticipation of the chase to come was fuel for Billy and Pete. They were back in their element.

"Shush!" Billy covered Pete's mouth. Pete looked as if he had a month's worth of pent-up conversation. "We gotta get Sal."

"How do we get her down?"

"There's a huge tree beside her window," Billy whispered. "We have to put this board from a branch over to the windowsill."

Pete looked leery. "Think she'll do it?"

"Sure she will...you know Sal."

Carrying the plank, they skirted the tree line heading for the side of the old mansion. From the conversation he had overheard with the Russians, Billy figured that they had maybe fifteen minutes to get Sally and go. They held up at the trunk of the sycamore and resorted to sign language to formulate a plan. Billy headed up the tree first and stopped about ten feet off the ground. Pete lifted the plank up to him and started up the tree, and they slowly relayed the plank upwards until they were level with the third-floor window.

Sally was in a frenzied state, waiting for Billy and not knowing the fate of her friends. The thought of impending freedom had overwhelmed her, and if Billy did not show up by morning, she thought that jumping might be a better alternative. The house had fallen into an unbearable silence after she had heard the muffled footsteps. When the three o'clock chime rang out, it hit Sally like an electric jolt and she bolted upright from her chair.

Suddenly there was motion outside the window and a soft clunk onto the windowsill. She tiptoed to the window and parted the sheers. Sally had never seen a prettier or more welcome sight in her life—Billy and Pete smiling back at her and seven feet to freedom. For several seconds she revelled in the honour of being rescued and the bravery of her friends.

The plank that she had to cross was six inches wide and balanced precariously between a branch and the windowsill, thirty feet above the ground. Sally grasped both sides and carefully placed her left knee on the board. It rocked despite Billy's best attempts to stabilize it, and she instinctively pulled back into the room. She could see the look of horror on Billy and Pete's faces as she collected herself. Sally knew that she had to do this—not just for herself but for her two buddies as well. She started out again with renewed determination and concentration. When the plank rocked this time, she was expecting it and did not retreat. Soon both knees and arms were on the two-by-six plank, and there was no turning back. Billy had a death grip on the board as he straddled a limb, holding on with his legs. Pete leaned out over the abyss, stretching his free arm towards Sally. She slowly slid her left arm down the plank, following it with her left knee and pulled herself into a prone position in the middle of the board.

Nothing that Billy had ever done risking life and limb had ever matched the fear that he felt now. He looked at Sally in desperation, unable to assist her. She needed one more foot of progress along the board and Pete's arm would be in reach. Her left arm moved along the plank again followed by her left knee. The board rocked, and Sally's right arm flew up in a desperate attempt to regain her balance. Pete had one chance to save her, and he didn't miss. His free arm grasped her right hand, and he yanked her seventy-pound body violently towards the tree. She grabbed the limb with her left arm and straddled it with her legs as she crashed into the branch. The plank fell to the ground.

"What the hell was that?" Petar asked, hearing the plank hit the ground. Both he and Dimitri paused, looking in the direction of the house, but nothing else stirred. "Let's get this over with." They unbolted the door and entered the room quietly, hoping that Billy had not awakened. The job would be a lot less messy on a sleeping body. Dimitri flipped the light switch. "Why, that little bastard!" Petar was livid, looking at the empty bed. "That little bastard!"

Chapter 68

Out of the Frying Pan, Into the Fire—August 1964

Billy, Pete, and Sally dropped silently off the limbs of the old sycamore tree and froze instantly in their tracks as they hit the ground. Petar was charging towards the house, frantically yelling for Jebb to wake up as Dimitri struggled to keep up. "Jebb, get your butt down here!" He screamed in a blind, out of control rage. The intensity of his anger sent chills through Billy, Pete, and Sally as they lay motionless on the ground.

Soon lights began to illuminate throughout the house as Jebb and his cronies struggled semi-conscious from their beds, confused and in a panic from all the commotion. One by one they came staggering out of the rear kitchen door, rubbing their bloodshot eyes.

"They're gone! Those two little beggars are gone!" Petar started his tirade directed at Jebb. "And it's because you didn't have the guts to do what needed to be done."

"Mike, get upstairs and see if the girl is there," Jebb commanded, ignoring the caustic comment. This was a Petar like he had never seen before. The amiable, good-old-boy camaraderie was gone, replaced by a cold, viscous killer.

"You said you had dogs in a kennel in the drive shed. Go get them," Petar commanded. Jebb nodded at Butch to comply. "And get me two rifles...Frank and I will do the job you should have done."

Billy listened in horror. He knew from bad experience that trying to outrun a dog without a good head start was futile. He tapped his two buddies on the shoulder, nodded towards the tree line and the threesome took off in a flat out sprint. "There they go, Jebb! There they go!" Larry yelled as they all turned to see the tail end of Billy disappear into the woods. Billy heard bullets whiz over his head as Petar emptied his revolver into the darkness.

Butch opened the sliding door to the drive shed and was greeted by three yelping, slobbering, coon hounds all in a state of serious agitation. He struggled to get a rope leash on each one before they were released from the kennel and was unceremoniously dragged out of the shed with both heels digging into the dirt. Jebb took the two deer rifles from their rack on the parlour wall and grabbed a box of shells. *Damn dumb kids,* he thought to himself, *I can't help them now.*

The threesome tore through the forest, leaping over logs and roots and dancing around the eerie, low-lying branches burdened with a cloaks of hanging moss. The ground was soft and damp and felt as if they were running on a sponge. It was not the boreal forest that they were used to, and it had a looming, intimidating feel—as if they were being swallowed up. They ran aimlessly in a blind panic, guided only by the moonlight and fuelled by fear. Outrunning grown men usually ended up in their favour, but Billy knew that you needed more than speed and stamina to escape dogs. For now all they could hope to do was push on through the jungle-like undergrowth and put as much territory between them and their pursuers before they could rest to plan a strategy.

Petar and Dimitri were armed and ready to go, impatiently waiting for Jebb to round up two flashlights. "Go get some of their bedding and give those mutts the scent." Petar barked out orders to his resentful hosts. Their plan was unravelling, and he knew it. By now Dimitri and himself should have been headed for a remote airstrip to board a waiting Cessna Caravan.

"Okay, okay, let's stop for a second," Billy said through his panting. Pete and Sally pulled up and dropped to the soft forest floor, gasping for breath on all fours.

"Listen," Pete uttered between breaths. "They're still on the leash...running hounds don't yelp like that...I know from when we go deer hunting."

"Billy, we can't outrun them...we need a plan!" Sally said desperately. Billy did not respond. He was lost in his thoughts. "Billy what are we going to do?"

"Wade in the water."

"Billy, are you nuts! What are you talkin' about?" Pete grabbed Billy by the shoulders.

"Wade in the water...we need to find a stream or a swamp...it's what the slaves did. The dogs will lose our scent."

The idea silenced both Sally and Pete. They looked on at their comrade with astonishment.

"Honestly, Billy Parker. Sometimes—" Sally let the sentence hang unfinished.

"They're off the leash now," Pete said. He was right—the yelping had changed in tone and volume. "Let's get outta here!"

Chapter 69

The Hunt—August 1964

Petar and Dimitri, with rifles slung over their shoulders and flashlights in hand, stumbled through the undergrowth, following the yelping of the hounds. The going was tough for two middle-aged guys who, despite their KGB training, had let their conditioning slip. Every root that they tripped over, every low branch that clipped them brought forth a tirade of the very best in Russian cursing.

Petar silently berated himself for his weakness. Sentimentality had no place in espionage, and yet when he had his chance to deal with these kids back at the Northern camp he got soft. Now he was chasing three individuals who knew enough to blow KGB operations right out of North America, and his window of opportunity to make a clean escape was closing fast. His frustration level and anger at himself was spinning out of control.

Dimitri was relieved to hear the sound of the hounds getting closer, and they appeared to be stationary. It could only mean one thing: the kids were treed and now it would just be a duck shoot. He thought about how badly he wanted to get out of that bush, out of this country, and back to the homeland. *This was the end of my duties as a KGB officer,* he thought. *I have done my bit—made the sacrifices—and now a flat in central Moscow and a boring pedestrian life will be paradise. All we have to do is eliminate those damn kids.*

The hounds ran up and down the edge of the swamp without direction, and their yelps of excitement had turned to whimpers of frustration. The trail had gone cold. They looked to Petar and Dimitri for some sort of guidance as the pair staggered up to the swamp. Petar knew immediately what had happened. "They're running in the water, but they have to come out somewhere. You take two hounds and go upstream, and I'll go down. If you get a scent, fire off your rifle three times," he commanded Dimitri. "I won't be outfoxed by some twelve-year-old punks."

The tough running through the bog of the swamp began to ease up as the kids neared the mouth of a creek. Running in the creek bed was fast, but tough and treacherous. With each step came the possibility of twisting an ankle on an unseen rock, and a twisted ankle meant the end of the line. Billy followed close behind Sally, trying to assist her whenever she stumbled, which was becoming more frequent now. She was out of her element, and Billy was worried. If they were caught this time, he knew what was in store for them.

No matter which way he cut it, in his mind, he came up guilty. None of them would be in this mess if it were not for him. He could live with the fear but not the guilt. Billy was starting to come apart. They were in the last laps of a life-and-death race that they were certain to lose. There was no time to think, to put together a plan. Just run and run some more—until exhaustion ended it. He could barely put together a coherent thought through his rising panic. Visions of Aunt Emily and of the Reynolds plantation tormented Billy. He fought to stay focused, to find that miracle he needed, but the visions just became more strident. And then the revelation came to him. He had found his miracle: *Aunt Emily was trying to help them.*

"Pete! Cross the creek here and climb up the bank," he yelled at his partner in the lead. The creek was deeper than they had anticipated, and it was almost over their heads in the middle. They struggled against the current and scrambled up the opposite bank with renewed energy after losing the burden of the water.

"Where to now?" Pete screamed at his partner, his composure long since gone.

"Follow me."

"Follow you to where?"

"To the Reynolds plantation,"

"How do you know about a Reynolds plantation?"

"I don't know how I know...I just know, so let's go!"

Billy was navigating by instinct now, like a migrating bird. He made inexplicable course changes as if he was following some internal compass, dragging them through thickets that tore at their clothes and skin. Their route was no longer the path of least resistance, and his intuition seemed to always pick the worst terrain. Pete and Sally followed along, loyally giving their leader the benefit of the doubt.

A rifle cracked three times, so close that Billy expected to hear bullets piercing through the forest. The hounds were howling again, closer than they had ever been before. Billy led his exhausted, bedraggled charges through a hedge so dense that he had to drag Sally through. They came through the other side to a small embankment and up to a gravel road. "We're almost there!" Billy cried, trying to rally his flagging troops. They started into a sprint, but Sally's legs were spent and she immediately fell back. Billy and Pete each grabbed an arm and dragged her along. She stumbled and fell several times, further damaging her wobbly legs that now only had the strength of rubber. Two hundred yards down the road, the hounds had cleared the thicket and howled in glee at the sight of their prey. They broke into a sprint.

The oak-lined laneway of the Reynolds plantation was now in sight. Sally was like a rag doll, with a boy on each shoulder taking most of her weight. "We'll be safe there!" Billy yelled. It made no sense to Pete, but there was now no alternative. They stumbled up the laneway of the planta- tion. It was exactly as Billy remembered it—*from his dream.*

The dogs were now closing in on the old gate posts to the lane. Pete looked futilely at his friend who had promised them safety. "Billy, they're going to catch us! What now?" he pleaded. Billy said nothing and reduced his gait to a calm walk. "Billy, are you nuts! Did you hear me? Run for it!"

Suddenly the howling stopped and the once-blood- thirsty hounds turned tail on a dime—as if they had come up against an *invisible wall.* They headed back up the road in a flat-out run, whimpering and yelping in fear.

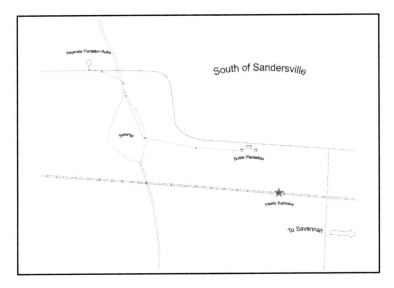

Chapter 70
Reynolds Plantation—August 1964

There was magic in the air of the old Reynolds plantation; they could feel it as they walked beneath the majestic oaks bathed in moonlight. The halcyon days of the Old South had ended over one hundred years ago, but Dixie lived on in the spirits and ghosts that still wandered the grounds. All that remained of the great house was remnants of the stone foundation overseen by a National Historic Site plaque that itself seemed antique. But the proud old mansion was still there in spirit—in all her grandeur and glory.

Billy, Sally, and Pete crept silently towards the remains of the plantation home, each one awash in the ambience. They felt safe and calm—as if they were in some sort of protective bubble.

"Billy...what happened there?" Pete stared back up the laneway, shaking his head in bewilderment.

"This is Aunt Emily's home," Billy seemed oblivious to his comrades.

"Don't you mean *was* her home?" Sally replied.

"No, I mean *is* her home...she's here now...and she's looking after us." Sally glanced at Pete, looking for some sort of plausible explanation to Billy's strange behaviour. "There are four huge pillars right across the verandah here, that go up two floors and hold up the roof." For Billy, the house still existed—he had seen it in his dream. "And when you go inside, there is a huge round staircase that goes up to the bedrooms, and off to the right is a parlour and the kitchen is in the back." He continued the tour, pointing out Mammy's bedroom and Aunt Emily's room and all the little idiosyncrasies of the house as his two pals listened with rapt attention.

As they lay down exhausted on the lawn, Pete and Sally tried to make sense of the strange events that had just taken place. Too much had happened too quickly, and the terror of the dog chase started to seem like a bad dream. The boundary between fantasy and reality was no longer clear on this ethereal property. The only one that it made sense to was Billy. He knew they had been helped by his fellow prisoners in the old slave quarters. He knew that Aunt Emily had guided them to her plantation and protected them from the dogs. There was no question in his mind.

"Billy, what did your Aunt Emily look like?" Sally asked.

"She's beautiful...long black hair...pure white skin...like an angel."

"But wasn't she very old?" Sally was puzzled.

"She's young forever now."

"Do you really think that she's here?"

"Of course she is," Billy chuckled at her question. "This is her home."

Questioning Billy was starting to seem very futile to Sally. She knew Billy Parker was not a guy prone to fantasy, and the supernatural was becoming the only feasible explanation for the events of the last half hour. Even Pete knew when to quit. The threesome lay back, quietly lost in their thoughts for several more minutes.

"Pete...we have to go back," Billy said circumspectly, not sure how to break the news.

"Back...where? Why? We're doin' great right here."

"There's something that I didn't tell you guys," The reverie of the moment was quickly slipping away for Sally and Pete, who were now both sitting defiantly upright. Leaving this idyllic setting seemed absurd.

"When I heard the Russian guys talking...they're going to do something really horrible."

"What, Billy?" Sally asked.

"They're going to blow up a train."

Pete was now on his feet gesturing with his hands. "So what are we supposed to do about it?"

"The wife of the president of the United States is on the train."

"This is too weird. Billy, are you sure?" Sally shook her head in amazement.

"They're going to blow it up and blame it on Jebb and his guys."

The whole thing was starting to seem surreal to Sally and Pete. For several minutes no one spoke.

"When is this supposed to happen?" Pete finally asked, much less animated.

"The train goes through...behind Jebb's house at seven o'clock in the morning. We have to stop it."

Pete glanced at the fading darkness on the horizon. "I don't know why I ever follow you, Billy Parker." He wrapped his face in his hands and slowly shook his head. "But the sun's coming up and it must be getting close to seven."

"So you're in?"

"Sometimes I hate you, Billy...but yeah...I'm in."

"Great. Sal, you'll be safe here...and we'll come back to get you."

Sally was afraid now—afraid for her friends. She took Billy and Pete by the hand. "Will you guys please be careful?"

Chapter 71
The Presidential Train—August 1964

Old Sam polished up his General Motors F-40 locomotive with the reverence of a guy that lived for his job. The F-40, especially *this* F-40, was the Cadillac of locomotives—the first generation of diesel-electric after the steam engine. His patriotic heart felt a kinship with this stars and stripes-adorned train.

Sam waited for the go ahead from the secret service man in charge of the twenty or so secret service agents onboard. He had been handpicked by the agency, after an exhaustive search into his background and record as an engineer, to take the Lady Bird Special on a tour of the South. This was the crowning achievement of Sam's long career. He was a proud man.

The train was parked on a well-guarded siding just outside the Macon central station. Most of the agents had taken up positions at regular intervals along the length of the train, while overhead a helicopter approached and began to circle.

"Come in, Lady Bird One," the walkie-talkie of the head secret service man crackled to life.

"Go ahead, Sky Watch," the agent answered.

"Track looks clear...depart when ready."

"The first lady is doing whatever it is that first ladies do when they wake up. We are awaiting word from her valet...shooting for a zero-six-thirty departure."

"Lady Bird One...you had better count on a zero-six-thirty departure...otherwise you will mess up the entire Norfolk–Southern Macon-to-Savannah schedule. Kind of defeats the purpose of the trip, don't you think."

"We'll do our best."

Chapter 72

Back on the Trail—August 1964

Petar looked like a crazed man. The hounds had lost the trail again and were wandering aimlessly. It appeared that he had been outsmarted again. His years of training and experience had not prepared him for this looming failure. Fierce pride in his own abilities would not allow him to tolerate defeat. It now became a vendetta.

"Peter, let's give it up and head to that airfield," Dimitri begged.

"Shut up...I don't want to hear that again."

"But the plane will leave without us if we're not there by sun up."

Petar was now livid at his comrade's willingness to give up so easily. "I said shut up! What kind of a spineless KGB man are you? We leave when the job is done. Do you understand?" Dimitri exhaled audibly but knew better than to reply.

♦ ♦ ♦

It took a great act of will for Billy and Pete to leave the tranquility of the Reynolds plantation and head back into the swamps—like leaving the ceasefire zone to head back into battle. *How many times can you push your luck until your luck finally runs out?* They both struggled silently with the question, not daring to verbalize it—as if to say it would somehow make it happen.

The boys were now running on empty, but a greater purpose that they sensed the importance of but did not fully understand pushed them onward. The wife of the president of the United States was within one half hour of being obliterated, and that was somehow going to plunge the country into chaos. It seemed like a fantasy beyond their wildest dreams.

The horizon was beginning to lighten, revealing an eerie shroud of mist covering the countryside. Billy knew that they had to somehow retrace their steps from the night before and find their way back to Jebb's place in order to locate the railway line. They left the road and ploughed back through the underbrush, looking for the only landmark that they were sure of—the creek. The forest felt like a much more foreboding place in the early morning light, now that they could see the terrain and were not being pursued. It was a bit like their myriad chases through the valley. They would think nothing of tumbling down a cliff side to escape. The greater danger always made them oblivious to the lesser danger.

"This place has got to be full of snakes...maybe even alligators," Pete said with a touch of contempt in his voice.

"Yeah...and they won't be garter snakes like at home...maybe even pythons," Billy replied, "and I read about these black panthers—"

"Shut up." Pete had heard enough and regretted initiating the topic. "Which way do we go?"

"We've got to follow our tracks back to the creek and then walk up the creek to where we went in at the swamp. At least all this muck makes it easy to see footprints."

The white noise from the flowing water made the creek easy to find but *creek* was no longer an accurate name. A small hydro dam upstream had released its pent up waters, and it had morphed into a small, rapidly flowing river. Billy and Pete stood on the banks looking in amazement.

"Sure wasn't like this last night," Billy said.

"We try to swim across this, and we'll end up five miles downstream...if we don't drown first." Pete knew from experience the power of flowing water and its ability to carry you for miles. Billy knew he was right. He scanned up and down the riverside looking for a solution.

"You see what I see," Billy said, looking at the huge old oak clinging to the embankment, branches reaching out in all directions.

"Yep...just like the swing across the Don River." Pete knew instantly where he was going with the idea. "That one branch almost reaches the other side...should hold our weight."

They easily ascended the moss-cloaked oak tree, and Pete took the lead shinnying out the limb that almost spanned the river. As he reached the farthest end of the branch, it began to dip under his weight and nicely lowered him within eight feet of the river's surface. He dropped effortlessly into the shallow waters of the far side and scrambled up the bank. Billy followed confidently, handling the climb like an acrobat. As he approached the drop zone, his partner on the shore suddenly froze.

"Billy...don't move!" Pete was bug-eyed, staring at his partner.

"What...why not?" Billy stammered. He knew that it took a lot to shake up his normally unflappable buddy.

"Don't look up—there's a snake right above you." All the commotion in the branches had disturbed the slumber of a poisonous cottonmouth that now had Billy in its sights. Billy clung frozen to the branch, fighting his rising panic and waiting further instructions from Pete. The serpent had now come to life and was slowly, meticulously slithering towards Billy.

"Billy, jump!" Pete screamed, recognizing an animal stalking its prey. Billy was in the air in an instant, and the rebounding branch catapulted the cottonmouth into flight, following Billy to earth. Billy hit the shallow river bottom running, with the startled snake splashing down beside him. Both prey and predator happily parted ways as Billy scrambled up the embankment and the serpent sped away like a dart across the surface of the river.

"Holy crap, Billy...did you see the size of that thing? It could have eaten you whole!" Billy did not respond and lay panting on the embankment. "You sure that this thing is worth doing? Maybe you didn't hear those Russian guys right."

"I heard 'em right...and we have to stop that train." Billy was adamant. "Let's get going."

They followed the shoreline of the swollen creek, now vigilant of every movement in the bush. This time they followed the tracks of the hounds that had pursued them a few hours earlier. The trail led them to the point at the swamp where their own tracks had disappeared into the waters. Billy knew that they had to get within sight of the old plantation to get a bearing on the railway line just to the south. He also knew that they would probably be getting dangerously close to the hounds again.

Chapter 73

RCMP–FBI Raid, Georgia–August 1964

The four Dodge Polaris squad cars sped along the back road with only the lead car visible. The other three were enveloped in a cloud of dust. In each trailing car rode four camouflaged FBI agents well versed in early morning raids. Inspector Callaway drove the lead car with RCMP Sergeant Bryce riding shotgun. An arsenal of high-powered rifles filled the trunks.

The plan was simple. A half mile shy of Jebb's plantation, twelve agents from the trailing cars would hit the bush and form a ring around the perimeter of the big house. When everyone was in place, Calloway would get the okay by radio and he would proceed with Bryce up the plantation drive to start the operation. They would announce their intentions to Jebb and his colleagues with a bull horn and then let the boys decide on their next move. If they chose to flee, they would run right into a tightening noose of FBI men. If they were very foolish and decided to fire on the FBI, then a withering volley from sharpshooters would soon silence them. If they were smart, they would file out the door, hands on heads, and neatly line up in front of the house. Callaway had seen it all, and it didn't matter to him much what they did.

The whole thing seemed a bit surreal to Bryce. One afternoon he was sitting in his office in Ottawa, and the next morning he was on an operation with a famous police force in the Deep South. He mulled it over in his mind as he enjoyed watching the rural Georgia countryside slip by, past antebellum mansions—some restored, some dilapidated, and some missing altogether, thanks to Sherman.

"Hey Callaway...pull over a second will you," Bryce asked.

Callaway complied, and the entourage came to a halt. "Better make it quick, Sergeant...sun's coming up," Callaway said, thinking that this was a pit stop for his colleague.

"No, it's not that," Bryce corrected him. "Unless I'm hallucinating, I saw a little girl waving in the laneway of that old ruin back there."

"What the hell is a little girl doing up at this hour in the middle of nowhere?" Callaway replied. "We'll have a look."

Chapter 74
The Final Chase Begins—
August 1964

"What kind of goddamn tracking dogs are these?" Petar mumbled out loud. "They're just taking us back to Jebb's." Sure enough, the frustrated hounds were just backtracking on the original scent. Petar knew that their time was running out. Their escape aircraft would be taking off shortly without them, and there was no sign of the kids.

"Peter...let's leave it and get out of here," Dimitri begged one last time.

"I don't want to hear Peter or Frank again!" Petar barked back. "I'm sick of these bullshit American names. From now on it's Petar and Dimitri...understand?" Dimitri nodded meekly—a man almost spent. He considered making a break for it and leaving Petar behind, but he knew full well that Petar would not hesitate to put a bullet in the back of his head. He plodded on with resignation.

"You know what, Dimitri?" Petar asked as they entered the grounds of the plantation. He sounded calm now, almost philosophical. "When the FBI get their hands on those kids, all KGB operations in America will be blown out of the water. Jebb and the boys won't talk because they know what the penalty for treason is...but the kids..." He shook his head, not completing the sentence.

"But Petar...we have sacrificed immensely for the motherland...surely Moscow will appreciate that."

"When you and I get back, Dimitri, they will treat us as traitors...and you know what that means. No sir, there will be no cushy retirement for us."

"But we could stay in Cuba, Petar."

"Cuba takes her orders from Moscow...and if we get caught here, we get to see the inside of an American prison for the next twenty-five years. No, it does not look good, my friend."

Petar's equanimity was suddenly shattered by the yelping of the hounds that were unanimous on the direction they should take. The two Russians struggled to hold them back. "Dimitri...look over there!" he commanded. On the horizon were the silhouettes of Billy and Pete bounding across a field, like scared deer. "They're heading for the railway tracks...we've got them this time!"

Petar's assessment of their dire prospects began to sink in with Dimitri. *But if the kids are not around to tell their tale, the outlook is not nearly as bleak,* he thought to himself. *And what if our explosives went off and the first lady of the United States is no more, supposedly assassinated by Southern rebels. That great evil power, the United States of America will be thrown into chaos, and we will return to KGB headquarters like conquering heroes.* Dimitri began the chase with renewed vigour.

Chapter 75
Stop the Train—August 1964

Old Sam released the air brakes and started to throttle up the F-40 as they pulled out of the siding. The diesel threw out a blast of black soot and began to roar as the couplers banged together down the length of the short train.

"Easy partner...we've got the first lady onboard," the secret service guy admonished. Sam was not used to pulling only a light six-car load. He sheepishly backed off on the throttle. "She's got to be in good shape for a nine o'clock speech in Savannah this morning."

"I really don't follow politics much myself," Sam replied, "but what does she hope to gain by all this running around the South?"

"She doesn't hope to gain anything. It's her husband, President Johnson, who has something to gain. He needs the South in this fall's election...and you know how popular he is down here." The secret service guy rolled his eyes.

"They don't like him in the South?" Sam asked naively.

"Man...you sure don't follow politics. President Johnson inherited the Civil Rights Act from President Kennedy. The South hates it and him for pushing it. He sent Lady Bird down because she's a Southerner...try to smooth some ruffled feathers."

Old Sam shook his head in bewilderment. "I'll stick with locomotives." The short Lady Bird Special made its way through a maze of tracks and switches towards the outskirts of Macon.

♦ ♦ ♦

Billy and Pete ran up the embankment and onto the mainline between Macon and Savannah. They had been running on and off for most of the night, and they were hitting the limit of endurance for their twelve-year-old bodies. The urge to lie down in the soft grass beside the tracks and give their hearts a chance to catch up with their legs was overwhelming. But they instinctively resisted—knowing that getting going again would be even tougher.

Billy looked in both directions up and down the track— confused—not knowing what direction the ill-fated train would be coming from. "I don't know which way we should be going," he stammered between gasps for breath, but his partner did not hear. Pete was fifty feet away jogging down the track.

"Billy! Look at this!" Pete yelled to his buddy. Billy sprinted to catch up with him. "I think you heard right...I think this is a bomb." Billy looked down at the device sitting on the railhead and the two wires leading to a package partially buried by the ballast.

"Jesus...it's like one of those in the war movies," Billy said incredulously. The stuff in the movies never seemed real, but this was real. "Don't touch it...it might blow!"

"Billy, we gotta stop that train!"

Billy put his ear down on the rail—using a technique that they had used time and time again, waiting for trains to hop down to Bond Park. "There's one comin...and not far away!"

Chapter 76

Two Deaths—August 1964

Old Sam was now in his personal nirvana. Free of the city limits with his brand-spanking-new F-40 gliding along at track speed through the Georgia countryside. His brakeman in the left seat and the secret service guy behind him were starting to nod off, which was also a good thing because Sam did not like to talk much.

"Lady Bird One from Sky Watch," the radio cackled. The secret service man who was somewhere between sleep and awake mumbled something unintelligible.

"Lady Bird One from Sky Watch...come in."

"You should think about answering that, partner," Sam said giving him a bit of a nudge.

"What...what was that!" The secret service man tried to shake himself back into consciousness.

"The guys upstairs want to talk with you."

"Why didn't you say so?" the secret service man replied indignantly. "Go ahead, Sky Watch...I was just dealing with another matter."

"Lady Bird One...keep your eye out for a couple of kids on the track about four miles ahead. We don't see a problem...keep your track speed."

"Roger, Sky Watch...will do."

"We're going to head closer to Savannah...call if you need us."

"Will do, Sky Watch," he replied putting the mike down. "Need those guys like I need a headache."

Billy and Pete were running full tilt down the track-side ballast, but the footing was bad, giving way frequently and sending one or both of them hurtling into the ditch. They knew that they had to put as much distance between them and the explosives if the train was to have a prayer of stopping.

Old Sam had the F-40 cruising along at the track speed of sixty miles per hour just as Billy and Pete came into sight.

"Have a look at this," Sam said to the secret service man. "You sure we should keep going?" Billy and Pete were waving frantically.

"Slow her down," the secret service man ordered as he stared intently at the two youths. With both arms waving frantically, Billy lost his balance and tumbled into the ditch once again. As he struggled to get up, he heard the ping and unmistakable whine of a bullet ricocheting by his head. He turned and in horror watched as the three hounds mounted the rail bed one hundred and fifty yards down the track. Sensing victory, they broke into a gallop for the final chase.

"Pete! Get outta here!" he screamed at his partner, "into the woods!" When he turned to see the pursuing hounds, Pete knew in an instant that they were finished— the game was over. They might get another few hundred yards before the hounds would be all over them. Billy and Pete tore into the bush at the trackside and for the first time; in a blind panic. They ran like they had never run before—as if they had fresh legs. Like the final sprint of a deer about to be taken down by a pack of wolves.

"Dump the brakes!" the secret service man yelled at old Sam. "Those hounds are after those two young guys, and the hunters over there have no control over them. Hope the little beggars are smart enough to get up a tree...should be able to control your animals. I'm going to give those two hunting bastards a piece of my mind!"

Sam reined in the F-40 and brought the Lady Bird Special to a gentle stop to avoid upsetting the first lady. The secret service man climbed down the cab ladder onto the track ballast, muttering about irresponsible hunters. Being a hunter himself, he was astounded and livid that anybody could have so little control over their tracking dogs. With his patent leather shoes offering next to no traction on the loose rocks, he gingerly made his way to the front of the locomotive. He scanned the track for the hunting party, but the only sign of them now was the yelping of the bloodthirsty hounds tearing through the bush. *Goddamn bastards,* he thought to himself. *I'll report them when we arrive in Savannah.* The secret service man knew better than to leave his post, and he started back to the locomotive. As soon as he turned, something very interesting on the rail head caught his eye.

♦ ♦ ♦

The hounds had now closed the gap with Billy and Pete to one hundred feet. This was not a practice for the dogs, to be given up once they had run down their prey. All they saw was game to be killed—their rightful reward.

"The tree, Billy!" Pete screamed as he tore up the pine almost as fast vertically as he had been going on the flat. Billy was right on his heels just as the lead dog made a last-gasp flying leap and caught him by the foot. He wailed in pain as the animal's teeth ripped down his foot slowly losing their grip. For several interminable seconds, Billy supported his weight as well as the weight of the hound until the dog dropped back to the ground. The frustrated hounds circled the base of the tree, growling and making mock charges. The kill would be left to their masters.

Billy and Pete instinctively climbed higher as Petar and Dimitri arrived—as if the extra height would somehow afford them some safety. It was the only option that they had.

"Dimitri...you take the other one...I want Master Billy." Petar was a man obsessed—his cold penetrating eyes fixated on Billy. Billy and Pete looked down, paralyzed with fear and disbelief that these would be their last few seconds alive. The two Russians slowly raised their rifles. The crack of two rounds echoed through the woods. Petar and Dimitri fell dead as the FBI sharpshooters lowered their barrels.

Chapter 77

Recovery, Macon County Hospital, Georgia—August 1964

Sergeant Bryce of the RCMP and Detective Callaway of the FBI paced the floor in the waiting room of the Macon County Hospital like expectant fathers. They were tough cops, but the sight of the three ragtag, busted-up kids brought out the protective father in them. It had been twenty-four hours since they had checked in Billy, Pete, and Sally, and they still had not heard a word about their condition.

"I never saw more tired, scratched, and torn-up kids in all my days," Callaway exclaimed.

"Me neither," Bryce replied, "and I hope I don't see any again."

"You know what, Bryce...those kids are made of the right stuff."

"Sure are a far cry from most the punks I have to deal with these days," Bryce said. Just then the doctor wandered into the waiting room, trying his best to slide by unnoticed.

"Oh, Doctor," Callaway beckoned.

"Yes, Detective?" replied the doctor, knowing full well what he was going to be asked.

"Can we have a word with the kids? Nothing stressful...just see how they're doing."

"Look, Detective...I told you...they are the three most exhausted children that I have ever seen in all my days in practice...they need sleep. In fact, they have been sleeping for most of the last twenty-four hours. And when they're not sleeping, they're eating and that is what they need...not pressure."

"We'll save the interviewing for later...just a social call," Bryce interjected.

The doctor paused for several seconds and gave a resigned sigh. "Okay. The one young guy...Billy, I think his name is. He was awake a few minutes ago, reading. His room is 104. Go see him."

Bryce and Callaway slipped quietly into room 104. Billy was sitting up reading old *National Geographic* magazines. His right foot was heavily bandaged, lying outside the sheets.

"Hi kid...how you doin?" Callaway asked.

"Pretty good, sir."

"You three sure had your share of excitement, didn't you?"

"I guess so, sir." Billy was a bit intimidated by the two heavy-set cops looming over his bed.

"Your parents are coming tomorrow, Billy," Bryce informed him. "You'll probably be heading home in a few days."

"Any idea how your partners are doing?" Callaway asked.

"I haven't seen them yet, sir."

"Just call me Callaway. Everybody else does. Nobody seems to know my first name."

"I thought that was your first name," Bryce kidded. The two detectives had developed quite a friendship in the short time they had been together.

"It's a good thing that Bryce here...isn't that your first name?

"Cops don't have first names," Bryce chuckled.

"It's a good thing that the detective saw your friend Sally. She told us one doozie of a story...about you guys and the train. We changed our plans and headed for the railway."

"I'm sure glad you did," Billy replied. The whole thing seemed surreal to him—like he was living a movie.

"You made the headlines of the *Macon Register*, Billy. Have a read of this," Bryce said, handing Billy the paper.

Three Missing Canadian Kids Found Outside Sandersville

Yesterday police found three twelve-year-old kids, who were missing from their homes in Toronto, Canada, for over a month, wandering the backwoods outside Sandersville. Their story is so incredible that it barely seems believable. They became involved in a pursuit between some Southerners and some foreigners of the supposedly missing Confederate gold...

Billy carried on reading every word of the article. "But it doesn't say anything about the Russians or the bomb on the railway track."

"Billy, we may as well tell you now...there were no Russians or explosives," Bryce answered his query.

"But I met them...a guy called Petar, another one called Dimitri...and Ivan...and I saw the bomb!" Billy pleaded with them.

"Billy, I will say it again...there were no Russians or explosives."

"Look kid," Callaway interjected, "do you know anything about the Cold War?"

"I've heard of it,"

"Well, the Russians and us are enemies, and we came very close to nuclear war not so long ago. If it got out that the Russians tried to kill the first lady of the United

States...we could be very close to nuclear war again. Don't get me wrong...you and your buddy are heroes and we are very grateful for what you did...but this incident has to be hushed up, as we say."

"Don't think for a moment that the Russians will get away unscathed," Bryce continued. "Things like this happen fairly regularly on both sides, and the public never hears about them. They get used as levers...levers in negotiations—and you gave us one huge lever."

"Aren't you worried that we might say something?" Billy asked.

"Kid, feel free to say whatever you want...but we and the Canadians will have to deny any knowledge of what you are saying."

"I won't say anything," Billy replied meekly.

"You're a good man, Billy," Bryce said. "We'll be on our way now...you have to rest up for the reunion with your parents."

The two detectives headed out of the room. "Oh...and kid," Callaway said, stopping short of the door. "You may be meeting some very important people." Callaway winked at him as they left the room.

Chapter 78
Reunion, Georgia—August 1964

Billy, Sally, and Pete felt like caged animals as they stood under the canopy of the Macon County Hospital with a fancy, gold braided rope separating them from a throng of press from all parts of the United States and Canada. Burly policemen prevented any microphones from being thrust into the faces of the three reluctant celebrities. Bryce and Callaway stood on the sidelines with a State Department PR man. Everybody wanted to capture the moment of reunion between the kids and their parents. It was great press for two countries now fascinated by their story, or what they knew of it.

"The two officers told me they're not going to say anything about the Russians...like they weren't even there," Sally said as they chatted among themselves.

"Me too," Billy replied.

"And me," Pete said.

"It's really serious...something about a war with the Russians," Sally continued. "They said that probably nobody would believe us even if we talked about it. And they called us heroes." Sally started to blush.

"Without you, Sal, Billy and I wouldn't even be here."

"I was just so scared for you guys. I decided I had to find somebody...then these cars went flying by."

"Buddies forever," Billy said as he put his hand out for a group handshake. The cameras whirred as they clasped hands.

The crowd in front of them began to part as the police cleared a path for three limousines crawling up the driveway. They came to a halt, and the three chauffeurs, with great pretense, marched around their cars to formally open the rear doors. Formalities were not foremost on the minds of the Parkers, Mills, and Olmsteads as they let themselves out in a scramble to reunite with their children. Sally uninhibitedly rushed to embrace her parents while the boys held back, a bit recalcitrant to show emotion in front of a crowd and a bit wary of what was to come when the show was over. Flashbulbs went off like a fireworks display as the two boys were being crushed in bear hugs from their mothers. It was the perfect fairytale ending for the fascinated press, who peppered them with questions that went unanswered.

The love-in went on for several minutes until the State Department PR man took the hastily set-up microphone. "Ladies and gentlemen, would you kindly clear a path for the three youngsters and their parents to get into the cars. There will be no interviews with the kids, but the two detectives will take questions after they depart. They will be taken to the airport for a return flight to Canada on a government-supplied airplane...as a gift to our Canadian friends. Please clear the way now."

Billy sat with a parent on each side of him on the ride to the airport. For the first time in his life, he appreciated his parents—just for that warm, safe, and secure feeling that he got sitting there between them. For the first time in his life, he was not struggling to be free of their grasp. He could not wait to get home, to his own bed, his own backyard and all the little things that meant nothing to him before.

"Son...you've been through an ordeal that I don't know all the details of, and I don't really care...it's just great to have you here," Bert Parker said as he struggled to hold back a tear. Crying did not come easily for men who had been toughened by World War II.

Barb Parker had no such inhibitions about showing emotion. "Oh Billy," was all she could get out between hugs and tears.

The Lockheed Electra sat on the tarmac with its auxiliary engine whining as the three limousines pulled up to the air stairs. The plane with its paint job and decals looked like the flying embodiment of the United States of America. The crew gave a warm greeting to the three families as they boarded the aircraft. Pete, partly up the stairs, glanced back, beaming at Billy on the tarmac, and muttered some unintelligible words. Billy understood.

The brand-new turbo-prop aircraft was empty except for the three families and the crew, who seemed to outnumber the passengers. The captain, who had been part of the greeting party, came onto the PA system. "I would like to welcome once again all our Canadian friends onboard and hope that you enjoy your flight on this state-of-the-art aircraft." He too had that Southern drawl that Billy, Sally, and Pete had become so accustomed to. Now their parents even sounded as if they had accents. "Please buckle up for takeoff...oh, and I forgot to mention...we will be making a brief stopover at Dulles Airport in Washington, DC."

Chapter 79
Important Meeting, Washington, DC—August 1964

As it taxied off the main runway at Dulles International Airport, the Electra headed for a hangar at the far end of the airfield. Billy was in a state of hyper exhilaration after the takeoff from the Macon airport. He used to love it when his dad would kick the gas pedal down on the Parisienne, and the two-hundred-and-eighty-three cubic-inch V8 would rev up and push him back into the seat. To Billy, the Lockheed Electra takeoff felt like the Pontiac's acceleration times ten.

The first inkling Bert Parker had that this was more than just a stopover was the sight of three limousines lined up on the tarmac. The aircraft pulled up beside the waiting cars and the pilot shut its engines down.

"Ladies and gentlemen...and kids...please board the three limousines. We'll see you back here in a bit," the captain said giving no reason for the stop over.

There was no time for conversation as the three families were whisked into their respective cars. The escort of police motorcycles did not escape the attention of Bert, who was by now getting very curious as to their destination.

"Bert...what is going on?" Barb Parker asked as if her husband was party to the unfolding events.

"Barb," Bert began his reply with a touch of frustration. He stopped himself in mid-sentence and redirected his attention to the driver. "Excuse me, driver. Could you tell us where we are going?"

"You will find out shortly, sir," was the curt reply.

The rules of the road obviously did not apply to their motorcade as they sped through red lights and the traffic conveniently parted as they approached. When they turned onto Pennsylvania Avenue, the picture began to become clear to Bert Parker. He strongly suspected where their destination would be but was still in a state of disbelief. "Billy! What have you been up to?" he asked his son, slowly shaking his head as the White House came into view.

The motorcade came to a halt directly in front of the East Wing of the White House. The chauffeurs opened the doors of their limousines simultaneously as if it were a maneuver on a parade square. This time no one leaped from the cars. One by one, they slowly appeared and surveyed their surroundings with great circumspection. At the top of the stairs stood an impeccably dressed gentleman, and looking a touch amused, he greeted his astounded guests.

"As special assistant to the president and on behalf of the president of the United States of America, I would like to welcome the Parker, Mills, and Olmstead families to the White House. Please follow me...when you are ready." Not a word was said as they climbed the stairs and followed the special assistant, who was doing his best to make them feel at ease, but with little success. His questions and comments seemed to fall on deaf ears, and even the most talkative members of the three families were very reserved and reticent.

They gathered, after a short walk down halls adorned with massive portraits, in some sort of elegant parlour.

"Please make yourselves at home here. The president has requested that he see Miss Sally and Masters Billy and Pete first." Billy could not decide when he had been more scared—running from the Russians or meeting the president of the United States. Even blustery Pete seemed petrified. This was a different kind of scared—one where escape was not an option.

They entered the Oval Office under the close scrutiny of an avuncular, yet dour-looking man seated behind a large desk. The threesome lined up stiffly in front of the desk, which to Billy and Pete felt very similar to the many times that they had stood in front of the principal at school awaiting the tongue lashing.

"Mr. President...may I present Billy Parker, Sally Olmstead, and Peter Mills."

"Thank you...that will be all, Tom." The special assistant left the office. For several interminable seconds, there was silence as the president surveyed the three of them. Then to the relief of all, he broke into a big smile. "Well, welcome, my friends," he said with a Texas drawl. The president stood up and made his way around the desk. To Billy he looked like a giant. "You three have had quite an adventure, haven't you?"

They stood in stunned silence, no one wanting to be the first to reply. Finally Sally took the lead. "Yes, Mr. President."

"My friends call me LBJ...please call me LBJ." He went down the row and meticulously shook the hand of each one of them. "Billy and Peter...I want to thank you from the bottom of my heart for saving the life of my wife...and Sally, I want to thank you for saving the lives of your two comrades here."

"You're welcome, Mr. President." This time the reply was almost in unison.

"I would love to make this an official event...a public event...but I think that it was explained to you why it cannot be. But you are no less heroes...a tribute to Canada. Now what you have also done for me...besides saving my wife...is given me a very large club in our dealings with our adversaries. I cannot go into any further details, but again I thank you. Now I would like to meet the parents of my three heroes."

Chapter 80
Back Home, Don Mills—September 1964

"Billy, stop puttering and come eat your breakfast...you're going to be late," Barb Parker yelled down the hall. This was a familiar refrain for Billy, who heard it pretty close to every school day of the year. Any little distraction was enough to divert his attention from the unfortunate inconvenience of having to go to school.

Today was different. Billy sat on his bed reflecting back on the events of the summer. It barely seemed real to him, and he found himself questioning whether it really actually had happened. *Maybe it was a dream. How could everything be so normal now?* he thought. Billy pulled on a T-shirt and the same beat-up jeans that he had been wearing for the past week, then laced up his PF Flyers.

On the calendar, summer was not over, but for every school kid, on the first day of school—summer was over. Normally for Billy, the first day of school was the worst day of the year, just like the last day of school was the best day of the year. But this year was different. He felt like a condemned man granted a reprieve. Just being alive felt wonderful.

"I don't need any breakfast today, Mom," Billy said as he sailed through the kitchen, grabbing his lunchbox along the way.

"Billy, you need your breakfast...get back..." Barb Parker was drowned out by the slamming of the screen door. "And stay out of the valley!"

Billy jumped the hedge and cut across the two lawns separating his house from Sally's. Like clockwork, old man Clark banged on his living room window at the damn Parker kid cutting across his lawn, and the Coulters' dog crashed into the back gate, yelping at the intruder on his territory. He banged on the aluminum screen door at the Olmstead residence, forgetting for the umpteenth time to use the door bell. *Ahh geez,* he thought to himself. *Four, three, two one,* he counted off until the door opened.

"Billy...there is a doorbell for a reason," Sally's mom reprimanded him. He knew exactly what she was going to say. Things felt just downright normal. Sally bade her mother farewell and started out the door. The rough and tumble tomboy was now a prim and proper young lady— cute as a button in her red checkered dress and braided hair. For a few stunned seconds Billy just stared at her.

"Well, come on, Billy...we have to call on Pete."

"Gee Sal...you look really good."

, "Well thanks Billy," she replied beaming. Sally thought about returning the compliment in kind but decided that it would be too much of an exaggeration since Billy looked like he did every other day of the year.

"Sal, does it feel weird to you...I mean, like you just had a dream or something?" Billy asked as they wandered off down the street. Sally knew exactly what he was talking about.

"Really weird, Billy...but I feel different now. All the things that I used to worry about...things like being late for school, or my homework, or not getting an 'A'...I don't think they're going to bother me anymore."

"Yeah...and maybe I'll start to worry about those things now," Billy replied as they both shared a chuckle.

"I doubt it, Billy."

As they made their way up the front walk of the Mills residence, they could hear the usual ruckus from the vestibule. "Yes, Mom...yes, Mom," Pete repeated as he stumbled out the door, trying to put some breathing space between him and his mother. Glasses half cocked on his head, held together with hockey tape, his hair looking like a wheat field after a tornado, and tripping over his undone shoe lace—Pete Mills presented himself to the world. He made Billy look like a Rhodes Scholar.

"Good morning, Peter...trouble with Mother today?" Sal was back to her sarcastic best.

"Geez...all that stuff about being happy to see me...that sure didn't last. But you know what? I didn't get grounded...and I thought I'd get a life sentence this time." Pete Mills was a happy guy.

And off they went, down the street towards Bedford Park Senior Public—Billy and Pete nattering on about why it must be some sort of trap that they did not get grounded and Sally amusing herself going over her "What I did on my summer vacation" speech.

After the boys had pretty much beaten the "trap conspiracy" topic to death and Sally had gotten over her amusement of telling the class how she had been kidnapped for her summer vacation, there was a brief silence.

"You know what I never told you guys?" Billy broke the silence.

"What, Billy?" Sally was first to reply.

"You know how the FBI and the RCMP don't think that we were really on a submarine. They think that we were in the hold of some kind of boat...it only felt like a submarine."

"Yeah...that's what they told me too," Pete replied.

"They said that if there really was any gold, it's probably in Russia now."

"Maybe it is," Sally said.

"It's not."

"What!" Pete and Sally stopped dead in their tracks.

"When I was trying to get off that submarine, I tripped over one off the boxes and the lid came off...it was full of gold." He paused. "And you know what? We're the only people who know where it is." Billy had that twinkle in his eye that usually meant trouble.

Sally slowly digested what she had just heard. "Oh no you don't, Billy Parker...not again," she said, slowly shaking her head.

"No way, Billy...you got me in enough trouble already." Pete was adamant.

Billy just smiled.

CPSIA information can be obtained at www.ICGtesting.com
Printed in the USA
BVOW03s1000230614

357117BV00020B/833/P